Last Will
and
Testament

by
Evan Charles

To Judy,
What a priveledge to meet a fellow
artist such as yourself. Much love
a you this  *New Years Eve.*

PublishAmerica
Baltimore

Cheers
Evan Charles

Dec. 31, 2004

ISBN: 1-4137-2521-X
PUBLISHED BY PUBLISHAMERICA, LLLP
www.publishamerica.com
Baltimore

Printed by Houghton Boston, Saskatoon, Canada

To Jerry:
for always knowing

A special thanks to George Pearl for providing me with knowledge in the field of handwriting expertise, my Mum for making enough sense of my hundreds of pages of notes and longhand to type the whole thing, and every individual responsible for bringing me the inspiration to write this story.

Last Will
and
Testament

A Fictional Novel
Based on a True Story

by
Evan Charles

PROLOGUE

"Push harder! Harder, Daddy! Make me go up real high! Ha ha ha ha! This is fun. Ha ha ha ha!"

Darryl giggled with delight as her father pushed her on the swing set he had so ardently designed and welded together for her.

"Daddy, there's nobody better than you! I'm gonna marry you one day. You know it?" she said with all the confidence in the world. Darryl loved her father, and it was very clear.

Even now, it was apparent while she reminisced, looking through her childhood photo album. It was a habit of hers. Somehow, looking at old pictures made the stresses of her everyday life disappear.

"I'd give anything to go back there."

Ring. Ring.

The phone abruptly began ringing, interrupting her train of thought.

"Hello? Hey, Daddy. I was just thinking about you! Dinner on Saturday? You bet. You pick the place, Daddy. Ha ha ha. You know the West Country Steak House is one of my favorite places to eat with you. It's about the only place to get a decent piece o' meat. Six-thirty? Sounds fine to me. See you then. 'Bye, Daddy."

CHAPTER ONE

Daddy was a businessman by the name of Clinton Lee. He was a lower-middle class man, born in the small southeastern town of Stoweville during the thirties. His actual date of birth was November 22, 1933. He got a kick out of telling people his birthday. "One one, two two, three three," he would say.

Clinton was the first-born son of Ruby Lee. His birth would be the beginning of a trend for Ruby. She began making young 'uns so frequently that everyone in town started calling her "Rabbit." There wasn't a single person in town who didn't know who Rabbit was, even Ruby.

When it was all over, Ruby had twenty-two children. Twenty-one boys and one girl.

Ruby felt like her hands were too full after Clinton's birth, and decided to let Sadie Lee, his grandmother, have sole custody of him.

Clinton never knew his real father. Fritz, they called him, died from a strike of lightning. He was out during a summer rainstorm plowing in the cornfields he'd worked hard to build, and in one single flash, it was over.

Ruby took it hard because she was young and they had been married for only ten months. It wasn't long, though, before she struck the fancy of Darwin Chandler, another corn farmer, and they married the next spring. Ruby was eighteen.

Across town from his mother, Clinton began his life with Sadie Lee. "MaMa," he called her.

He was the sort of boy who entertained himself by being mischievous. It seemed, however, that he didn't have to find trouble; trouble found him. That's why Sadie insisted on pulling him out of school after he'd finished the third grade.

She thought putting him to work on the Chandler Farm would teach him a lot more values than the schoolhouse ass-whippings would.

He'd had more broken bones and bloody noses than any other kid in town.

The town doctor, Arthur Peterson, always cringed when Sadie came around hauling in her grandson from a recent beating.

"He's diggin' his own grave, Ms. Sadie," Peterson said. "One day he'll dig too deep. What you need to do is teach this boy how to be a man."

And that's exactly what Sadie did. Clinton started his first day of work at the age of eight.

Working hard was quite an adjustment from the almost carefree life Clinton was accustomed to. He soon got the hang of it, though.

Working on the Chandler Farm gave Clinton the opportunity to meet his half-siblings. Of course, not all of them had even been born yet. Less than half. But every year, like clockwork, there was always a new addition to the litter. Clinton was aware of the fact that Ruby was his real mother. For some reason, though, he never once carried any ill will toward her for not raising him. He knew that she chose to let Sadie raise him out of love. For him, what was done was done.

Surprisingly, everyone on the farm got along with one another reasonably well. It was a quality rarely seen in siblings.

Clinton was closest to Ruby's two oldest boys, Martin and Massey. Supposedly, the closeness in their ages had something to do with that. The three did nearly everything together. They worked and played. They literally grew up together. Each one, however, took on his own individual interests, even though they were reared under the same situation.

One by one Clinton, Martin, and Massey came of age and were able to make important decisions for themselves.

Clinton grew up to be a bright young man who knew what it meant to earn an honest living. He understood the value of money too.

One evening, after plowing in the cornfields, Clinton and Sadie sat down for their usual Wednesday night fish dinner.

"MaMa, I've been thinkin'," he said. "I've been working on the farm just about my whole life. But I know that farmin' ain't the kind of work I wanna do for the rest of it."

Sadie took a sip of tea, and looked at her grandson. "What is it that you think you might wanna do, Clinton?"

"Well, I've thought about it a lot, and I think I'd like to do something where I can work with money. Well, MaMa, I ... I think I'd like to become a banker."

Sadie responded with a long silent pause. She stared at the pitcher of tea sitting at the edge of the table, as if to appear she was making an important decision.

"Boy," she said, "I think you'd make a fine banker."

The conversation ended with that. Two months later, Clinton would enlist in the army.

Farming had blessed Clinton with an immense amount of physical strength. He had come a long way from the stringy runt he once was. At five foot six inches, he was quite a manly man. He was very popular with the ladies, too.

A week before he was shipped off to boot camp, he and his two oldest half-brothers, Martin and Massey, went out for an evening of carousing on the town. They headed into a local saloon called Hampton's.

Martin and Massey had one particular goal in mind for the evening. Their plan was to initiate Clinton into the club of manhood the old-fashioned way: get him drunk and find him an easy woman.

The three brothers sat at the bar, where Hampton himself poured the first taste of whiskey the boys would ever taste. That first taste was the beginning of a sort of kindred friendship for Clinton.

Not knowing any better, he and his brothers indulged in one shot after the other, as most inexperienced drinkers do. It hadn't even been an hour since the three had walked through the door, and they were knee-slapping drunk.

About that time, a young woman by the name of Margene Wilkot eased her way through the door. She was an unsightly female, to say the least. But nevertheless, she was a female, and that was all that mattered to Martin and Massey if they were going to find their brother a woman.

Margene was about four feet ten inches tall, and carried every bit of a hundred and ninety pounds on her hips. Her lips were about as plump and round as her face. She had eyes that might've reminded one of a Pekinese dog. They protruded from her head so far, they could have easily rolled out into your lap if she sat down next to you. When she smiled, anyone around her would stop what they were doing to take notice. Right between those lips, in the exact center of her head, was one tooth. She and that tooth managed to repulse anyone who was ever unfortunate enough to eat a meal with her. Nevertheless, she was female, and qualified for the task set out by Martin and Massey.

Margene sat down at the bar with a confident expression on her face. Down deep inside, though, she possessed not one ounce of self-esteem. She knew she was ugly, but tried to make a conscious effort not to let anyone else know this. Little did she know, they did.

"Hey, Massey," whispered Martin, "look at that. I do believe the winner just walked through the door. What d'ya think?"

"I'd say you just might be right," replied Massey.

Clinton's two brothers knew that Margene Wilkot was known for her familiarity with the opposite sex. In other words, she was loose. Margene was the kind of woman who knew that it was nearly impossible to find a man who would court her. No man was that desperate. So she just took what she could get.

"There's one for ya, Clint," said Martin.

"You boys must be crazy," he said. "I think I'll just wait for something better to come along, if you don't mind."

It wasn't as if Clinton needed any help from his brothers to land a female. Better yet, he didn't have to settle for a whore. Clinton courted his fair share of young women. Nice young women, to be exact. The difference in this situation is that Clinton needed the type of woman who would show him just why God made him a man. Clinton knew that his brothers didn't have to do too much persuading. The situation was foolhardy– but it was also fool proof.

"Hampton." said Clinton, "could you pour me another shot? I think I'm gonna need to be a little extra numb for this one."

Clinton downed his shot of whiskey, took an unbelievably deep breath, and jerked himself off his bar stool. He had to move fast, otherwise, he would changed his mind. He slid onto the empty bar stool next to Margene.

"My name's Clinton."

Margene looked at him, shocked that he would actually come within ten feet of her. She was accustomed to men approaching her, but for all the wrong reasons. She was also used to the homelier type. The type who couldn't get any better.

"I'm Margene," she said. "Do you wanna buy me a drink?"

Of course, Clinton graciously accepted the favor.

The two began talking, which led into what seemed to be a never-ending conversation for Clinton. He tried to block out most of her yapping, but the blistering twang of her voice wouldn't allow it. Clinton related to Margene about as much as a rock relates to another rock.

With the booze still flowing, after awhile Clinton couldn't even tell what she looked like.

Which explained why he romanced her into the bed of his 1950 model Ford truck.

In the meantime, Martin and Massey were in the saloon, busy celebrating the birth of Clinton's manhood.

When all was done, the three brothers had to stumble their way back home. None of them were able to hold the key still enough to insert it into the ignition of that 1950 model Ford truck.

The next morning Clinton woke up with the sun blaring in his face. He opened his eyes, only to find that he hadn't quite made it to bed the night before. There he lay, underneath the window of his bedroom on the cold hardwood floor.

When he was able to make some sort of comprehension as to his whereabouts, he immediately closed his eyes again to keep the room from spinning. His head hurt something awful. He now knew what people were talking about when they referred to the term "hangover." About that time, Sadie slung open the door.

"What in the world did you get into last night, boy?" she yelled. "I didn't see that truck of yours drive up last night. I thought maybe you'd gone and gotten yourself killed or somethin'."

"Well, I uh..."

Sadie interrupted, because she knew the smell of whiskey was lingering about.

"Do I smell whiskey in this house?" she shouted. "Boy, you know what I told you about that evil poison. It's what put your grandfather in the graveyard."

Clinton's grandfather, like his own father, died before Clinton turned a year old. After having one too many, his grandfather had somehow managed to stumble over the side of a bridge and plunge to his death into the Shay River.

So after being reminded of this particular tragedy for about the five hundredth time, Clinton vowed never to touch another drop of whiskey.

He would eventually inherit the name "Milk Baby."

The day Clinton headed off to boot camp, he had a particular aura about him, the kind that only a proud man could have. He knew that he was going to make something of himself.

Sadie never let on how proud she was of him, but Clinton knew it anyway. The glimmer that shined through her tear-filled eyes as she hugged him goodbye said it all.

As he drove off to face the new life that would await him, he knew that he had some very big shoes to fill.

Life for him during the first two weeks of boot camp was challenging. Strangely enough, though, it wasn't too terribly different from the strict and rigorous life he knew on the Chandler Farm.

When boot camp was finally complete, Clinton was anxious to face the world as a bonafide soldier. Everything seemed to be in order for him. He was popular with his bunkmates and received the utmost respect from his superiors due to his candor and dedication. The world was on his side.

That is, until he got an unexpected bit of information contained in a letter that he received one day during mail call.

Trying not to acknowledge that the name "Margene Wilkot" appeared in the upper left-hand corner, Clinton opened the letter and read, "Dear Clinton, It took me awhile to find out just where you were. You wouldn't believe the folks I had to go through to find you. Well, I just know that our baby will be real proud of his papa, seeing that you're a soldier and all..."

A million and one chills scattered through Clinton's entire body like tiny daggers. He was so dumbfounded that the letter slipped out of his hand and landed on the floor.

If he had been smart, that's exactly where he would've left it. But after giving himself enough time to overcome the initial shock, he knelt down to pick it back up.

"What kind of mess did I get myself into?" He was completely beside himself for the next several days.

The truth of the matter is that the letter Margene sent him was a fine example of white lying at its finest. Margene not only looked like one of God's ugliest creations, she had a soul to match. She was one deceitful hussy, and was proud of it too.

It appeared that while Clinton was working his way toward becoming a soldier, Margene was working her way into the trousers of Tom, Dick, and Harry. The fact is, she didn't know who the father was. One thing was for sure though. It wasn't Clinton's. The math just didn't quite calculate.

The way Margene figured, Clinton was the best candidate to be the daddy of her bastard child, considering who her other choices were.

It was a brilliant plan. Who would've ever thought you could be a whore and a genius too?

Poor Clinton. He simply didn't know any better. He was smart, but he wasn't used to the con artist type. Those types weren't a popular breed in the neck of the woods that he grew up in.

So Clinton did what any true gentleman did in those days. He asked for Margene's hand in marriage.

The situation was a shameful one, considering that Margene wasn't the bride-to-be he'd always dreamed about.

He caught an unbelievable dose of hell from Martin and Massey. Never mind Sadie's reaction.

Ah, Margene looked as lovely as someone like her could on the day of the wedding. That tooth of hers gleamed through the smile that was plastered on her face. All Clinton could do was bite his tongue and try to make it through the service without running for his life. But by that afternoon, Clinton and Margene were good and married.

"May I present to you Mr. and Mrs. Clinton and Margene Lee," announced the minister.

It was the beginning of a very long and bumpy ride for Clinton.

His new life with Margene was far worse than he ever imagined it being. Fortunately, though, he had his military life to escape to. But the bad news was that Margene had relocated to live with him on the military base, and was ever present at the end of every long day, which made for an even longer night.

More than likely, it was this fact that lured Clinton back to the bottle. It was the only solace he could find to help ease the presence of her in his life.

When nine months had come and gone, Margene looked like she was ready to pop. The hundred and ninety pounds she once carried around with her seemed surprisingly unnoticeable compared to the water buffalo sized figure she now possessed.

When the baby came, Clinton, the doctor, and nurses were in complete disbelief. Not one soul was able to speak. They all just stared.

They stared in shock at this young life they saw before them. In their stares, it was evident that they also felt some sort of sympathy. This child that Clinton believed he had a part in making was the spitting image of Margene. Tooth and all. What made things worse was that "Margene Junior" was a boy.

A boy they chose to name Earl. Actually, this was Margene's choice of names.

Clinton spent a lot of time helping to raise Earl. When the boy reached the age of two, Clinton was called away to serve in the Korean Conflict.

While he was off fighting for his country, Margene moved back to Stoweville and took over the task of raising Earl.

During this time, she managed to brainwash her child into becoming the same class of person that she was. Margene taught Earl very early in his life that it was normal behavior to lie, cheat, and even steal, as long as you got what you wanted.

In Clinton's absence, Margene also felt the need to go astray. In the Biblical sense. One of the men she had formerly hussied around with had agreed to take her out for a night of sinning.

"Mum's the word," she insisted.

Of course, given Margene's pattern of luck, she wound up getting herself pregnant again. She had to think about the situation long and hard before she came up with a lie to cover this one. How she put it in the letter that she wrote Clinton was: "Oh, Clint, I've got some news for you, honey. Remember the night you went out bowlin' with the boys and came home so drunk? Well, when you walked through that door, you started coming on strong to me. Remember that, honey? I just didn't know what to think. Well, anyway, it seems that we've got another young 'un on the way..."

Receiving the news that he would share a second child with Margene was upsetting for him. More so now than it was the first go round. It wasn't that Clinton didn't want children. He did. He just didn't want anything else connecting him to Margene.

Clinton bought the story that she fed him. He knew what his drinking habits consisted of. Falling down drunk could easily describe it.

For the life of him, though, he just couldn't quite remember the night in question. You see, sex between Clinton and Margene was completely nonexistent. He married her out of responsibility, not for love. And certainly not for lust.

After grasping the news and letting it sink in, he made a vow to himself. He decided to give up drinking for good this time. He didn't want to bear any more children with Margene in the name of a good bottle of whiskey.

Back home, Margene made herself busy, preparing for their young 'un to be.

She was out shopping one afternoon when an interesting situation caught her eye. She saw the City Judge, Arnold Lanford, smooching with some sweet young girl in the alley behind the local drugstore. Seeing this created a spark in Margene. She was the type who took a bad situation and made it worse. Her motto was "Your loss, my gain." She knew exactly what she would gain from all this. And all it would take would be a little harmless blackmail.

CHAPTER TWO

Arnold Lanford was a happily married man, or so his wife thought. He was well liked in the community, and as a Man of the Law was very respected too. He was in his mid-fifties, had two teenaged kids, a white picket fence, and a dog in the yard. The whole nine yards.

As a whole he was a decent man, he just had a slight problem controlling his wandering eye. His problem was a secret that was very well kept. The young girls he pursued had no problem keeping their lips sealed. Arnold Lanford managed to take care of his girls in more ways than one. The fancy vacations and jewelry, among other things, was all it took to buy their silence.

This pattern of secrecy would soon change, given Margene's eye-popping experience.

Her first plan was to scheme her way into a hired position at the Judge's office. She would accomplish this the very next morning.

That morning she groomed herself as best she could, as to make the best impression possible on Judge Lanford. She sashayed through the front door, walked right up to the secretary, and said, "I need to see Judge Lanford."

"Do you have an appointment?"

"I don't believe I need one, Miss," she demanded.

The secretary got wide-eyed and hesitatingly eased from her roller chair to walk toward Lanford's office. She poked her head in the door. "There's some lady who insists on seeing you. I don't know what it's all about."

"She didn't say what she wanted?" Lanford asked.

"No, sir."

"Well, for heaven's sake! I can't get a damn thing done around here without being interrupted by some "Do-gooder" trying to collect brownie points!"

Though annoyed, the Judge stood up from his desk and went to see who was trying to hinder him.

"Come on in," he said, after seeing who the hinderer was.

Margene helped herself to the Elizabethan chair sitting diagonally from the Judge's desk. There was a moment of silence before she opened her mouth to speak.

"I swear, Judge Lanford. You need a real secretary in this office. You know, one who will at least water the plants and such. That geranium looks half dead. And for goodness sake, you'd need a chisel to scrap the dust off the furniture in here."

Judge Lanford slumped over his desk.

"What do you have up that sleeve of yours, Margene?"

The Judge knew better than to think Margene had come by for an innocent social visit. When it came to her, nothing was as simple as it seemed.

Margene looked toward the office door, making certain that it was closed. She didn't want a third party involved. Especially if it could ruin her chances of a successful blackmailing plot. Noting that the door was indeed shut, she proceeded to carry on with the show.

"Yesterday, I was out and about, doin' my usual shopping, you see, and I got a peek at a most interesting situation," she explained. "I just happened to see a well known fellow, married at that, neckin' with a certain young girl. I do believe, if I'm not mistaken, that this girl is about high school age. Yes, oh, yes. I'm pretty positive that she must be about high school age. Well, Judge, I'm going to make a long story short. You have two days to come up with a good excuse to relieve that secretary of yours from her duties at this office. Yes, sir, I believe I'll take over that job in two days. Unless, of course, you'd like all of Stoweville to know that their judge likes romancing the young girls in this town. Why, I don't believe you'll be able to find one father of a teen-aged girl who wouldn't want to snap your neck in two. Never mind next year's election."

With that earful of information Judge Lanford had only one response: "Consider it done."

Margene graciously excused herself, leaving behind a middle-aged man who looked like a frightened little boy who had just seen a ghost.

Lanford sat in his chair for the next three hours, trying to come up with a legitimate excuse to dispose of his current secretary. His final decision consisted of making a few phone calls to several high class comrades, persuading them to hire her. Two days later while the former secretary found herself being initiated into the position of Office Manager for the Stoweville District Attorney's Office, Margene was busy molding her derriere imprint into the roller chair at Lanford's secretarial desk.

Needless to say, as far as political intelligence went, Margene was clueless. She couldn't tell a court order from a short order. When it came to brains, though, Margene was no dummy. Anybody who was born with a natural talent for conniving had to possess a moderate amount of brain cells.

She was able to catch on to the most pertinent details of the job, but never managed to lose sight of the reason she actually put herself there. To gain power.

Over the next few months she figured out who the Who's Who were in Stoweville. She also discovered a great deal of information about such individuals, both professionally and privately. Margene was now sitting on a gold mine.

In the meantime, Earl, who was now nearly three years old, spent his days home alone without any supervision.

Without an adult in his life, Earl learned absolutely nothing about common sense, with the exception of the immoral teachings his mother drilled into his young head.

Margene left for work in the morning, only to return late in the evening. She wasn't much of a mother for one child, much less for a second one on the way.

"Keep yourself busy," she would say to Earl every morning before she took off, as if a three year old could understand what that meant.

Some days he busied himself by playing with the skimpy selection of toys he had to choose from. Other days, he wandered off into neighbor's yards as a means of finding something of interest. On one particular day, he humored himself by tossing around a cola bottle which he thought was filled with cola. Nope. That cola bottle was not filled with cola. To this day, Margene can't come up with an excuse that explained how gasoline ended up in that bottle on her front porch.

You see, in all of Earl's mischief, he somehow grew very fond of matches, and the neat little flame they created. So after he managed to spill "cola" all over himself, the young boy decided to entertain himself by striking matches from the matchbook Margene had left lying around. In the blink of an eye, the child had turned himself into a human flamethrower. He ran around the yard, screaming furiously.

Fortunately, a neighbor gentleman had come home for lunch just in time to see all the commotion. He ran over to Margene's yard and rolled the boy on the ground until the flames were smothered. After successfully "puttin' the boy out," the neighbor contacted Margene, informing her of the incident and explaining that he had taken her son to the county hospital.

She in turn conducted herself as any calm person who didn't give a damn would do. She waited until it was time to "clock out" for the day, and then picked up her son up from the hospital.

As a young boy, Earl not only had the misfortune of experiencing life outside of his mother's presence, he was also missing a father figure as well.

Clinton remained in Korea, fighting for his country. He sent letters home to Margene, thinking she would have the decency to read them to Earl. Margene's usual habit, though, was to read the letters to herself and promptly wad them up to kindle the fire each evening.

Earl was very unfortunate in more ways than one. He was under-educated in comparison to every other child his age. And having no adult mentor in his life, he also didn't possess an ounce of common sense. Most people thought he was retarded. This was mainly due to his lack of proper behavior, but it was also because of his physical appearance.

Though he was an ugly baby at birth, his lack of good physical genes started to catch up with him the older he got. Together with the fact that Margene was his mother and his real father was an unbelievably homely looking joker, he didn't stand a chance.

Back at Lanford's office, Margene made a habit of eavesdropping on personal conversations between the Judge and a few of the local attorneys. Her goal was to find out as much dirt on the town's high-ranking officials as was humanly possible. She bragged to anybody willing to listen about her job at Lanford's office. "I didn't get this job for nothin'," she always said. And she meant just that.

It wasn't her goal in life to be Lanford's secretary forever. She had bigger and better plans in mind.

One Friday afternoon, Margene was packing up to leave the office for the week when she overheard boisterous laughter in the Judge's office. Even though the door was closed, Margene was able to understand quite clearly the words being uttered by one loud-mouthed D.A. Guy Saunders, the local District Attorney, was infamous for his loud, obnoxious behavior and his ability to convince himself that he was perfect. And as notorious as he was, he was undeniably the greatest talent ever to appear in the Stoweville courtroom. Saunders had inherited the name Ace, because everyone knew he was an "Ace in the Hole." Not once had he ever lost a case and his legal fees tended to mirror that fact. Not many individuals could afford to retain him. Not many, that is, except for the well to do and those with a background of crime and power.

The conversation that was currently being tossed back and forth attracted Margene's curiosity due to its interesting and very incriminating contents.

"A.D," as Saunders commonly called the Judge, "I'll tell ya, this was one bastard of a case. I don't want to see another one like that for a while. I think it's best for me to take on a few low profilers for the next couple o' years. This last one nearly exposed me for the crook I really am!"

The two men chuckled. "I got a pretty penny outta that Yankee," Ace boasted. "I don't think he was too happy about it either. Nope, but I'll tell ya, he knew there wasn't a chance in hell that he was gonna get outta this one unless I pulled a few strings."

The "Yankee" was a local restaurant entrepreneur who migrated from New Jersey to seek out his fortune in Stoweville. It was part of a cover-up operation.

He moved from New Jersey to the unlikely town of Stoweville because he thought it would be the perfect hiding spot to run his money laundering operation. The restaurant, of course, was merely part of the cover-up. The Yankee was affiliated with the Greek mafia back in Jersey and was under a great deal of scrutiny by the Jersey P.D.

When he moved to Stoweville, he opened the most elaborate eating establishment in town. The menu offered at least a dozen pages of domestic and foreign cuisine. Those who frequented the restaurant were amazed not only by the wonderfully prepared dishes, but the price tag attached to them.

No one ever understood how a five-course meal at a fine restaurant could put them back a mere buck-twenty five per head. Lanford knew. Saunders knew. The Stoweville Sheriff's Department knew. Now Margene knew.

"How in the world did you convince the Sheriff that he didn't have enough evidence to press charges?" asked Lanford.

"I pretty much grasped at straws," said Saunders. "But mainly, I reminded him of how powerless a small town Sheriff is against the Mob. You know, as big of an organization the mafia is, you'd think they'd be a little less paranoid when it comes to the law."

Lanford sat calmly in his chair and nodded in agreement.

"The only reason I even considered representing that Yankee is because he offered me a piece of the action."

"Well, how in the world do you plan on keepin' your new found fortune a secret? You know good and well that if folks start findin' out that your bank account has quadrupled in the past two months, they're bound to start askin' questions."

"No, no! You know me better than that. I got it all under control. I did some homework and found a nice private bank account in Switzerland. I don't guess the Swiss care enough to expose me as a front page headline, do you, A.D.?"

The two men began laughing again.

Margene had heard all she needed to. She quietly tiptoed out of the office so that neither gentleman would be aware of what she had heard.

She carried that earful of knowledge around with her for the entire weekend, trying to decide what her next step would be.

On Monday morning, Margene went straight to the Post Office before work. She mailed an extensive letter, written over the course of the weekend, addressed to one Guy Saunders. It mentioned the dirt she had on him and the favors she would expect in return for the sealing of her lips.

Margene was clever. She never let on that she had eavesdropped on the conversation between the two men, because that would simply be her word against his. She wanted Guy Saunders to think she had some sort of inside information. A leak, a trail, anything to keep him on edge.

Saunders received his ill-fated doom in the form of this letter the next morning. There was no return address marked on the envelope, so he more or less assumed it was literature of a simple nature. He proceeded to open the letter and read it. By the time he made it to "Sincerely, Margene," his face had turned from a flesh-like color to more of a purplish one. As angry as he felt that moment, he was also humoring the feeling of defeat. Saunders immediately reached for his phone and called the Judge's office.

"Mornin'. Lanford's office," greeted Margene in her usual unprofessional manner.

"Ms. Margene, I think you and I outta have a little sit down today. How's about lunch time?"

Margene played dumb.

"Well, who in the world is this?" she asked.

"I think you're smart enough to figure it out, Margene."

"Well, Lordy me, is that you, Mr. Saunders? You'll have to forgive me. I'm just terrible when it comes to distinguishin' people's voices. Did you say lunch time?"

Margene began to giggle as she continued her naive routine. "You know I'm a happily married woman, Mr. Saunders. I just don't think that would be an appropriate thing for us to do, Clinton being overseas and all."

"Cut the crap, Margene. Let's just get to the bottom of things here. Meet me in my office at noon today. I've asked my Office Manager to take the day off, so you and I won't have any problems as far as privacy goes."

"I'll have to ask Judge Lanford about leavin' the office. 'Cause usually I stick around here to eat a bite and then I get straight back to work."

"Let me talk to Lanford. I'll handle things."

Margene put him through to the Judge.

"I need Margene to take some dictations," he explained. "My girl took the day off."

Saunders didn't want Lanford to know anything about what was really going on. The whole idea of being outsmarted by someone like Margene was something he found to be a complete disgrace.

Right about noontime, Margene packed up and headed for his office. She had every last detail carefully arranged in her head.

When she arrived, there were trails of scuffmarks on the floor from where he had been pacing. Neither of them really knew what the outcome of all this would be. All they could do now was to put on their masks of confidence and hope everything would go their way.

"Mr. Saunders, I'm gonna make this real simple," she said. "I know what you've been up to, and I don't think folks in these parts'll take too kindly to the idea of the local district attorney helpin' in a cover-up. Especially for the Mob. Wouldn't you agree with me on that?"

The D.A. simply stood there giving every effort he possibly could not to break his straight face.

"Now, supposing I was to inform some of the local business owners in town about you and that Yankee. How do you suppose that would look?"

"What is it that you want from me, Margene? Is it money? What?"

"Nope. Better. I want you to render your services any time I need 'em. You know. Be there at my every beckoning call. That sort o' thing."

"What in the world does that mean?"

"Oh, you don't need to worry with that right now. I'll let you know when the time comes."

Saunders didn't seem one bit pleased with the idea of kissing ass with Margene, but it did seem more appealing than losing everything he'd ever worked for. So he agreed to her terms.

He didn't quite know what to expect from her, though. But one thing was certain. He would never again have the pleasure of experiencing something as simple as life without looking over his shoulder.

In the meantime, while the war in Korea was nearing its end, Margene was nearing the end of her pregnancy. What that meant was that Clinton would more than likely be back home in time to witness the birth of Margene's second illegitimate child.

Clinton arrived back in Stoweville in mid-summer of '53, and like clockwork Margene went into labor shortly after. She was about a week early having her baby, but the child just wouldn't wait any longer. It weighed a total of twelve pounds and three ounces. And to top it all off, it was yet another Margene look alike. Even more so than little Earl. Thus the name "Earlene."

It was about as brilliant as icing on cornbread. Something about having children named Earl and Earlene seemed a little too much. Especially to Clinton. Everyone else seemed to think so too. Perhaps that would explain why Margene was the butt of every joke in town for about a month or so. The sad news was that the two children, as well as Clinton, were also part of the jokes.

Even though Earl and Earlene didn't understand the act of being ridiculed, Clinton did. For the life of him, he couldn't quite figure out how a man could spend almost three years fighting in hellish battle conditions, only to come home to this. He wanted to go back.

Margene didn't care, though. She was about as proud as she was corrupt. Her impression was that she had done a fine job in choosing names for her children. And that was that.

But now that the birth of Earlene was over with, she was ready to get back to work at Lanford's office. Somehow the life of a deviant secretary to Stoweville's finest was more appealing to her than the life appropriated to motherhood. In better terms, Margene was afraid that she might miss out on something juicy.

Clinton was an excellent money manager and had been able to put the half of his military income that he had not sent home to Margene into savings. He decided that it would be best to take some time off and learn once again how to live and act like a civilian. He could afford to.

So for the first few years of Earlene's life, he took on soul responsibility of raising her. Of course, Earl would be a part of that too.

He did a pretty decent job of taking care of the two young 'uns. You might say that he was a natural father. He spent a great deal of time with Earl, trying to undo what Margene had done. Earl was a very stubborn little boy, so trying to teach him anything at all was a real challenge for Clinton. It seemed as though Margene's traits had rubbed off too much on Earl. Clinton tried his best to be patient with Earl, but he found himself cursing under his breath a good bit of the time.

He didn't give up, though. One of the traits he had learned from the Army was perseverance. A real man could endure almost anything. So while Clinton occupied his time playing the role of Mr. Mom, Margene happily faced the work grind, knowing that she wouldn't have to take on the task of sitting babies.

One day, while working at Lanford's office, Margene heard a loud commotion coming from the Judge's study. Lanford was having a coughing fit. Margene was not in the least bit concerned, but she felt it was her duty as secretary to see just what was going on. "Judge Lanford, you all right?" she asked.

"Oh, I'm fine," replied the judge. "I just got a little choked. This dang lump in my throat..."

"Ah, it's just the change in the seasons, I guess."

With that, she went back to her business.

For the next several weeks, however, the so-called "lump" in Lanford's throat didn't seem to be going anywhere. As a matter of fact, it appeared that Lanford had been having his coughing fits on a routine basis. So Margene decided to do something about it. And again, it wasn't that she cared or anything, she just wanted the coughing to stop. All that noise and commotion was getting on her nerves.

"Judge," Margene said as she approached him one day, "I think you outta have that cough of yours checked out. Whad'da say I make you an appointment with Doc Peterson?"

"Oh, Margene, you know I don't have time for that. My schedule's full enough as is."

"Now, Judge. You can't be walkin' around here, chokin' yourself to death. You 'specially can't be sitting up on the stand and interrupt the courtroom with all that racket. I ain't takin' no for an answer."

The next day, Lanford went to Dr. Peterson to have the lump examined.

"This is some kind of lump, Arnie," said Doc Peterson. "I don't believe I've ever seen one this size. Hmm. Well, Arnie, this one might be a little out of my league. I think we'll need to get you in to see a specialist."

Hearing those words wasn't exactly the breath of fresh air Lanford had anticipated. As a matter of fact, it made him downright uneasy. And rightfully so, as it turned out.

A tumor slightly larger than a mothball was the specialist's conclusion.

Trying to take in that sort of news was difficult for Lanford. He began to mentally plan out the remainder of his life in a sort of fast-forward motion. In summary, the man thought he was going to die.

But, in fact, it wasn't really as bad as all that. The specialist explained that Lanford could certainly live a somewhat normal life after a few operative procedures.

But there was another catch, as well. He would have to give up his chair as Judge.

"Retire!" yelled Lanford. "Me? Why, you've got to be out of your gourd."

The idea of giving up such an elite, social career was more troubling than having his throat dissected. All he could think about was what life would be like as a regular person. A civilian. The man had honestly devoted the better part of his life to the law. Everything before then was a blur. Lanford soon broke the news to a few of his closest friends, mainly lawyers and his faithful secretary. The murmuring between all those members of the legal fraternity could've woken the dead.

Who would replace Arnold Lanford?

With all the chatter going on, Margene began churning out conversations of her own.

Hers, though, were kept to herself. She had a pretty strong prediction of who the future judge of Stoweville would be.

When she was finished with her brainstorming, she immediately got on the horn with her newest "best friend," Guy Saunders.

The D.A. heard her voice on the phone and knew instantly that trouble was brewing.

"For some reason, Margene, I thought it might be awhile before I would hear from you again."

"You pegged wrong. I'm thinking that you're aware of the Judge's plans to retire..."

Saunders crossed his fingers, thinking that maybe Margene might say something other than what he, in the back of his mind, thought she would.

"Well, you know I been workin' for the Judge for a pretty good spell now, and I know most of what it takes to fill the shoes of a judge in a town like this. What kinda strings do I need to have pulled to get a position like that, Guy?"

Knowing that she had enough dirt on him to completely ruin his career, he found himself agreeing to do whatever it took to see that she was satisfied. Even if it meant helping to land Margene into the Judge's chair.

When the conversation between the two was over, Margene displayed the widest grin she ever had. But not Saunders. His reaction was slightly different. While repeatedly beating his head against the wall, the only words he could muster out were "Favor number one, favor number one..."

CHAPTER THREE

Life wearing the Judge's hat was a very fulfilling one for Margene Lee. Not one day went by that she didn't relish her upgraded role in society. She had the perfect life. For now, anyway.

As far as her job performance, Margene was lacking. She knew it too. But that didn't matter. She knew that she wasn't going anywhere.

Strangely enough, most people in Stoweville were of the opinion that Margene was perfect for the role of Judge. That was mainly due to the popular belief that all politicians are scoundrels. Whether that belief has any truth to it or not remains to be seen.

The town of Stoweville had certainly undergone some changes. For one, no one had ever experienced seeing a judge bow out before the end of a term. And second, Margene had given a bit of variety to what had formerly been an all male local government.

With her hands as full as they were now, Margene spent even less time at home with her so-called family. That was fine with Clinton. The less time spent with Margene, the better.

After a few months at her new job, Margene started to become abnormally irritable. And after a few years, she became even worse. It seemed as though the pressures that came with the job had taken their toll on her. Those who had the misfortune of working with her began walking on pins and needles. They knew that one wrong word or move would make her snap. And she had every bit of power and authority to put anyone who dared to oppose her down to size. Margene had finally lived up to her life long dream. She had become a "Bonafide Bitch."

The undesirable personality that Margene displayed around her legal colleagues was mild in comparison to that displayed in her home life. It was one thing to be slightly crude in the work place, but was it was downright necessary at home. That was Margene's theory, anyway.

In a strange sort of way, the bitterness that Clinton had to endure from Margene was a blessing in disguise. It's what inevitably led to the beginning of the end of their relationship.

One evening Margene came home from the office as she normally did. This particular evening was a little different from all the other evenings. It was almost as though she had an agenda in mind.

She slung open the front door and walked into the house. She slammed the stack of files that she had carried home with her down on the dining room table as hard as she could. It was her way of getting attention. It didn't really matter if the attention she got was good or bad, as long as it was attention. And she usually got what she wanted.

The butcher knife Clinton was using in the kitchen dropped from his hands onto the floor when he heard the slam. He rushed into the dining room to see what was going on.

"Margene, are you okay?"

"What in God's name do you care?" she responded. "I don't suppose you give a rat's ass about me anyway, do you Clint? When was the last time you bothered to ask me about how my day went?"

Clinton stood still in amazement. He couldn't believe what he was hearing. It was a fact that asking Margene about her day was part of his daily routine. He knew it. She knew it. Which lead back to the fact that Margene was simply trying to attract attention. Having made her unnecessary accusations, Margene stormed to the bedroom and slammed the door behind her.

Clinton bit his tongue and tried to pretend that the last few minutes never even happened. He was still a bit flustered, though. Enough so that he completely forgot about the fact that he had dropped the butcher knife onto the floor. So he opened the utensil drawer, pulled out another knife and continued preparing dinner.

Almost an hour had passed when dinner was finally ready. "Supper's ready," Clinton hollered.

Earl and Earlene eagerly scampered into the dining room and took their seat at the table. Clinton then joined them. The three sat there staring at their steaming meal, which would soon be cold unless Margene decided to hurry and join them.

"Where's Mama?" Earl asked.

He was the impatient one of the two kids.

"I'm not sure what's taking your Mama so long," Clinton responded.

"Can we start without her?"

"Earl, you know better than that. I have taught you a few manners, haven't I?"

Taking her dear, sweet time, Margene finally scuffled into the room just about the time the food had reached room temperature. When she took her seat, Clinton said Grace and then everyone helped themselves to dinner. Margene took one bite of her meal and immediately dropped her fork on the table.

"What's the matter?" asked Clinton.

"What's the matter? What's the matter? What's the matter is this food is no good!"

"What seems to be the problem, Margene?"

"For one thing, it's cold. And another thing, it just don't have a dang bit of flavor to it. How do you expect anybody to be able to eat this food, Clint? It don't have a lick o' salt in it, does it?"

Clinton shook his head and sighed. The children looked at him thinking he would respond to her. But he didn't. He didn't say a word for the rest of their dinner. Margene mumbled a few times to herself, but never really loud enough for anyone to understand what she was saying. Ironically, she ate every bite on her plate.

When everyone had finished, the children went back to their rooms and Clinton headed for the kitchen. Margene remained in her chair at the table. To look at her, one would think that she was staring into space. But in reality, she was actually conjuring up the next argument that she wanted to have with her husband.

Clinton stood at the kitchen sink. He rolled up his sleeves and began dunking dirty dishes in the sudsy water. About fifteen minutes had passed before Margene crept in behind him.

"So," she said. "What have you been doing all day besides playin' maid?

You know, you outta start wearin' an apron. If you wanna play the part, you may as well go all the way."

Clinton didn't respond.

"Gosh, you'd think there was something awful funny going on here. I mean, look at me. I go out and work every day to support this family. I must be the man of the house, I guess. Right? And you. Look at you. All you do is hang around here all day and clean and cook. So what d'ya 'spose that makes you, huh? The woman? What I need is a real man!"

Margene stared at Clinton, hoping he would break away from his dishwashing and respond to her, but still he didn't. He remained at the sink with his back to her the entire time.

This was a major disappointment. In fact, she was nearly speechless. But not entirely.

"You know, Clint, I could get me a real man. I been noticing how the fellows around town tend to look at me. I think down deep inside, every man has a cravin' for a powerful woman. I can only imagine what must be goin' through their heads when they see the likes of me!"

This time Clinton did respond. But not in a way that Margene could see. Because his back was facing her, Margene never even caught a glimpse of the facial expression he made that was somewhat of a grin.

Margene continued on with her spill.

"What if I was to find me a real man? What would you think about that? I bet that'd eat you up, wouldn't it, Clint?"

Witnessing no response from her husband, Margene began to get infuriated. There was a reason, however, why Clinton chose to ignore her. It was because he had become too familiar with her routine. He knew it like the back of his hand. He could even time it, almost. Clinton was fully aware that she was merely trying to "pull his strings."

In the past, Clinton had made the mistake of falling for her act. He consoled her when she griped. Tried to please her when she wasn't satisfied. Turned the other cheek when she slapped him. Basically, he kissed her ass. It never seemed to get him anywhere, though. Usually, it got him into more trouble than it was worth. So, by now, Clinton had learned the hard way how to "keep his head above water." Ignore Margene. It was as simple as that.

"Clinton, are you even listening to me? You know what? I think I will go out and find me another man. Maybe just for a night. Maybe even longer. 'Cause you know what, Clint? You ain't nothin' to me! You're more replaceable than the filthy water you got your hands in."

Last Will and Testament

Those particular words made Clinton realize that to continue ignoring her was no longer an option. He felt as though he'd had enough verbal abuse. For one session, anyway.

He calmly shook his dripping hands over the sink, reached for the towel on the counter beside him, and one by one, wiped off each finger until both hands were perfectly dry. He stood very still at the sink and took a moment to collect his thoughts. Remaining calm, Clinton looked Margene dead in the eyes and made his response in the most collected manner that he could.

"Margene, if another man is what you want, then you're more than welcome to seek him out. But, of course, that will happen after our divorce."

Those were the last words Clinton said to Margene that night. As it turned out, those would be the last words he would ever say to her again.

Margene was stunned. She couldn't believe that a mere mortal would, or even could, attempt to threaten her. And her own husband was no exception.

"How dare you make such a threat to me! Not one soul in this town has the right to speak to me in such a manner! Especially not you, Clint. And I mean, especially not you! You are nobody compared to me. Are you forgettin' that, Clint? You can't divorce me! No, because you see, I'm the one with the power here. What are you thinkin', huh? You think you're more powerful than me? Is that it?"

About that time, she spotted the butcher knife lying on the floor that Clinton had dropped earlier.

"I think maybe it's about time I show you who's got the power here."

She immediately reached down for the knife and clinched it tightly in her hands. Before Clinton had even realized what was going on, it was too late to do anything. There he was, with Margene pressing the razor sharp knife against his neck. He wasn't exactly sure how he'd managed to get himself into this situation. But one thing was for sure. He definitely needed to find a way out of it. And quickly.

For nearly thirty seconds, Clinton stood still as a rock. As still as he was, however, his mind was quite active. When a person's life is in danger, they manage to think a bit more creatively than usual.

Clinton eyeballed the doorway in the kitchen. He didn't blink. Not for a second. He wanted to give Margene the impression that someone was there, witnessing her behavior. It took a moment before she fell for it, but when she did, Clinton didn't hesitate to make his escape.

When Margene turned around to see who was watching, Clinton ducked down and inched his way out of the corner Margene had positioned him in. He darted through the kitchen and made his way out of the house, slamming the front door behind him. He didn't come back for the rest of the evening.

It was a rough night for him. Between sleeping on the cramped seat of his truck and worrying what do to next, he didn't get very much rest. He had the same thoughts, over and over, in his head.

He repeatedly mumbled to himself, "I've got to see a lawyer. I've got to go back to the house..."

All in all, his fate could be summed up on one word. Divorce. But divorce was just the beginning of the nightmare he would soon face.

The next morning, he awoke to the sound of a tractor plowing . Somehow, in his frantic state of mind, he had managed to park his truck at the edge of a corn field the night before. The sound began to get louder, so Clinton knew the tractor was heading closer in his direction. He rubbed his eyes and blinked several times until he could focus, then peeked out the window.

The tractor seemed to be far enough away for him to make a departure without getting noticed. So he sat up in the seat, cranked up the truck, and drove off without leaving a trace.

He wasn't exactly sure where he needed to go, so he drove to the nearest diner to have a cup of coffee and collect his thoughts.

After taking a quick peek at himself in the rearview mirror and patting down his cowlick, he got out and walked into the diner. He seated himself at an empty booth and ordered one cup of coffee after another.

He couldn't figure out how things had ended up the way they did. He had tried to live a decent life, but somehow a dark shadow seemed to follow him everywhere he went.

He was determined, though, to make his life a better one. And he knew that he would have to make some serious changes in order to accomplish this. So he came up with a plan of action.

First, he would go back home and gather his belongings, then he would seek out the best lawyer that money could buy.

After he had finished his last cup of coffee, he left twenty-five cents on the table and walked out. He stopped for a moment to look up in the sky. "Today, I'm starting my life over."

Having made that promise to himself, he got into his truck and drove off. He took the long way home, in order to build up his savvy in the event that Margene was there. And sure enough, as luck would have it, she was.

CHAPTER FOUR

It was the very first time that Margene had taken a day off from work since she had become judge. So obviously, everything that had happened the night before had taken a serious toll on her.

She was both stunned and offended that her own husband had the audacity to desert her. But due to the fact that she was an extremely stubborn individual, Margene was determined not to let on that she was the slightest bit hurt.

Instead, she wore a stern expression on her face and chose to act as morally bad as possible. She had taken it upon herself to contact the Sheriff's office that morning. The load of crap that she fed them was the exact opposite of what had actually taken place.

Margene's version was that Clinton had held the knife to her throat and had threatened to kill her if she left him.

Poor Clinton. It seemed as though he really did get the raw end of the deal this time. So, without a doubt, this occurrence made every other scam that Margene had pulled seem nonexistent.

As usual, Clinton was unaware of what was happening behind his back.

When he drove up in the yard, he got out and walked through the front door of the house with a great deal of confidence.

He had seen Margene's car outside so he was fully aware of her presence.

But he was most determined not to let anything hinder him from doing what he needed to do, which was to collect his personal items and spend a few brief moments with the children. After that, he planned to go straight to town to retain a lawyer.

So first he walked over to his favorite spot in the bedroom. There stood a bureau filled with all of his most prized and valuable possessions.

He opened the bottom drawer first, which was where he kept his coin collection. He pulled out a drawstring pouch made of sacking and bounced it on the palm of his hand.

As he continued to scramble through the bureau, he was suddenly interrupted.

Not able to contain herself any longer, Margene decided that it was time to make her appearance.

"You know you ain't s'pposed to be here don't ya? I've done called the Sheriff and told 'em what happened. They said that you were not to come anywhere near this house, or else they'd slap you straight in jail. Now, I think if you know what's good for you, you'll just find your way outta here this instant."

Clinton didn't bother to look at her. Her words seemed to be cruel enough, without having to look at her face too. So, with coin pouch in hand, he left graciously and virtually empty-handed.

For some reason, the idea of walking away with almost nothing didn't affect him. The only thing that really concerned him was getting out of his nightmarish marriage to Margene. But on the other hand, she wasn't so eager to end it. Other than acquiring the position of Judge in the town of Stoweville, her marriage to him was the only thing that was decent and worthwhile in her life.

"I can't believe he's wanting to leave me."

Margene stared out the window and watched him walk to his truck. For a brief moment, she let her guard down and acted in a manner that most anyone would in her position. She began to cry. Her eyes were so full of tears, that her view of Clinton soon became a blur.

When she heard his truck crank, she opened her tear-stained eyes and formed a frown on her face.

"Well, we'll see who's leavin' who."

As Clinton backed out of the yard, the names of every lawyer he knew began racing through his mind. Obviously, Guy Saunders was out of the question.

And given the fact that his attorney would more than likely be battling Saunders, he would need to find a real dandy to represent him.

He made his first stop at the office of Clive Parker, Attorney at Law. Mr. Parker was considerably the next best thing to Saunders. He figured his chances of getting a reasonable and fair divorce settlement were good with Parker on his side.

He walked in, and after apologizing for not having an appointment, sat down and began to tell his story.

Parker listened patiently.

"Uh huh," he said.

The lawyer put both hands on the edge of his desk and pushed himself up from his chair.

"Can't take the case. There's simply too much muddy water involved. And, believe you me, I do sympathize with you. I really don't know what to tell you, Mr. Lee. But I suppose that I should be brutally honest here. I don't think there's an attorney in this town who wants to get involved in a contest against your ex-wife to be, and Guy Saunders. Let me tell you, I know what a conniving woman Margene Lee is. I know first hand. Do you know, I believe that woman has an agenda to dig half the graves of everyone in this town. Nope. Can't take it."

Clinton's confidence began to dwindle.

"The only thing I could suggest to you, Mr. Lee, is to retain an out-of-town lawyer. One who isn't fazed by Stoweville's politics. You may as well get used to the idea of dealing with out-of-towners, anyway. If I had to guess, and I'm probably right in assuming this, your wife is not going to give you a peaceable divorce. She'll fight you tooth and nail for everything she can. So you'll most likely go before a judge. I'd be shocked it you settled this out of court. You are aware that any judge likely to be appointed to you will be an out-of-towner, aren't you?"

Not knowing what else he could say to Clinton, Parker grabbed the paperweight sitting on his desk and began fidgeting.

Clinton, being no dummy, realized that their meeting was all but adjourned. So he politely shook the attorney's hand, thanked him for his time, and excused himself.

"Good luck," said Parker.

Clinton hurried to his car because he didn't want to waste any more time than he had already. He knew that Margene had made good use of her time pulling strings and doing just about anything to make sure that he was left helpless, penniless, and without legal representation.

He drove forty miles until he reached Groverton, a city comparable in size to Stoweville.

Everything there was unfamiliar to him. Given this fact, he did the only thing he knew to do. He winged it.

He parked his car downtown and walked around, keeping his eyes open for signs that read "Attorney at Law."

He had walked for all of twenty seconds before he stumbled upon what he was looking for. The sign read "Law Office of Burtus O'Kelley, L.L.D."

"L.L.D." said Clinton. "Maybe this fellow is worth checking out."

Though he knew nothing about this man called Burtus O'Kelley, L.L.D., he took his chances and made his way through the front door anyway. He sat in the waiting area for half an hour before O'Kelley even showed up.

"Sorry I'm late, Eloise," O'Kelley said to his secretary, rushing through the door with an untidy stack of papers tucked under his arm. "Oh, do I have a client meeting already?"

O'Kelley turned to look at Clinton.

"Well, don't just sit there. Come on into my office," he said.

O'Kelley was a short man with a giant voice. He spoke so fast that Clinton found it to be a challenge just to understand him. Nonetheless, the attorney did talk quite convincingly. Enough so that Clinton decided that he was the best lawyer for the job.

He began to tell O'Kelley his story.

"Now, let's go back a little bit here. I wanna get this straight. Your wife is the judge of Stoweville?"

He burst into a fit of laughter.

"Mr. Lee, you've gotten yourself into one fine mess."

Clinton gritted his jaw, as he was most uncomfortable with the attorney's behavior.

"What a pompous ass," he thought.

Indeed, O'Kelley was a pompous ass, but in a charming sort of way. He had a gift of making everyone like him, even in his crudeness.

"This has got to be the most interesting case I've seen. And I can honestly say that you've gotten my attention."

Clinton clued the attorney in on the rest of his story, then both men stood up.

"It's going to be a pleasure to have you for a client, Mr. Lee. Now it looks as though I've got some work ahead of me here, so.... no time like the present."

Back in Stoweville, Margene sat in Guy Saunder's office rehearsing her act. She explained to him how Clinton had threatened her life and how she needed to be out of "that God-forsaken marriage" as soon as possible.

"I'm afraid for the children," she said. "What if he tries to harm them?"

Saunders didn't know what had really taken place, but he had a slight hunch that she may have fabricated her version. Even so, Saunders was indebted to Margene Lee in a way that ran thicker than blood. So, as much as he despised representing her, it was his obligation to do so.

"I wanna see to it that the children are well taken care of, Guy. I don't know if you are aware of this, but did you know that Clint saved every penny he earned while he was in the service? Can you believe that the entire time he was supposedly fightin' for our country, it was me who was takin' financial responsibility of the young 'uns? Have you ever heard of such, Guy? I think you outtta see to it that Clint takes responsibility of the children's financial upbringin' from here on, wouldn't you agree? Not to mention all them doctor bills that I had to dish out when poor little Earl caught himself on fire."

Saunders rolled his eyes, disgusted.

"I'll do everything I can," he said.

Gleaming with delight, she walked out.

"Good Lord," he said. "If I wasn't experiencing it myself, I'd never believe it. How in the world does that bitch manage to have such control? Damn, I hate her!"

He walked over to his office door and peeked out through the crack. He wanted to make absolutely certain that Margene wasn't still lingering about. Once he saw that the coast was clear, he walked back over to his desk.

"DAMN! I HATE HER!" he yelled.

He worked meticulously for the next several days, planning out every detail of the divorce trial. But unbeknownst to him, Margene had concocted something of her own. She had worked nearly as ardently on the case as he had. But unlike Saunders, she had decided that legal hoopla wasn't enough. She had to take it that extra mile by planning not only to take every bit of Clinton's money, but every bit of his self-esteem too. And she had chosen to use her young son Earl to do it.

"Now, cry like you mean it, Earl," she said to her son.

"Why, Mama?"

"Don't you be questioning your Mama, Earl. Do you want me to take a switch to you?"

Earl's eyes got very big and round.

The small child was deathly afraid to get a switch beating from his mother. He knew that she and her switch were to be taken very seriously.

Trembling, he looked up at her. "No, Mama. I don't want a switchin'."

"Well then, you'll do what you're told."

"Yes, Mama."

"Now, let's see if you remember everything I told you. What are you gonna do when you see your daddy in that big courtroom?"

"I'm gonna start cryin' and screamin'. Like I did when I got all those burns on me."

"That's good, Earl. Now what else did I tell you to do?"

"Come runnin' to you and crawl in your lap? Is that right, Mama?"

"My goodness, you have certainly turned out to be an intelligent little boy. You remembered everything just like I told you. Now, don't you forget it. Go on out and play, now."

Earl went outside, and Margene proceeded to get on with her so-called important things.

An hour had passed. Then the phone rang.

"Yes, hello?"

"Margene, we've got a court date lined up," responded Saunders on the other end of the line.

"Well, let's have it."

"It's set for August the twelfth, which is two weeks from tomorrow."

"Now, let me think for a minute. Will that give us plenty of time to prepare? I mean, I do plan on walkin' out of this marriage with everything."

"Margene, relax, there's no need for you to get yourself in a frenzy. We've got all our bases covered. All right?"

"Okay then," she said. "Well, give me some of the specifics. Who's been appointed judge for this affair?"

"Gus Mosely. Do you know him? He's judge in Groverton. But listen, I do need to inform you of something, but it's not anything for you to get concerned about."

"Why do I get the feeling that whatever it is you're gonna tell me is something I don't wanna hear?"

"Just listen, damn it! It appears that Clinton has retained a lawyer in Groverton."

"What? Do you mean to tell me that this case has been rigged? How in God's name could you let a disaster like that happen?"

She continued her yelling until Saunders couldn't take it anymore.

"Excuse me,"he said. "Could you hold on for just a minute?" Saunders laid the phone down. He kicked the waste basket sitting beside his desk as hard as he could, then picked the phone back up.

"Okay, now, where were we? Oh, yes. I know Gus Mosely from some of my dealings. And one thing that I know for certain is that he is very fair. He's not one who can be persuaded in his decision making. Believe me, I've tried it myself. The man has always delivered an unbiased verdict. And as far as I'm concerned, Margene, there's not a chance in hell that you won't get exactly what you want. I've already consulted with Clinton's lawyer. His name is Burtus O'Kelley. He does seem to have all his ducks in a row, but let me just say, he ain't no match for Guy Saunders. So, with that having been said, you just need to carry on like you normally do, and stop wasting your time being anxious over this mess."

"I'll do as I see fit, Guy."

"Have it your way."

The two hung up their phones at exactly the same time. There were no goodbyes said. But they both knew the conversation was over.

Back in Groverton, O'Kelley was preparing his debate for the case. And he did so in what he considered to be a legitimate manner. But he also convinced himself that if pure facts weren't enough to gain the judge's favor, he'd have to rely on the second best thing. His salesmanship.

CHAPTER FIVE

Burtus O'Kelley was indeed a remarkable salesman. He could've sold domestic rifles made in Yugoslavia to the President of the United States. So when all else failed, he relied on one particular theory: "Mouth Over Matter."

It seemed to work quite well for him. So much, in fact, that he was fixed on the idea that he would be the first ever to defeat the "Ace."

"Ace," he mumbled. "We'll see who the Ace is."

The over-confident attorney called out for his secretary.

"Eloise, bring me those journals that I told you about."

She hurried into his office with a load of law books.

"Here they are, Mr. O'Kelley. This case must be real important."

"Why do you say that, Eloise?"

"Because I don't think I've ever seen you put so much work into a divorce trial."

"Let me explain a thing or two to you, Eloise. When you're fighting in a battle, and your opponent has never been defeated, and I mean never, it makes you have a tendency to prepare yourself as much as possible. Now that's not to say that your opponent won't ever be defeated. Because there's always a first time for everything. But the bottom line is, you don't stand a chance unless you're prepared. Does that make sense to you, Eloise? Eloise? Are you paying attention to me?"

During his mind-boggling explanation, she had briefly begun staring off into space.

"Eloise, you all right?"

"What? Oh, umm, yes, I'm fine. I think I might of had a bit of a dizzy spell, or something."

"For a minute there, I was about to get concerned. Why don't you go and take a break for a little while. It would probably do you some good."

"If you insist."

"Oh, I insist! I can't go around having a secretary who drifts off on me. We need all the brainpower we can get in this office."

She walked out, slightly embarrassed.

"Now, where was I?"

As the day progressed, O'Kelley eventually lost track of time. Even when dawn began to shine through his window, he didn't seem to notice. He was so absorbed in his own little world of debates and cross examinations that if it weren't for the growling of his stomach reminding him that it was way past dinnertime, he would've been at his desk all night.

"Good gracious, stomach. Are you trying to tell me something? What time is it, anyway?"

He reached down in his pocket, and squirmed around till he was able to locate his pocket watch.

"One-forty-five! For Heaven's sake. Where on earth did the time go? Guess I'll call it a day. There's no tellin' what folks would think if they saw my light still burnin' at this hour. They'd probably think I was up foolin' around with my secretary or something. Glad I'm not a married man."

The next day he showed up at his office door bright and early. Never mind the fact that he didn't get an ounce of sleep. After making his way inside, the first thing that he did was make a phone call to his client.

Clinton had been lodging at an inn in Groverton. He found it to be the most suitable place of residence, given the fact that it was conveniently located less than a quarter mile from his attorney's office. It was also far enough away from Stoweville that it allowed him the freedom to come and go as he pleased, without the possibility of Margene knowing his whereabouts. There were no phones in the rooms of the inn. The sole telephone was located at the front desk, with the inn clerk.

As the phone at the inn began to ring, the clerk immediately answered and said, "A good morning to you. This is the Main Street Inn of beautiful, downtown Groverton. What may I do for you today?"

"I need to locate one of your guests," replied O'Kelley. "His name is Clinton Lee."

"I'd certainly be happy to help you, sir. May I inform Mr. Lee who is trying to reach him?"

"Burtus O'Kelley. Mr. Lee is my client."

"Your client? I'll certainly page him this instant."

The clerk headed up the hardwood staircase then walked down the dimly lit hallway until he reached room number twelve.

Clinton, who was awakened by the knocking, called out, "One minute, please."

Wearing only his trousers and undershirt, Clinton quickly grabbed a shirt to put on.

"Where in the world did I put my shoes?"

He looked around the room, then remembered that they were under the bed. "Here they are," he said, lifting up the bed skirt.

Stumbling to the door while he tied his shoes, he called out again, "I'm coming."

He was out of breath by the time he made it to the door, so he just stood there and smiled.

"Hello there, Mr. Lee," said the clerk. "I'm terribly sorry to inconvenience you at such an early hour, but it seems you have a caller. He's waiting on the telephone, right now as we speak."

"How long have they been waiting?"

"Oh, I'd say a good five or six minutes."

"It's my attorney, isn't it?"

"Yes, sir, it is. So what sort of business do you have with your attorney? I mean, it's not too often that we have guests in our inn who receive telephone calls from attorneys."

It was quite obvious to Clinton that the clerk was desperate to know a good bit more information than was necessary, but he managed to act as polite as possible.

"Oh, it's just some minor legal matters," he said. "Nothing that would be anything more than a bore to a fellow such as yourself. I picture you as the type who likes a little excitement."

The clerk, who was somewhat of a nerd, blushed. "Oh, yes sir, you've figured me out."

The two walked down the hallway and headed down the stairs to the telephone.

"Mr. O'Kelley, are you still there?"

Irritated by his wait, the attorney began to spout off.

"Mr. Lee, we don't have time to pussyfoot around here. What in the world took you so long? Having trouble buttoning your garters? For Christ's sake, I know it doesn't take a man that long to dress himself and go retrieve a phone call!"

Clinton was insulted. His manhood had been challenged.

"Now, you listen here. No man talks to Clinton Lee like that! I don't give a damn who he is. Are your hearing me loud and clear?"

"Well done," said O'Kelley. "That's the man we need to have in court. One who won't be intimidated by a little finger pointing. Some aggressiveness won't hurt you either. But not too much, though. Clinton, you need to prepare yourself for just about anything because your wife and her attorney are gonna throw every curve ball at you that they can. Now, why don't you get over to my office so we can work out a few particulars."

"You're about as conniving as Guy Saunders."

"Listen, whatever it takes to get you motivated."

"I'll be over in a few minutes."

He hung up the phone and a few minutes later appeared in O'Kelley's office.

"Good, you're here. Now, here's what we have to work on."

Clinton slid a chair from the corner of the room right in front of his desk and sat down, hovering over the mess of papers in front of him.

"This bunch, over here, deals with the welfare of your children. Now, I know that you intend to take your share of financial responsibility. Basically, what it boils down to is that if you and Margene have joint custody, you'll both be responsible for Earl and Earlene's expenses. That's pretty standard in divorces. I don't expect any surprises pertaining to that. Now, where I do expect all the curve balls is when it comes to Margene herself expecting more than she deserves. To put it bluntly, she'll take everything you have, if you let her."

"I believe she's already done a good job of that. I'm not even allowed to go in my own house to get my belongings. The only thing I've managed to get my hands on is my coin collection. And knowing her, she'll probably go after that too."

"Don't be so negative, now. What we need to focus on is a positive outcome to all this. The truth of the matter is that Margene threatened your life. Unfortunately, though, we can't prove that."

"I'm gonna end up without a pot to piss in, aren't I?" Clinton scooted his chair away from O'Kelley's desk and walked over to the window. The rage in his face was apparent.

"Okay, Lee, that's enough You have one of two choices. Work with me and you get what's yours. Don't work with me and you get nothing. Which is it gonna be?"

Clinton hesitated for a minute. "All right. Show me what you've got."

"Now, going back to what I said earlier, there's no way you can prove that Margene threatened your life. I don't suppose either of your children witnessed it, or you would've told me. Not that they would be very credible witnesses, anyway. But the fact of the matter is this. She can't prove anything on you, either. Her word against yours. Given that, I think you're in fair shape here. What we're going to claim to the Court, is irreconcilable differences. The mere fact that you can't be accused of any wrong doings means that you can walk out of the marriage with what you walked in with. Does that sound suitable to you?"

"I can live with that."

"Good. Now, I can focus my attention on any unnecessary garbage that Guy Saunders has in store for me. Most divorce cases of this nature are cut and dried. But this one is different. I have a feeling he'll try and create sour grapes, if you know what I mean. Now, as for you, go spend some time relaxing. Do something you enjoy. The worrying is my job."

"I'll do my best."

"So, I'll see you in court in three days," said O'Kelley. "Actually, why don't you meet me here at eight-thirty on the morning of? We can ride together."

"All right."

On his way down the sidewalk, he began to think. "I don't have a decent thing to wear to court, since all my good clothes are at the house. I think maybe I should buy myself a new suit."

He continued walking till he spotted a sign that read "Nalley's Tux and Tailor." As he walked in, a gentleman walked from behind the counter to greet him.

"You Nalley?"

"Yes sir, I am."

"I need a nice suit to wear to an important occasion."

"Well, you've certainly come to the right place. Browse around a bit, why don't you? Then if we need to take your measurements, we can."

Clinton spent half the afternoon in that men's shop, and by the time he walked out, he had a handsome suit draped across his arm.

For the next two days he tried his best to relax, but he just couldn't manage to. He read newspapers, fumbled through a few books, but nothing seemed to cure his anxiety.

Finally, he decided that he would just sleep the rest of the time.

The clerk from downstairs woke him once, being the inquisitive busybody that he was.

"I've got an important trial coming up," he told the clerk. "Just do me the honor of giving me some peace and quiet, so that I can get some rest?"

"Well, forgive me, sir, but I noticed that you hadn't stepped foot out of your room the entire day. I only wanted to make sure that there was nothing wrong."

"Take a good look at me," said Clinton. "Do I look fine to you? Well, do I?"

"I....I...." the clerk stuttered. "I just thought you might like to come out for a breath of fresh air."

Clinton stood in the doorway of his room and stared angrily at the clerk.

The pencil thin young man looked back at him with wide bashful eyes and hesitatingly said, "Not even one small breath of fresh air?"

"Go away!"

The inn clerk darted down the hall as fast as he could.

There were no more interruptions for the rest of his two day nap.

CHAPTER SIX

Clinton woke up at seven forty-five on the morning of the trial. His heart immediately started to thump. Still uneasy, he feared it would be a day that would end in disaster.

He wanted to trust his attorney's confidence that the case would be a successful one. But down deep, his intuition told him that something was going to go wrong.

As he began to clean himself up, he began thinking about his atrocious behavior toward the poor inn clerk.

"What in Heaven's sake was I thinking? That poor little runt must be terrified of me. I definitely owe him an apology. I guess Margene has the talent to bring out the worst in people, whether she's around or not."

As he dressed himself, his hands began to tremble. He felt butterflies fluttering in his stomach, almost to the point that it was nauseating to him. Clinton was undeniably experiencing his first panic attack.

"What's happening to me?"

He walked over to his bed and lay down to take several deep breaths. Then he closed his eyes and began to pray.

"Dear God, please grant me the strength to make it through this day. I know that I haven't lived a perfect life, and I don't know if this is your way of punishing me. If it is, all I ask is that you have a little mercy on me. I know that you will do what's best for me. Just help me to remember that."

He opened his eyes and began to feel a calmness throughout his body. "Thank you, God."

Eight-fifteen rolled around and he headed out the door. When he reached the lobby, the clerk was nowhere to be found.

"Gosh, I hope I didn't scare him out of a job."

He looked around but never saw him, so he gave up and headed for O'Kelley's office.

When he got there, he found that O'Kelley was more than ready to go. He had parked his car in front of his office, and was there sitting behind the steering wheel with the engine running. At first Clinton didn't recognize the car, much less who was in it, so he simply walked around it.

O'Kelley rolled his window down. "Lee, what are you trying to do? Make us late?"

"Oh, it's you."

"Of course it's me. Well, what are you gonna do? Stand there all day? Get inside, for Pete's sake."

Clinton opened the door and took a seat. He was barely able to close the door before O'Kelley stomped on the accelerator.

"What time is it? About eight-twenty?"

"Maybe. But what does that matter? Hasn't anyone ever told you that the early bird gets the worm?"

Clinton rolled his eyes.

"So, are we gonna win this thing?"

"Did you hire Burtus O'Kelley?"

He didn't respond to the question in a matter of words. He just quietly nodded.

"Well, that's what I thought," he said.

The trip to the courthouse took about five minutes, so needless to say, the two men arrived before the front doors were opened.

"We'll just sit here for a while and wait. Is that all right with you, Lee? Now, I'm gonna explain something very important to you. It is absolutely crucial that you conduct yourself in a manner that is not only strong, but a wee bit humble. What you're after is getting the judge to like you. So what you need to do is act modest. Show the judge that you aren't here to fight a battle, but are simply here for justice on your behalf."

"That's exactly why I am here, O'Kelley."

"I know that and you know that. But does Judge Gus Mosely know that? That's what you need to concentrate on."

"All right. I guess my only question to you now is, do I need to be on the lookout for any cruel or unusual surprises?"

"Lee, just be the straightforward man that you are, keep your thinking cap sharp, and tell your story the way that it happened. Remember, you aren't the one at fault here. You haven't done anything wrong. Think positive, and everything should turn out fine. Have a little faith in your old attorney. Can you do that, Lee?"

Clinton nodded.

The two men waited in the car until a guard in uniform opened the front door of the courthouse.

Given the fact that they were the first to arrive, O'Kelley took it upon himself to give Clinton a short tour of the place. After making their way inside, O'Kelley poked his head in the empty courtroom and pointed out to Clinton where they would be stationed during the course of the trial.

"See that table in the front, on the left? That's where we'll be sitting."

The hollowness of the courtroom made their footsteps on the hardwood floor echo, and Clinton began to get that nauseating feeling again as he made his way down the isle.

After they took their seats, O'Kelley flipped open his leather portfolio and rifled through his notes. Clinton sat with his hands under the table, so his lawyer wouldn't notice how badly his hands were trembling.

For the next several minutes the room remained silent, then the door was flung open.

It was Guy Saunders. He wore a grin on his face that could've put a laughing hyena to shame. For him, this day didn't represent his desire for winning Margene's case. It represented just one more day that he could add another digit to his win count. He noticed O'Kelley brushing over his papers as he walked past.

"You know a real lawyer don't need notes, don't ya?"

"Didn't they teach you in law school that 'smart' isn't the same as 'smart ass'?"

"That's good. I'll have to remember that one."

Somehow, the immaturity of both lawyers didn't make Clinton feel anymore at ease.

The guard, who had unlocked the courthouse doors earlier, walked in the courtroom from a side entrance. He walked through the room, slapping the concealed weapon strapped to his waist in a means to look intimidating.

Within a few minutes, the room began to fill with local townspeople who had nothing better to do with their time than to spend the day being entertained by anyone's life, but their own. The sound in the courtroom had gone from dead silence to noisy chatter.

Saunders checked his watch for the time. When he saw that it was five minutes until nine, he began to panic. He turned to scope the courtroom for his client, but no Margene.

"Where in the world is that woman?"

He wasn't the only one who noticed that she wasn't there. O'Kelley had been keeping a lookout for her too.

"Looks like your wife is gonna be a no show," he said.

" I don't think that I could be that lucky."

The ticking on the clock that was hanging on the wall at the rear of the courtroom became louder and louder as nine o'clock approached.

At one minute until, the bailiff entered the room and the guard took his position by the entrance.

Still no Margene.

When the hand struck nine, the bailiff stood to introduce the judge to the court. Everyone there stood in honor of Gus Moseley as he entered the room.

"Be seated," he said.

Saunders turned around, yet again, to see if he could spot his client. When he didn't, he immediately stood up and said, "Your Honor, it seems as though my client, Margene Lee hasn't arrived yet. I'm certain that there must be a terrible problem. You see, my client is the judge of Stoweville, and she is fully aware of the importance of timeliness in a matter such as this. May I ask, Your Honor, for a brief recess, until I get to the bottom of this?"

"I am completely aware of who your client is, Mr. Saunders. Your motion for a recess, I must unfortunately say, is denied."

Saunders plopped back into his seat.

"Mr. Saunders," said Moseley, "do you know what the absence of your client means to this court?"

"I do, your..."

He didn't even finish his statement before the courtroom doors flew open.

"Mr. Moseley, I'm terribly sorry for the delay," Margene said walking in.

"Mrs. Lee, you'll address me as 'Your Honor' as long as you're in my courtroom."

"Oh, forgive me. I guess I'm just not used to addressing other folks of my significant ranking."

"Do you have some sort of excuse for your tardiness?"

"I do, Your Honor. My boy took ill late last night, and I spent all evening and the better part of the morning trying to doctor him back to health. He's much better now, though, thank the good Lord. He's actually here with us today. But I told little Earl to sit out on the front steps for a while. I thought the fresh air might do him some good."

"Sit down, Mrs. Lee. You've wasted enough of the courts time, I believe."

"What in the world was that cockamamie story all about," whispered Saunders after Margene slid beside him.

"I'm supposed to give the right kind of impression, aren't I?"

"What kind of impression do you think you made by walking in late?"

"Well, now the judge thinks I'm a good mother, silly."

"Uh, huh."

About that time, Moseley cracked his gavel.

"This court is now in session."

"Your honor, I'd like to call my client to the stand," said Saunders.

Margene stood up and walked as sassy as she could toward the witness stand. After she swore to tell the truth, the whole truth, and nothing but the truth so help her God, she cleared her throat and gave her attorney a confident smile.

"Could you please state your name to the court?"

"Of course. My name is Margene Lee. But I believe most everyone already knows that."

"There's no need to elaborate. Just answer the questions, pure and simple."

"Well, all right."

"Now, can you explain to the court why we are here today bringing your divorce case to trial?"

She pointed her finger to Clinton and said, "It's because that man threatened my life."

"Objection, Your Honor," said O'Kelley. "There is no evidence to support Mrs. Lee's comment."

"Well, there is one witness," spouted Margene.

"Overruled," Moseley said.

Saunders continued.

"Why don't we back up a little bit here. Now, you pointed your finger at someone who you claim threatened your life. Can you state the name of the person to whom you are referring?"

"I most certainly can. His name is Clinton Lee, my soon to be ex-husband."

"So what exactly do you mean by the term 'threatened'?"

"Well, that's simple. He grabbed me and held a knife to my throat, telling me that if I ever left him, he'd kill me. And that was after he'd picked a fight with me."

"Objection!" said O'Kelley. "Where is the so-called witness to support this accusation?"

"Your Honor, may I have a moment to consult with my client?" asked Saunders.

Moseley looked at Margene, who was clearly trying to win his support.

"This court is already behind schedule, but I am interested in seeing what kind of witness Mrs. Lee is able to produce. You have two minutes."

"Thank you, Your Honor."

O'Kelley gave Clinton a look of concern.

"What do you know about this?" he asked.

"Absolutely nothing. There wasn't anybody in the kitchen that night. Nobody."

"Well, maybe she's pulling one of her usual stunts. Who knows?"

"I just don't know how she thinks she's gonna be able to pull this off."

So while Saunders was quietly consulting with Margene, Clinton and his attorney were busy being thrown for a loop.

"Margene, you'd better have something good hiding up that sleeve of yours," whispered Saunders. "Otherwise, you re gonna make me look like a complete fool."

"Don't worry. My witness is waiting outside on the steps."

Saunders paused for a moment.

"You don't mean..."

"Yep!"

"Absolutely not."

"Yeah, it's perfect. Trust me, I have all this planned out to a T."

The thought of Margene making him look like the courtroom dunce made Saunders twitch. Reluctantly, he agreed to let her proceed with whatever it was that she had planned.

"Your Honor, it seems as though we do have a witness present today who can testify to the threat made by Mr. Lee. I do have a few more questions for my client, though."

"Well then, let's carry on," said Moseley.

O'Kelley looked at Clinton, noticing how jittery he had become since Margene had taken the stand.

"You okay?"

Clinton was so wound up that he couldn't speak. He just sat watching Margene while she continued to answer questions. His heart began to beat rapidly, to the point that he broke out into a sweat. He had experienced most all of her shenanigans before, but never had he felt so ultimately betrayed by her. O'Kelley, however, seemed to be intrigued by the whole thing. He was anxious to see who Margene had brainwashed into backing up her bogus story.

"Your Honor, I don't have any questions for Mrs. Lee at this time," he said. "I'm ready to meet the mysterious witness."

"As well as I," said Moseley.

As Margene excused herself from center stage, Saunders said, "I need a moment to retrieve my next witness."

"Very well."

Saunders then made his way outside, where he found Earl sitting all alone on the steps.

"How you doin' there, buddy?"

"Fine. Who are you?"

"You don't know? Why, I'm the one who's helping your mother. What I want to do today is ask you some questions in front of a very important man. He's called a judge. Just like your mother. She's a very important person too. So when we go into that big courtroom, you just say everything that your mother told you to, and you'll do just fine."

Saunders reached down and grabbed his hand to lead him inside, where everyone had begun to whisper amongst themselves.

When Saunders and his young witness entered the room, he said, "Your Honor, I'd like to present my next witness, Earl Lee."

CHAPTER SEVEN

veryone turned to look at young Earl Lee, Clinton included. There were gasps and "Oh My's" from the crowd when they saw the little boy who would be the rap on his father.

Clinton suddenly felt dizzy, so he ducked down in his chair. He knew instantly that his intuition about the day ending in disaster was accurate. There was something stirring in him that he'd never quite felt before. Perhaps it was the thought of the son he loved so much turning on him. But whatever the case, he was certain that this was only the beginning, and things were sure to get worse.

Saunders and Earl walked slowly through the mass of faces that filled the room. Earl was completely overwhelmed by the experience. Being only accustomed to the sheltered world that he lived in with his immediate family, this was the first time he had ever seen so many people. He was genuinely spooked. Everyone there appeared to be a giant, in comparison to his small, child-sized frame.

When he and Saunders were almost to the witness stand, he failed to see his so-called father seated to the left. Margene was responsible for that. She made eye contact with him and gave him secret hand signals that she had taught him. So, the scared little boy wasn't able to tear his eyes away from his mother once he saw her.

Saunders bent over to Earl and spoke softly.

"We're gonna have you sit up here in this big chair. But don't you get scared, because I'll be close to you the whole time, all right?"

Earl didn't make a response. The whole situation just seemed so confusing for him.

After Saunders had helped him to his seat, Margene again, stole his attention. She gave him a look that instantly removed any and all confusion that he may have had. It was the look that she gave him before every switching he'd ever gotten. So without any doubt, he was instantly able to remember what she had not only taught him to do and say that day, but what she had taken great pleasure in expecting of him, as well.

Moseley leaned over toward Earl.

"Hello there."

Earl was still locked in a stare with his mother.

"Hello," he said again. "Can you look at me for a minute, son?"

About that time, Margene gave her son a cue to look at the judge. He turned his head and stared at Moseley bashfully.

"How you doin'? You're a brave little lad for coming up here in front of all these nice people."

Moseley gave him a big grin.

"I promise this won't take too long. Now this nice man here is gonna talk to you for a minute, then you'll be able to go down and sit with your mother."

Moseley nodded at Saunders. Earl managed to make eye contact with Saunders for a mere second, then they wandered back over to his mother again.

No one in the room was able to see that Margene was making her secret gestures since she was sitting up front. That included Moseley. His eyes were completely glued to Earl.

Margene opened her lips and began mouthing certain words to Earl. The show was about to begin. She pointed her finger over to Clinton. It was then that Earl finally saw him. At first he sat motionless in his seat. Then he began to shake in a nervous fit. His behavior was phoney, but no one else seemed to be aware it. They were all just taken in by the boy's obvious display of nervousness.

He continued on with his routine, which got progressively more outlandish.

"No, no, no!" he screamed. "Please don't let him hurt us! He's gonna hurt us! Please don't let him do it anymore."

Moseley was flabbergasted. All he could do was look at Clinton with a demeaning expression.

Saunders walked toward Earl and said, "Son, are you okay?"

"Mama, I'm scared," he said, looking at Margene.

"Calm down, Earl," said Saunders. "Tell me something. Are you afraid of your daddy?"

"I'm scared of daddy. He's gonna kill us."

Everyone in the room suddenly began chattering amongst themselves. The ruckus became so loud that Moseley found it necessary to crack his gavel several times.

"What in God's name, is going on here? This isn't a three ring circus. This is a court of law, and anyone who wishes to remain in my courtroom will act with proper behavior."

The noise then softened.

"Son, nobody in this courtroom is going to hurt you. We're just going to ask you a few questions. You're not scared of me, are you?"

Earl nodded no.

"You're not scared of Mr. Saunders here, are you?"

Nodding again, Earl gazed over at Saunders with a pitiful expression that Margene had taught him to concoct.

"I hope you will trust me," said Saunders. "I'm your friend. I don't want you to be scared. Now, does your daddy frighten you?"

Earl began to shake again.

"Why don't you tell me what your daddy did to make you so scared of him."

"I'm too scared to say," he replied.

About that time, O'Kelley intervened.

"Your Honor, I hardly think you could classify this boy as a credible witness. I believe that he may have possibly been coached by his mother, considering the outrageous behavior we have all witnessed here. I'd like to request that we dismiss Earl Lee and get to the important issues. Your Honor, this is not a murder trial, and we shouldn't treat it as such."

"Objection," said Saunders. "I do agree that this situation is unusual, but I believe Earl Lee can inform this court of the behavior that took place in the home. With the information that he is able to provide, we can determine whether Mr. Clinton Lee can have custodial rights. We can also determine what financial responsibilities Mr. Lee will render to my client if he is declared to be an unfit husband."

"I'm in agreement with Mr. Saunders," said Moseley. "Though our witness is a little younger than what we're normally accustomed to, his testimony is pertinent to my final decision."

"Yes, Your Honor," said O'Kelley.

"I can't believe this is happening," he whispered to Clinton. "Your wife is one more piece o' work. It's as clear as day that she told that boy what to say. I've never, in my life, seen a child act in such a manner."

"I've gotta be honest with you," whispered Clinton. "I'm feelin' some more kinda' nervous right now. It's almost like I can't breathe."

"Let's just wait and see what Earl's gonna say before you start getting too overwhelmed. It does appear to be a little on the bleak side, I know. But you never know what can happen. As the sayin' goes, 'It ain't over till it's over.' "

Saunders continued.

"What did your daddy do that made you so scared of him? Did he try to hurt your mother?"

Clinton watched, wondering how far things would go. He wondered if all his dignity would be lost.

And, as fate would have it, those were the last thoughts that would enter his mind that day.

His heart was beating so hard that it made his face flush. His temperature began to rise so quickly that his vision blurred. The beads of sweat dripping off his brow splattered onto his lapel, staining his new suit.

Earl never did get a chance to answer the question. When Clinton dropped sideways out of his chair and onto the floor, he immediately stole everyone's attention away from the witness stand. There were a few screams. And nearly everyone jumped up from their seat and rushed toward Clinton to see what had happened.

"Is he dead?" asked one gentleman.

"Just stay back!" yelled O'Kelley, crouching over him.

No one seemed to hear, though. Everyone began shoving and pushing in an attempt to get in front of the huddle that had formed around him.

"Stay back, I said!" he yelled again. "This man is not dead, but he's going to be if you all don't give him some breathing room."

With everything as out of hand as it was, Judge Moseley decided to take control of the situation. He walked down from his platform and over to the herd.

"Quiet down, everybody," he said.

It appeared that no one was interested in following any type of command, so out of desperation Moseley chose to go to the extremes. He instructed the court guard to fire his gun.

When it fired, everyone dashed out of the courthouse in fear. A few onlookers were left, though, along with Moseley, the attorneys, Margene, and Earl.

Margene looked over at her half dead husband.

"This court isn't being adjourned, is it?" she asked. "Surely you're not going to fall for this stunt, are you?"

Infuriated by Margene's tasteless lack of respect, O'Kelley yelled at her. "Why don't you just shut the hell up! You've done enough damage, don't you think? Right now might be a good time for you to leave. And take your little trained puppet there with you."

Those who were left all stared at Margene, hoping she would follow his orders.

"Fine," she said.

She grabbed Earl's hand and bitterly pranced out of the room.

"Can somebody help me get my client to a hospital, already?"

Moseley and Saunders both volunteered.

Once they got to the hospital, no one was able to explain to the doctor what had actually happened. All they knew was that Clinton had collapsed in the middle of his divorce trial.

"He did mention that he was having a hard time breathing," said O'Kelley.

"Well then, we need to get this man stabilized immediately," said the doctor. "You folks can mind yourselves in the waiting room, hmm?"

After being wheeled into the intensive care unit, Clinton was hooked up to various medical contraptions and IV's.

"Vital signs don't look too good," the doctor mumbled to his nurse. "His blood pressure is through the roof. They said this man was in the middle of a divorce trial? My goodness! That must've been one heck of a trial. Looks like Mr. Lee here was going through too much anxiety to handle. Yep, he up and had himself a heart attack, all right. It's lucky that he got here when he did. Much longer, and they could've gone straight to the coroner. Well, in any case, he'll be in our care for a while until he recovers. Why don't you go outside and tell the gentlemen waiting what's going on."

"How long will he need to stay here?" O'Kelley asked the nurse.

"It's hard to determine that right now. All I can say is that Mr. Lee won't be going anywhere until we feel that it's safe for him to leave. In the meantime, if you have any further questions, you can find me right down the hall."

"Thank you, miss. Listen, why don't you two just go on home." O'Kelley looked at the gentlemen accompanying him. "I'm sure you have other responsibilities to take care of. I'll stay here for a while to see if there's any improvement."

"You'll let us know if there's any change?" asked Saunders.

"I'll do it."

Since both Saunders and Moseley had ridden to the hospital in O'Kelley's car, they had no other choice but to walk back to the Groverton courthouse.

Several hours had passed while O'Kelley remained patient. He began rehashing the day's events and tried to convince himself that it was all just a bad dream. Watching a divorce trial turn into a serious tragedy was anything but normal.

By sundown, he began to nod off. The sound of his snoring caught the attention of the nurse, who rushed to nudge him awake.

"Sir, why don't you go home. It's getting late. I promise I'll give you a call if there are any changes."

As exhausted as O'Kelley was, it didn't take too much persuading to get him to leave.

Early the next morning, Saunders drove to Margene's house to accomplish two things. To bless her out, and to figure out what in the hell they were going to do next. When he knocked on the door, she answered it, a bit surprised.

"This is certainly unexpected. You don't normally make house calls do you, Guy?"

"You'll have to overlook my casualness this time, Margene. I think you and I need to get some things squared away while Clinton is still in the hospital."

"What's going on with him, anyway?"

"It seems that your beloved had a heart attack, and will more than likely be hospitalized for an uncertain amount of time. But that's beside the point. I need to know what was going on in that thick skull of yours, to bring your child in as a witness. And without telling me about it. Not a good move, Margene. I think you stirred up a bigger mess than what you were expecting. This little stunt of yours didn't help you out at all. Quite frankly, I believe it backfired on you. It doesn't take a genius to figure out that Clinton's little episode won him a great deal of sympathy. As a matter of fact, I'm under the impression that Judge Moseley might have already made a decision, with or without a courtroom wrapped around it. I already know that he'll discredit Earl's half-ass testimony. If for no other reason than because he never came out and gave any solid answers. Never mind the fact that he's not the brightest kid in the world."

"What's that s'posed to mean? That boy learned everything he knows from yours truely."

"My point exactly."

"How dare you come into my house and insult me like that. If you didn't owe me dearly, I'd just as soon have you taken out than look at you."

"Let's just get one thing straight here. I don't like you anymore than you like me. Has it ever occurred to you that I've become the devil's sidekick? Sometimes I think you spilling the beans on me would be a privilege. Then I wouldn't have to deal with you ever again. And I could tell the whole town every one of your dirty little secrets."

"Oh, come on now. You don't mean that."

"Don't test me, Margene. I'm just about tired of you."

"All right, all right. Let's hear what you came all this way to tell me."

Shaken and angry, Saunders had to take a few deep breaths before he was able to calm down enough to talk about what was originally on his mind.

"I'm gonna suggest that O'Kelley and I meet with Moseley and settle this thing out of court. You'll do more harm than good, I'm afraid, if you're within ten yards of Moseley. Plus, we don't want to sit on this thing too long while Clinton is recovering. The sooner we take action, the better. Now, first of all, a seed has already been planted in Moseley's mind that Clinton tried to harm you. And the fact that he ran out on the night in question makes him look a bit on the guilty side. Another thing that you may be overlooking is that you did put a restraining order on him. That doesn't make him look too innocent either. So just let me handle this the best way I know how. I'll come up with whatever I can to make sure that you come out of thing with your pockets overflowing."

"Don't you think I should be involved in this thing somehow?"

"Hmm, let me think about that for a minute."

Saunders paused for about two seconds.

"Nope."

"Well, shouldn't I at least..."

"Nope! Margene, the only thing I need from you is your approval to let me handle this without you!"

"Do you really think..."

"Yep!"
"Well, I guess that's that."
"That's that."

He called up Moseley to suggest that the situation be handled out of court. Moseley, being somewhat annoyed by the whole ordeal anyway, welcomed the idea.

When the three met to settle the case, both Saunders and O'Kelley had opposite ideas of how things should be handled. Saunders pulled his usual stunt of finger pointing and stretching the truth. On the other hand, O'Kelley stated the facts as he knew them to be.

By the time both were finished, Moseley was so confused that he jumped out of his chair and ran for the door.

"Fellas, I'll let you know my decision soon as my eyes uncross."

CHAPTER EIGHT

bout three days had passed since the meeting. Moseley hadn't uttered one word to either attorney.

"What do you mean you haven't heard anything?" O'Kelley yelled to Saunders during a phone conversation.

"I'm serious," said Saunders. "Judge hasn't tried to contact me even once since we all met."

"Well, if you ask me, this whole thing is totally absurd. You know the stuff your client is made of. The fact that you could even represent a piece o' work like that says a lot about you. And I'm not referring to the lawyer in you, either."

Saunders, having only half a conscience, let the words go in one ear and out the other.

"We'll see who goes home draggin' their tail between their legs," he said.

"You better believe it!"

O'Kelley slammed the phone down. Desperate to get his mind off things, he decided to swing by the hospital to check on Clinton.

He arrived and found the nurse who had admitted Clinton into the Intensive Care Unit. She happily reported that due to the improvement in Clinton's health, he had been moved to a different room and was now eligible to receive patients.

"Yes sir," she said. "He's already gotten a visit or two."

"For crying out loud, missy, you should've called somebody. I swear. You can't rely on anybody these days."

Brushing her off, he went in search of Clinton's new room.

He opened the door just in time to witness Margene trying to smother her husband to death with a pillow.

"What in the hell do you think you're doin' woman?"

"Oh, um, I'm just tryin' to fluff up poor ol' Clinton's pillow here."

In an effort to camouflage her attempted act of murder, she quickly jerked the pillow off of his face, and shoved it under his head.

"I just felt so bad for him after what he went through that I thought I'd try to come down and see about working things out in a more peaceable manner."

"You get away from my client." O'Kelley rushed over to the bed and pushed Margene aside. He helped Clinton into a sitting position so that he could catch his breath. As soon as it was apparent that he was able to breath, the lawyer turned around and looked at Margene.

"You're mine," he said.

Her hands began to tremble.

"You can't prove a thing," she said.

And just like anyone who is aware that they have been caught red handed, she ran out of the room as fast as she could.

O'Kelley attempted to run after her, but Clinton unexpectedly clinched onto his arm to stop him.

"Are you all right?"

"Let her go. Just please keep her away from me. She's a dangerous woman."

Clinton was barely able to mumble those few words. He was still very weak. Not to mention the strain that he had experienced from his near suffocation. As O'Kelley looked into his eyes, what he saw was a man who was genuinely full of fear.

"What do you want me to do?" he asked softly. "I can have her put away, if you want me to."

"Just give her what she wants."

"Do you know what you're asking me to do?"

He nodded.

"I really hate to do this, but if you're absolutely sure it's what you want..."

"It's time I had some peace."

"I think it's past time for that."

And that was the end of it. There would be no more battles to fight. O'Kelley was disheartened, to say the least, but as a lawyer it was his duty to satisfy his client.

Though he tried to hide it for Clinton's sake, the frown on his face was more than apparent.

Leaving the room, he began to search the halls until he found the nurse again.

"You need to check on our patient. I'd also like to ask that you monitor his visitors. Could you inform the other nurses to do that too?"

He looked her dead in the eyes.

"It's very crucial that you do this."

"Of course."

After he left, he began to obsess about the reaction Saunders would have once he got the news. He could visualize his pompous gloating as plain as day.

Poor Burtus O'Kelley. He just wasn't ready to raise the white flag. He knew, though, that the sooner he surrendered the sooner he could get the whole mess out of his mind. And the sooner he could go back to his former opinion of thinking that he was perfect.

So about six o'clock the next morning, he called Moseley to surrender.

Moseley had just woken when he received the call.

Standing in the middle of his livingroom, still in his long johns, he said, "O'Kelley, can't this wait until I've gotten to work? I mean, at least let me get a cup o' coffee in me."

"I'm afraid it can't wait, Your Honor. Something has come up, and I don't think I can keep it in much longer. We need to meet as soon as possible. I can't wait around till eight or nine o'clock."

"I'll call Ace," he said, yawning. "Now, for future reference, unless you're callin' to invite me huntin' or to play a hand o' poker or two, don't disturb me in my home again."

"So, I'll see you in an hour?"

Around seven o'clock, he walked into Moseley's office. Saunders was there waiting with bells on.

"Fellas, my client has agreed to settle. He has agreed to leave her everything."

"Your client what?" asked Moseley.

"He has."

There was a brief moment of silence between the three men.

"I do think that personal items Mr. Lee accumulated before his marriage remain in his possession, said O'Kelley. "I also believe that he is entitled to custodial rights. You both know that boy was put up to that ridiculous routine."

"Sounds fair to me," said Moseley. "Saunders, I believe I've had all I want of this case, so I'll leave the rest to you boys."

"I think my client will be most pleased to hear this," said Saunders. "Oh, and, by the way, you are aware that there is an insurance policy that you'll be handing over, as well?"

"I'm afraid so."

"Looks like we've got a busy day ahead of ourselves. And since I've got most of the pertinent files stashed at my office, why don't you follow me back there."

"Fine."

Saunders got up to leave, but O'Kelley stayed a moment longer to collect his belongings.

"It's funny. Sometimes things don't exactly turn out the way you expect, do they?" he said to the judge.

Moseley nodded.

"I know what you mean. I had planned to rule in favor of your client."

CHAPTER NINE

Clinton eventually recuperated back to normal health and bid farewell to the Groverton Hospital. He left broke, alone, and without a clue as to where he was going. He left happy, though. He was a free man. That alone made him feel like the wealthiest man in the world.

With all of the freedom that he now had, achieving a new and improved life was certainly a possibility. And what better place to start than with the family that he had been deprived of for so long.

His first stop was to his grandmother's house. When he drove up to the yard, it was as though he'd never left. Everything looked exactly the same, only more beautiful. Though the scenery hadn't changed, he had. So everything he once let slip into the past had now become a sight for sore eyes.

He hopped out of his truck and began walking through the yard. The smell of late summer filled the air. It was a scent of crab apples ripening on the trees and marigolds waving in the warm breeze. Clinton stood with his face to the sky and became intoxicated by the essence.

Sobriety hit with the sound of his grandmother's screen door flinging open. It made a distinctive creak, which also brought back fond and familiar memories.

Sadie Lee had heard Clinton drive up, so she hurried out of the house to greet him.

"Oh, my boy," she said. "I knew it was you. I'd recognize the sound of your truck anywhere. I've been thinkin' about you a lot lately, and now here you are. Tell me, how are the children? Better yet, how are you? And tell me about that God awful divorce trial? I heard it was a doozie."

"One question at a time, MaMa."

Clinton put his arm around her and walked her back to the house. They spent the next few days catching up on all the things that had happened since they had last seen each other.

It was a given too that he would make some time to visit his favorite siblings, Martin and Massey. Each had a great deal of hell to pay for the oh, so famous night they had coaxed him into making that first encounter with Margene.

"I don't think I'll ever forgive myself for that one," said Martin.

"Yeah, I've been struggling with it myself," added Massey.

Clinton placed a hand on the shoulder of each brother.

"Boys," he said, "I'm free from the old hag now, so consider yourselves forgiven."

For Clinton, those were more than just words. He really meant it. The way he saw it, the whole marriage thing to Margene was an enormous learning experience. And now, he could honestly say that he knew exactly what not to look for in a woman. What's more, he gained the wisdom to focus on his own happiness rather than letting it slide for the sake of someone who didn't deserve it in the first place. He had enough love in him to share it with someone. But for the time being, he simply wanted to go back in time and be that eighteen year old who was full of hopes and dreams. The one that existed before Margene. "B.M.," he called it. And though his heart attack had somewhat aged his twenty-five year old body, he was still young enough to start everything over from scratch if he wanted to.

While he was at Sadie's, he began trying to focus on what his next step would be. He began to humor the idea that he once had of becoming a banker. And why not? The sky was the limit, now.

One morning he got into his truck and drove to the Bank of Stoweville. He was wearing the suit he had purchased for his court appearance, sweat stains and all. But he wore it proudly, as though it were perfect.

"I'd like to see about getting a job," he said, walking up to one of the teller booths.

"One moment, sir. I'll see if I can find someone to help you."

The teller disappeared, then returned with a distinguished, middle-aged gentleman.

"What can I do for you, sir?" he asked.

"I was asking this young lady here about a job."

"Why don't you come to my office where we can talk more appropriately?"

Grateful, Clinton followed him.

"Come on in and have a seat," he said, opening the door.

He sat in one of the plush, velvet armchairs located near the desk. He was a little nervous, but managed to conduct himself with an amazing sense of confidence. Then he remembered that he hadn't yet introduced himself, so he stood back up and reached out to shake the gentleman's hand.

"Let me introduce myself. My name is Clinton Lee. I am recently divorced from the honorable Margene Lee. I lost just about everything that I ever had. And right now, I'm here in your office asking for a job because I have absolutely nothing to lose."

It wasn't exactly the opener that the gentleman had expected.

"I did hear mention of our judge having involved herself in one more hell of a divorce trial. So you're the one. You know, I'm not really interested in all that. But I am flattered that you find me approachable enough to blurt out your personals."

He smiled at Clinton.

"Well, let me introduce myself. My name is Gordy Rutherford and this here is my bank. I opened this place thirty years ago when I was a little bit younger than yourself. I started with peanuts, boy, and I ended up with the whole damn farm. What I'm sayin' is that I worked long and hard, and it finally paid off. Now, tell me, do you have any experience with money? Other than slappin' it down on a poker table, I mean."

"Well, I can honestly say that the only experience I have with money is looking in from the outside of teller walls like these. I've owned a little bit of it. Spent some, too. Sir, to be completely honest with you, I've never held any kind of civilian job before. I served in the army for three years and then I became a family man so that my former wife could pursue her career. But, sir, I am a smart man and I'm eager to learn. I'll start at the very bottom and work my way up from there. I'll take any opening you have available."

Rutherford smiled again. "I'll be honest with you, son. At the time being, I'm fresh out of jobs." He stood up from his chair and slowly walked toward the door. Reaching out to open it, he looked at Clinton, who was preparing to leave disappointed.

"You can start today."

"I don't think I understand, sir. I thought you just stated that there weren't any jobs available."

"Well, yes, I guess I did say that. But that's not to say that I can't invent a new one, now does it?"

Rutherford patted him on the back.

"There's something I like about you, kid. I'm not sure what it is, though. But I think I'd like to see your face around here. So what do you say we go find somethin' useful for you to do?"

Overjoyed that he had made it to the bottom rung of the ladder of success, Clinton eagerly followed his new boss to see what his new career would be. "I already have one gofer, so we can't have you doin' his job. Hmm, let me see."

He stopped and looked over to the small utility room in the corner. "You know what? I have these large sacks of coins stashed away in that room there. You know, odd-ball coins. They're pretty useless, unless a person just has a taste for collecting things like that."

They walked into the utility room where Rutherford pointed out the sacks. There were four of them. Four canvas bags so full of coins that they would've been impossible for a soul to lift.

"I've been saving these over the last thirty years. I didn't really know what to do with them, so I just started my own collection in here. I doubt you can lift 'em, so don't worry with trying to maneuver 'em around. I bet they weigh a good four or five hundred pounds each. Mostly they're coins that are either out of circulation, or they're those aggravatin' foreign ones. Some people try to pull one over on you, by spending the foreign jobs as though they were U.S. Some of 'em do look a heap like the American ones...."

Not wanting to appear unappreciative of his new mystery job, Clinton tried to pull off a positive expression. He was a little turned off though, because he wasn't exactly sure what Rutherford was expecting him to do.

"Mr. Rutherford, what is it that I'm supposed to do here?"

"Well, for goodness sakes, son, what do you think? I want you to go through each and every one of these coins and put them into categories. I want all the ones out of circulation to be separated by year and size amount. The foreign ones, you can do the same thing with. Just separate these things. That's it for now. I'll figure out what to do with them when the time comes."

Clinton responded with a fake smile.

"One thing you'll learn about me, boy, is that I am one meticulous S.O.B."

Rutherford left the room. Clinton stared at the four sacks.

"This wasn't exactly what I expected."

But then he began to think about Margene. He thought about what it was like to listen to the sound of her voice. To eat a meal with her. To share the same bed with her. Then he looked at those four heavy bags and greeted them as though they were the best friends her ever had.

He took his jacket off and rolled his sleeves up. Then he got down on both knees and pulled the string to one of the bags. When he looked inside, what he saw was a mass of overwhelming monotony. There must have been fifty thousand coins.

He sat trying to figure out where he would place the individual piles of coins. And being somewhat meticulous himself, he decided to approach the situation by taking small scraps of paper and scribbling information about each type of coin: the date, amount, location of mint and nationality. He also noted any distinguishing markings.

By the day's end, Rutherford found him sitting in the middle of the floor surrounded by a circle of coin stacks.

"Well, I see you've made some progress," he said.

"Yes, I guess I have."

"I think you'll have this all done in no time. Now, when you come in tomorrow, plan on takin' some time off to eat a bite of lunch."

Clinton hadn't bothered to break for lunch. Somehow, he was a little more anxious to make a good first impression than to do something as petty as eating.

"Thank you. I'll keep that in mind," he said.

He stood up and looked over the circle. He payed particular attention to one of the stacks. It was such a small stack that it wasn't really a stack at all. It consisted of a single coin. He reached down to pick it up. It looked very familiar to him, but it didn't resemble any of the coins he had in his own private collection. So he studied it down to the tiniest scratch marks, then put it back in the circle.

Its image stayed on his mind for the remainder of the day, even on his way back to Sadie Lee's. But when he got there, the smell of home cooking pulled his focus away from it and on to more important matters. His stomach.

"Mmm, what you got cookin' Ma-Ma? A little yard bird?"

"Yeah, I found a special on chicken when I was at the market today. Thought you might like to eat somethin' good for supper."

"Are you kiddin'? Every supper you cook is nothin' but tasty."

"Go on and wash up, boy. Then you can set the table."

Clinton cleaned his coin-filthy hands, then hurried back to the kitchen. "Well," he said, "are you gonna ask me about my day?"

" 'Course I was. So what did you get into today? Obviously it was something pretty important given that good lookin' suit you're wearing."

"It was, MaMa. I've just gotten my first job since leaving the Army. And it's working at the Bank."

"Get out o' town! Boy, that's wonderful. So tell me, do you have one of those nice office jobs?"

Clinton was a bit hesitant to answer her, considering. "MaMa, the important thing to remember is that I got a job at the bank."

"Uh-oh. Don't tell me you're pushin' a broom around."

"No," he said laughing. "It's not that bad."

"Well, let's hear it. What is your new job?"

"You know, I really don't know the answer to that question. But today I worked with coins."

Sadie scooped the chicken pieces out of her cast iron skillet and placed them on a plate. She walked over to put it on the table, but didn't comment.

"To be honest with you, MaMa, what I did today was separate odd coins that nobody has a use for. I didn't do anything important. But the thing I'm trying to focus on here is that I got my foot through the door."

"If that's what makes you happy, then I'm happy for you."

On Clinton's second day of work, he arrived about twenty minutes early. The doors were still locked, so he waited on the back steps. A few minutes later, Rutherford drove up.

He looked at Clinton but hurried past him with no more of a greeting than tipping the brim of his fedora.

Clinton tried to be friendly by making small talk. "Boy, that sure is a beautiful automobile you're driving."

The man didn't as much as smile, but he did hold the door open for him.

"Brought my lunch today," he laughed, still hoping to get something out of him. Rutherford didn't budge.

Gosh, I wonder if he's changed his mind about me, he thought. Clinton walked to the utility room on pins and needles. He was disturbed by Rutherford's standoffishness, but was determined to do the best job he could while he still had a job. Even if it was insignificant. He got straight to work separating those coins. The familiar one he put aside, so he wouldn't lose track of it.

By lunch that determination seemed to have paid off, because he'd made it to the bottom of the first sack. He stopped only briefly to eat then went straight for his second sack. Hour after hour passed and without realizing it, the Bank had closed for the day. Yet there he sat, two hours after closing time in the middle of the floor, feeling mentally exhausted.

When he got up to leave, he didn't notice that everyone was gone until he tried to open the door, only to find it locked. Fortunately, he found another soul lingering about. It was the night watchman.

"Hi. You work here, I take it."

"Yeah. I watch after this get-up at night. You new?"

"Yeah. So new that I somehow managed to get locked in without realizing it."

The man laughed. "What'd you do, lose track of time? What's your name, anyway?"

"I'm Clinton. Clinton Lee."

"Nice to meet you. James Wiggins. But most folks call me Jesse. Well, here, I don't want to keep you. You're probably ready to get someplace."

He walked Clinton to the back door and let him out, then walked to over to Rutherford's office. Rutherford, it seemed was still there too.

"Looks like you got a night owl on your hands, Mr. Rutherford. And I thought you were the only one."

Rutherford nodded as he watched Clinton through the window.

The next couple of days consisted of the same routine. Clinton would arrive to work early and spend the day separating coins until he was completely finished with a sack. Rutherford kept up his act of indifference too. By this time, Clinton had become excessively paranoid about it, so by the time all the sacks were empty, he was a bit nervous to see what would be in store for him. He had run out of work to do, so he decided to walk around and browse at what he'd ignored during his first few days.

It was a beautiful bank. It had walls of oak and bold, dome-shaped windows inlaid with stained glass. The crystal chandelier hanging from the architectural ceiling looked like diamonds falling down from the sky. The giant sheets of mauve colored marble hanging on the wall matched the mauve and chestnut checked marble floors. It was undoubtedly a work of art.

He spotted a large globe sitting atop one of the tables in the lobby, and sat down beside it. He spun it with his thumb and watched as all the continents became a blur. When it stopped, he instantly fixed his eyes on the country of Korea. His mind went blank. Then his fact lit up.

"That's it!" he said. "That's where I've seen that coin before."

The odd thing was that the coin that had been eating away at his curiosity wasn't even Korean. It was German. He had seen one of his Army mates carry one identical to it. Clinton, being the coin fanatic that he was, had noticed it one day when his mate was sitting in his bunk polishing it. After inquiring about it, he found it to be peculiar in a special sort off way. Supposedly, it had circulated during World War I. It was recalled after only a few had been minted, because there seemed to have been an error in the production. On the tail side of it, the figure of the German flag had been imprinted rather than embossed. According to his buddy, the coin was very rare and worth a lot of money.

Of course, Clinton didn't know if the story was even true. And better yet, how did such a treasure end up at the Bank of Stoweville? But the mere idea of it seemed to give him a thrill. He began daydreaming about all the wealth it could bring.

Hearing footsteps behind him, he quickly snapped back to reality. It was Rutherford.

"Good morning, Mr. Rutherford. I'm just taking a peek around the place! I haven't really gotten a chance to until now. I've completed the job that you asked me to do. You know, the coins."

Rutherford was already aware that he had finished his task. And what was more, he was impressed by his timeliness. But as impressed as he was, he still kept his cool attitude of indifference.

"Let's go to my office. I think we need to have a little chat."

"Yes sir." Clinton smiled, but what he really wanted to do was ask him what the hell was wrong with him.

When they entered his office, Rutherford closed the door behind them. "Take a seat there."

Clinton sat down and leaned back in the chair. He wanted to ask why he'd spent the past four days doing the most ridiculous job he'd ever encountered. He wanted to ask his boss if he was pleased with the idea that he had an ache in his back from constantly stooping over, bruises on his knees from kneeling on the hard marble floor, and a twitch on his nerves for putting up with the annoying fact that his boss couldn't even crack a smile at him. But he didn't.

He just looked at Rutherford and said, "Talk to me. I am curious to hear what you have to say. After all, you have spent enough time keeping quiet. I don't know if you've changed your mind about hiring me, and just haven't figured out how to tell me, or what. I just don't know. But I sure would like to be clued in. I mean, I want to impress you by doing a good job, but all the silence has got to go."

Rutherford began to chuckle.

"What's funny? I don't think there's anything funny here." Clinton got irate.

"Calm down," he said. Don't get your shorts in a wad. I'm just amused at how defensive you are. I'll tell ya, that ex-wife of yours must have made a heck of a dent in your self-esteem."

Clinton looked down at his shoes. "You know, I guess you're right. I'll have to work on that. But tell me, why'd you call me in here?"

"It's pretty simple, actually. I've been watching you for these past four days, and I must admit there's never been one soul to walk through these doors whose loyalty has impressed me more. You took on a task that most people would walk away from. There might be a few people who'd tackle it for a little while, but you kept on. And I, for one, can't believe that you did it in four days. It would take anyone else two or three weeks."

"What's the point, Mr. Rutherford?"

"The point? The point is that I was testing you. I'd never ask anyone to do what you did unless I was interested in seeing what they were made of."

"I don't understand."

"Clinton, I've been looking for someone trustworthy, responsible, and intelligent enough to work along beside me. Someone who could fill the shoes of a Vice President."

Clinton's eyes lit up.

"Don't get too excited now. You're a far way from that. But you've impressed me, and I'd like to train you for that position. Do you think you might be interested in a job like that? I'll understand if you're not."

"Are you kiddin' me? Of course I am!"

"Well, keep in mind that you'll be working some pretty long, hard hours."

"It sounds perfect!"

"Then why don't we get started now? The sooner, the better."

Clinton beamed. But then got a puzzled look.

"Mr. Rutherford? If separating all those coins was just a test, what are you actually gonna do with all of 'em?"

"Beats me. I've been trying to figure out what to do with those useless things for years. I'm just about tempted to throw 'em away."

"Throw them away? If you're thinking about doing that, could I possibly keep a few?"

"Have 'em all, for all I care."

"You're sure?"

"Why not?"

Clinton smiled. He began daydreaming once again about that coin and all the wealth it could bring.

CHAPTER TEN

$\mathcal{A}$ few weeks had passed and the glitz of Clinton's prized coin began to fade. His job took up most of his attention. And what was left after that was spent relaxing. He enjoyed going to the secluded fishing hole that he went to as a boy. Eventually tangling bass became his favorite pastime. Indeed, he finally had the life that had been long overdue. There were a few things still missing, though.

For one, he didn't have a place that he could call his own. The room that he occupied at Sadie's wasn't exactly where he wanted to take root.

The other thing was that he missed the children. Somehow, the measly one day a month that Margene ever so generously agreed to allow visitation just didn't seem like a whole lot. And though she had completely distorted any normal concept they may have had of him, he loved them anyway.

In a nutshell, Clinton was happy and empty.

One day during his lunch break, he decided to take off in search of a place that he could possibly call home. Unfortunately, he found nothing but dead ends. There simply weren't too many possibilities for someone of his current financial means. He did come across a few affordable Room and Board situations, but after serious consideration decided that he was better off not returning to any kind of lifestyle that would remind him of his days at the Groverton Inn. Besides, he was a businessman now, and he needed to live like one.

He was in his office one afternoon, wrapping things up for the day, when he began talking to himself. Jesse, the night guard, had clocked in for the night shift, and inadvertently heard bits and pieces of what he was babbling.

"What am I gonna do? I've just got to get out of MaMa's and find me a place of my own. I hate it. I guess I'll just have to bite the bullet for a while."

"Huh hum." Jesse cleared his throat so that he could make his presence known. "Uh, you talkin' to somebody in there?"

Embarrassed, Clinton immediately clammed up.

"That's all right," Jesse snickered. "You ain't the first I've seen. But maybe for future record, you might outta consider lookin' around, just in case. To make sure nobody's a listenin'."

"Yeah, you got a point there."

"Sounds like you're havin' some trouble at home. From what I could make of it, that is."

"Oh, no. Uh-uh. It's nothin' like that. I just feel like I've outdone my welcome at the place I'm staying at now. You know what I mean."

"Yep. I know what you mean. So, how come you don't find some other place to stay?"

"It's a long story." Clinton went on to explain how he had to kiss all of his savings goodbye, and was basically giving up most of his current income to support the children that he had practically no custody of.

"Whoa, that's rough." Jesse shook his head. "Let me ask you something. How is it that a man such as yourself ends up in a mess like that? I mean, you seem like a nice guy and all."

"Bad luck is the only way I can explain it. But, you know, I've gotta be due for some good things to come my way, eventually. Hey, look at this job I have. Six months ago, you couldn't have convinced me that I'd be sittin' here in this office to save your life. I guess I outta be thankful, instead of complainin', right?"

"Naa. I don't have a lotta room to talk, myself." Jesse looked down at his watch. "Would you look at the time. You need to think about getting' on outta here, otherwise you may as well call this place Home Sweet Home."

Jesse moved out of the doorway, and disappeared down the hall. Clinton smirked at his comment, realizing he was right. He organized the papers on his desk into a neat stack, then grabbed his coat to leave. He walked to the back door, then reached in his pocket for his keys.

"Why don't you go check out the house on Old Jordan Road," Jesse called out from down the hall. "I hear it's up for sale."

"I might just do that."

Driving down the road, he began to humor the notion of taking a look down Old Jordan Road. *Naa, it's just one more thing to get disappointed about*, he told himself. So, he took his normal route back to Sadie Lee's.

When he came to a stoplight, he sat there trying to blow off the curious impulse he had to check it out anyway. It was as if there were a game of tug of war going on between his optimistic side and his pessimistic one. Should he go, should he not go?

His left foot began to tap, then he noticed the light turn green. Sitting there, he refused to press the accelerator. The car behind him began honking.

"Oh, what the heck?" Uncertain of whether it was a good idea or a bad one, he stomped the gas and made a U-turn.

He drove out of the city limits and through the countryside toward Old Jordan Road.

He wasn't familiar with the homes located on Old Jordan Road. But he had heard that it was a desirable location. A location he hesitated to believe that he could afford. That was all right with him, though. All he had to do was look at the house. No strings attached.

When he turned onto Old Jordan Road, he kept his eyes open for "For Sale" signs. The first house he approached was a beautiful antebellum estate with a well-groomed pasture occupied by horses. No "For Sale" sign, though. He drove further down and saw a house even bigger than the first one, with a stream running alongside it. Again, no "For Sale" sign.

"This is ridiculous. There's no way I could buy a house in this area. What in the world was that Jesse thinking? That smart aleck."

He continued on, rounding a sharp curve, then noticed a mailbox with a "For Sale" sign next to it. It was at the foot of a long driveway that was paved with flat stones. It stretched for a quarter of a mile through a healthy forest of hardwoods. When he reached the end, there stood yet another majestic home. It was crusted with the same flat stones that covered the driveway, and looked as though it had been plucked straight from the south of France. Even though he was fully impressed by its apparent beauty, he didn't get too excited.

As he got out of his truck, he heard the sound of water. He looked around, but didn't see any signs of a river. He walked up to the front door and proceeded to knock. A woman looking to be about in her sixties, opened it.

"Hello," she said.

"How do you do, ma'am? I was out in the area and thought I'd take a look at your house."

"Come in."

Clinton walked inside.

"My name is Clinton Lee."

"Mattie Arthur," she said. "So, you were out in the neighborhood?"

"Honestly? Well not exactly. A fellow I know recommended I come take a look."

Mattie called out for her housekeeper.

"Care for some tea?"

"Oh, I don't want to be any bother."

"Nonsense. Why don't you sit down for awhile and we can chat a bit. We can sit in this room over here." She led him into what she referred to as the Sitting Room, and poured some tea from her silver service.

"Now, what were you saying? You were in the neighborhood?"

"Ma'am, I'm going to be honest with you. A fellow that I work with mentioned that there was a house for sale here. But he obviously has the wrong impression of me, monetary speaking. You see, I have a job at the Bank of Stoweville, and I do plan to make my way to the top, but I'm afraid it's not going to happen any time in the near future."

Clinton hoped she was could understand what he was getting at. Somehow, though, she managed to overlook his point. She seemed more interested in Clinton Lee the man, than Clinton Lee the potential homebuyer.

"Working at a bank is a very noble profession. I'm sure you'll be very prosperous one day. So, Mr. Lee, are you married?"

Smiling, he said, "Funny you should mention. Divorced actually. But, I won't get into all that."

"Oh, please tell. At my age, what goes on in the world around me is the only thing that has much appeal anymore."

"I... really couldn't."

"Mr. Lee, you don't want to disappoint a little old lady like me, now do you? So tell me, who were you married to?"

Clinton hesitated. "Her name was Margene Wilkot. Now, she's known as The Honorable Margene Lee."

"What! That two bit hussy is a Judge?"

Clinton was a bit confused by her reaction. How could she not know that Margene was a judge? Everybody knew that. But, the even bigger question was how did she know that Margene was a two bit hussy?

"I take it you know Margene."

"Know her? Why, she went running after my son. Tried to convince him

86

that she was pregnant with his child. God only knows why he slept with her in the first place. No, but we put an end to that farce, right then and there. She wasn't any more pregnant than I am right now. Faked the whole thing. My beloved husband, God rest his soul, threatened her so fiercely you'd think she'd seen the devil himself when he got finished with her! Huh. So, you married the hussy. What'd she do? Hold a gun to your head?"

"No, actually. I'm the unlucky guy who did manage to get her pregnant."

"I wouldn't be too sure to bank on that one. No pun intended, of course. She's probably out for something. That was the case with my Junior, anyway. But nevertheless, Mr. Lee, you better make sure that the baby is yours."

Clinton scratched his head. He never once considered the possibility of Margene lying to him about the children.

"Ms. Arthur?"

"Call me Mattie."

"Mattie, she's had two children. Both she claimed were mine."

"Well, I'd look into it, anyway. You just seem a little too proper and handsome... a little too intelligent to get involved with someone like that."

Hearing her suggestion made Clinton start thinking. But then his mind began to focus on a former question he had. How could she be unaware of Margene's position as Judge of Stoweville?

"Not to sound disrespectful, but are you telling me that you didn't know that Margene was the Judge?"

"No. For a fact, I didn't. And to be honest with you, I think I would've been a lot better off not knowing. What a tragic disappointment to know that this charming town is being governed by trash. Anyway, you see, my late husband passed a few years ago. And my Junior, who moved down on the coast, insisted that I come and live with him. That's the reason I'm selling this place. I haven't been here in quite some time. I allowed the help to stay and care after things because I didn't have the heart to let it go. But now I feel like it's time. I know that I won't ever come back to live. There's just too many memories, and no one to share them with. Besides, I've grown quite fond of the ocean. And my boy enjoys having his mother around."

Clinton reached out to hold her hand.

"I'm sure you have more good memories than you can count. I think anybody would. Why, I'll bet the next family who lives here will fill these walls with as much love and happiness as you and your family did."

"You're a sweet young man, Mr. Lee."

"Please, call me Clinton."

The two sat quietly, sipping their tea and collecting their thoughts.

"Do you know what? I heard water coming from somewhere when I first arrived, but I couldn't figure out where it was coming from."

"Oh, well, let me show you. We'll have to hurry though, if you want to see it while it's still light out."

She led Clinton down the corridor to a large room, full of windows.

"It's okay, you can get a closer look, if you want." she said. "Walk out if you like."

Clinton walked through the French doors, only to be greeted by a terrace, some few feet from a breathtaking waterfall.

"I call it Shangri-la. See, over here. It's a sundial pattern that I had designed in the floor of the patio. See the words 'Shangri-la' inscribed underneath?"

"It's perfect. Please, finish showing me around the rest of your castle."

Mattie laughed.

"If this is a castle, then I suppose that makes me a Princess."

"And, I guess that makes me the court jester."

"You're a humorous young man. Do you know you've made my whole day?"

They walked back inside, while Mattie held tightly to his arm. "Do you know how comforting it would be for me to know that someone like you should live here? Why, I'd be thrilled. This place needs someone young and cheerful to brighten it up and make it a home again."

"Oh, Mattie, I don't think that I'm going to be that person. Remember what I told you about my friend at work misinterpreting my worth? But don't get me wrong. If I did have the money, I'd consider myself to be the luckiest guy in the world to live here. It's almost too much to imagine."

Mattie put her hand across his mouth.

"I don't want to hear another word. Clinton, you've probably figured out that I am rather well to do. And it's not that I need the money when I sell. Like I said earlier, I've kept this house because I didn't have it in me to get rid of it. My main concern is seeing someone live here who will give it as much appreciation as I did. Let me tell you something. There have been several couples who have come, interested in buying this place. I've put every single one of them on a waiting list. Do you know why?"

"I don't have the foggiest idea."

"I didn't feel that they were suited to take over. This house needs love and attention. Does that sound strange to you?"

"Not a bit."

"I feel something, having you here right now. There's a twinkle in your eye that makes me comfortable with you. But, do you know what's even better than that?"

"Tell me."

"It's that your ex-wife is Margene Wilkot. Wouldn't she just about lose her mind if you were to move in here? It's something she wanted a long time ago when she tried to land my son. And as bad as she wanted it then, she didn't get it. Tell me. Are you currently paying her any alimony?"

"No. She took everything I had. I am paying child support, though. But, of course, I don't mind that."

"I still think you should look deeper into that situation."

"I don't know about that. I don't even think I could comprehend the idea that they weren't mine."

"Suit yourself. But I wouldn't trust her."

"Oh, I don't. But, I'm not ready to humor that notion."

"All right, all right. Well, let's talk business, then. Clinton, why don't you tell me what you can afford to pay for a house?"

"Not what you're asking, I know. But realistically, if I got a loan right now, I could probably pay somewhere in the neighborhood of ten thousand for a house."

"It's settled, then. But under a few conditions. I want you to make this a real home. I'll expect that you care for everything the way my help has since I've been away."

"You couldn't possibly be serious."

"Oh yes."

Clinton looked up at the ceiling, and bit the inside of his cheek. His eyes started roving around as he tried to comprehend what it would be like to see such greatness on a daily basis. Then in almost a trance, he walked away from her as though she didn't exist, making his way through the beautiful mansion. He led his own self-guided tour through each and every room, which ended back at the window, revealing the waterfall.

Mattie walked in behind him, where he stood with his face smashed up against the glass. It pleased her to see his reaction, because she felt a certain humility coming from him.

"I think you'll be happy here."

Clinton turned around, with tears in his eyes. Not knowing the right words to say, he held his arms out and gave Mattie a warm hug. Afterward, they spent a little more time together, discussing all the details until Clinton left to go give Sadie the news.

CHAPTER ELEVEN

He had come a long way from the once wrecked individual that Margene had caused him to be. Now he was sitting pretty with a fine career and a house to match. A lot of people envied him. Margene was not excluded. Why, after wind got hold of Clinton Lee's new address, nearly everyone was convinced that he must have struck gold. How else could his rags to riches situation be explained?

At first, he didn't catch on to the fact that people were treating him differently. Perhaps it was because he had never noticed, or even cared what people thought of him. He had a unique and simple confidence about him. Always had. Even when he married Margene. It was just something that was always there. And as long as people were polite and respectful, he didn't ask for much more. The difference now, though, was the once polite disposition he got from others had merged into plain ol' suckin' up!

Everyone seemed to want to be his friend, his buddy, his pal.

The day he finally took notice of his mysterious new popularity was the day he ran into Guy Saunders at the bank. He had just finished his lunch at the downtown diner and was heading back to work. When he started up the bank steps, he heard the honking of a car horn and turned around to see if it was intended for him. Somehow, though, he kept walking up the steps, even though his head was turned. By the time he reached the top step, he bumped belly on into Guy Saunders.

"I'm terribly sorry," he said before noticing who it was.

He didn't appear to be the slightest bit pleased when he did.

"Well, looky here!" said Saunders. "If it isn't the newest slice of the Stoweville pie. Tell me, was ol' Mattie a hard one to handle, or did she swoon over you like a school girl? Why, I bet she melted like butter in the palm of your hand. I must say, Mr. Lee, I didn't think you had it in you. I figured after you'd finished lickin' your wounds, you'd go scamper out o' sight somewhere. But I had you pegged all wrong. You devil, you." Saunders nudged Clinton with his elbow.

Clinton felt the steam coming out of his ears.

"Guy," he said, "you seriously oughta consider steppin' out from behind all those law books and meet me someplace where I can teach you first hand how to get an ass whipping. Think about it. I'll be ready any time you are."

Saunders' smirk fizzled.

"You have yourself a good day," said Clinton just before he walked away.

Saunders was the first to blatantly confront Clinton about his monetary status, but there would be a lot more where that came from.

"Where on earth did you get the money to buy the Arthur house?" his boss asked him.

"I was wondering how long it would take you," he said. "Pretty much everyone else has already made their rounds."

"So...."

"The truth is, I struck a sweet deal with Mattie Arthur. I guess she likes me. Should I complain?"

"Heavens, no. If that ol' bat likes you, you outta be counting your blessings. All I can say is you must really have something special, 'cause the Mattie Arthur I know is one stuck-up cookie."

"Really? She didn't give me that impression. As a matter of fact, I found her to be quite the charmer."

"I guess you're entitled to your opinion. But, anyway, good job! It makes me look good when my right hand man has some prestige to him. Nope, don't hurt a thing."

"I'm glad you approve."

"Well, I do need to warn you, son. You're gonna have to start watching out for people's intentions from now on. It'll start out with a few questions here and there. But by the time it's over, every Tom, Dick, and No Good will be hounding you for money. And sometimes you gotta forget playin' polite. I've had to be dishonorable to folks sometimes, myself."

"But see, that's just it. I don't have any money. You of all people should know that."

"Clinton, let me tell ya, to anybody else but you and me, trust me, you have money. You may not know it, but you do. Speaking of which, I wanted to talk to you about a raise. You think you're to the point where you've earned a raise?"

"Always!"

"That's my boy. I'll tell what's her face in payroll that it's time that Clinton Lee earned a salary a little more fittin' for a Vice President."

"Thank you, sir."

"Oh, don't thank me. You've earned it."

Clinton walked away from Rutherford's office and did a Charlie Chaplin kick.

But, like his boss had said, it was only the beginning. The life he once knew, he would have to kiss goodbye.

His new world was very different from the old one. You might say that he had met Lady Luck. It seemed like it, anyway. But no matter what, he wasn't the type to let good fortune outweigh reality. A lot of people saw him as a man who carried himself with a great deal of humility. But, that only applied to those who knew or met him. Those who knew of him from the outside looking in assumed that he was just another privileged snob.

That goes to show that wealth and poverty has never, and probably will never, be able to fully mix. Together they're just too feared and misunderstood by each other to ever be comfortable.

Margene Lee, however, was an example of someone who couldn't be placed in either category. Though she did have a prestigious title under her belt, she didn't have the grace or dignity to be classified as well-classed. And though her wallet was a far cry from being empty, she neither knew how to spend or save money well enough to be considered rich. All in all, she was a lost cause. She was responsible for making her own bed. Even if she didn't like lying in it.

She envied Clinton. She still thought that she was somehow entitled to most, if not everything, he had recently achieved. But other than the children, she had no connections to him. The two never even spoke to one another. Ever. Even on visitation day. Usually Margene would shoo her children out of the house to wait on the front porch until Clinton arrived to pick them up. They never really came face to face with each other either. Sometimes she would secretly peek out the window at him when he came, just to remind herself of what he looked like. She had several photographs of him, but seeing the real thing was completely different.

Clinton seemed to get more and more handsome as the years went by. At one time, he was the most eligible bachelor in Stoweville. The ladies were certainly drawn to him. But as far as he was concerned, his disaster that most people referred to as a marriage had frightened him away from any serious relationships. The only person of female persuasion who had a place in his life, other than Earlene, was Mattie Arthur. They remained very close to each other by writing letters and making periodic visits. Besides, Clinton was just fine without a woman in his life. Or so he thought.

One morning he awoke, ate breakfast, and headed to work. He stayed cooped up in his office all morning, not allowing himself any goof-off time. As a matter of fact, he was so focused on his work that he hadn't even bothered to greet one soul that he passed by. He was too caught up with responsibilities to relax.

Eventually, he wound up with a splitting headache. And the longer he worked, the worse it got. When he got to the point that he couldn't bear it any longer, he jumped from his chair and hurried to the men's room to splash a little water on his face.

On his way there, he began to rub his temples in an effort to relieve some of the tension. His eyes were squinted to the point that he couldn't really see anything, so he just used his memory to lead him there. Memory got him there all right. Just not without bumping into someone in the process. Somehow, he had a habit of doing that.

"Excuse me, I'm sorry, excuse me." He tried to be polite, even though his headache had put him in a rather ill mood. Then he opened his eyes enough to see who the target was.

Clinton stood there awkwardly.

"Wha...whoa...uh...." is all he managed to get out.

The response he got was an earful of the sweetest laughter he'd ever heard.

He was embarrassed by his lack of composure, because it was the first time he'd ever been speechless. And, of all times to appear scatterbrained, this was certainly not the time. It was almost as though he had been instantly smitten. That, again, was a first.

As he stood trying to conjure up a complete sentence, he didn't take his eyes off the young woman, even once. She was very lovely to look at. She had long, sable hair that was pulled back from her face. Her blackish-brown eyes managed to hypnotize him. They were big and innocent, almost like a puppy. The dimples on her cheeks only got bigger when she smiled. Clinton felt like he had died and gone on to Heaven.

"Let me save you the trouble of trying to make the first introduction," she said. "My name is Julia Hallford. And, let me guess. You must be Mr. Lee. But, do you know what? I already knew that. I saw you sitting in your office earlier, and I noticed the nameplate on the door."

Surprisingly, Clinton managed to speak. "The pleasure is certainly mine. I don't think I've seen you here before."

"I just started today."

"Well, I certainly hope you'll enjoy working here. If not, then let me know and I'll see what I can do to change that."

She smiled bashfully, then excused herself. Clinton watched her as she walked away, and felt his knees start to wobble. He watched her until she was completely out of sight.

"Way to go, Rutherford!"

He turned around and started walking, once again, to the men's room. When he walked inside, he stood in front of the mirror. "Why was I coming in here? I don't have to use the restroom!"

Somehow, his run-in with Julia Hallford had made him completely lose his train of thought. He no longer had a headache either. So, without having any idea of why he went there in the first place, he walked out and went back to his office to fantasize about the newest employee of the Stoweville Bank. Actually, it was more like a state of coma. His mind had been officially altered. So much so that he spent the next hour staring into dreamland. Not the average behavior of an important executive. A few employees had walked past his office and noticed his far away stare. After awhile, Rutherford overheard a few bank employees snickering from afar.

"Did you get a load of Mr. Lee? He looked like somebody hit him over the head."

Rutherford walked straight to Clinton's office and found him in the same foreign trance he had overheard his employees describing.

"What in the world happened to you?"

"What?" he said.

"You heard me. What's the matter? Didn't get enough sleep last night?"

"No, that's not the case at all."

Clinton did seem a little concerned about how he must have looked, but for the most part, he didn't care.

"Gee, sir. I don't know what my problem is. It's probably something in the air."

Rutherford teased him. "I can't believe it."

"What?"

"Ha, ha, ha. It's so obvious."

"What?"

"You met her, didn't you. What am I saying? Of course, you did. You've got that sappy love nonsense written all over your face."

Clinton sat there, acting innocent.

"It's okay, Lee. Happens to the best of us. She sure is a pretty one, too!"

He tried change the subject, because he knew Rutherford had pegged him. Besides, grown men weren't supposed to turn into putty at the mere sight of an attractive woman. They were supposed to admire, perhaps, but not act like utter morons.

He went home that day, hoping to pull himself together enough to get Julia Hallford out of his mind, but with no success. He thought about her all night, and found himself eager to go back to work the next day. He didn't quite know what to make of it. It was all so new.

"Okay, Clint, just deal with this. Everything's gonna be fine. Tomorrow you'll see her. Might even say a few words. And that'll be the end of it."

As he had hoped, he went to work the next day feeling like his normal self. He had all but forgotten about the young woman who had taken such a toll on him the day before. Everything was fine and under control. When he arrived at the bank he walked inside, keeping his eyes down on his shoes. He wasn't going to chance the possibility of making a fool of himself a second time. A few people walked past, greeting him with their hellos and good mornings.

"Morning," he would say, keeping his eyes on his shoes.

But then one of those hellos was from the voice of Miss Hallford.

"Good morning, Mr. Lee."

His eyes instantly rolled over in her direction. It wasn't exactly how he had mapped things out, but what could he do, other than greet her back.

He spoke to her with a bashful type demeanor, saying as few words as he could politely get away with, then changed the subject.

"I've got a lot of work to do. Umm, uh, excuse me." He rushed into his office and began to search for something, anything, to do to preoccupy his mind. He was so flustered that he couldn't make sense of anything that he attempted to do.

"For Pete's sake! How in the world am I supposed to get anything done around here in this frame of mind?" Convinced that a little fresh air would solve the problem, he got up from his desk and walked outside.

Standing on the back door steps, he felt something nudge the side of his leg.

"What..." he said, looking around.

Seeing no one around, he eventually looked down, only to find the most pitiful little dog he'd ever seen. An obvious stray, it was thin as a rail and was covered in filth.

"You poor little puppy! Where on earth did you come from?" He reached down and picked it up and held it in his arms.

He had developed a strong love for animals back when he worked on the Chandler farm as a boy. The sickly ones always seemed to tug at his heart the most. And the stray little mutt was no exception.

He walked around to the front of the bank thinking that he would walk inside with it.

"I don't know if Rutherford's gonna like this." So he put it down on the steps.

"You stay right here now. All right, boy?"

He rushed inside and went straight to Rutherford's office.

"I'm gonna take off for about an hour."

"Trouble?"

"I just have something I need to take care of."

"You do what you need to do."

Clinton ran back outside as quickly as he could to grab his little friend and take him home. When he got there he saw Julia Hallford kneeling on both knees next to it.

"Hi again," she said.

"Hi."

"Do you know where it came from?"

"No, but I know where it's going. It's going home with me."

In a strange sort of way, the awkwardness he once had around her disappeared. And it was all thanks to one dingy, little stray pup.

CHAPTER TWELVE

Clinton and Julia had fallen head over heals with one other. The puppy that had inadvertently brought them together was appropriately named Happy. As a matter of fact, Happy was even on the guest list to their wedding. They were a charming trio.

Clinton maintained his upwardly spiraling career as the Vice President of the Bank of Stoweville, while Julia chased her dream to become a professional musician. The job she had taken at the bank when she and Clinton first met was merely a summer job to help make ends meet after graduating college. It was lucky for Clinton that they even had the opportunity to meet, because after only a month of working her bank job she was offered the pianist seat in the state orchestra.

At first, she wanted to decline the offer. But Clinton was most adamant in urging her to accept. Who was he to stand in the way of something she had worked so hard for, even if it meant spending a little time apart?

Julia kept an open mind about Earl and Earlene. At first, Clinton was unsure as to how she would react to that situation given that they had a less than stellar disposition. He soon learned, though, that the woman he had married was as beautiful on the inside as she was outside. She loved everyone within reason, no matter how ruthless, backward, or downright unappealing they were.

Now, as far as the whole marriage thing between Clinton and Julia went, Margene was none too happy about it. It made the bridge between her and Clinton seem even longer. She blamed him for getting on with his life–something she would never allow herself to do.

The first time that the children spent the day with Clinton after his new marriage, Margene was so bent out of sorts that she got in her car and drove as far away from Stoweville as she could. That way, if she decided to pout she could do it in private. To sit around and wait for his arrival was simply not an option.

What a tragedy it would have been if she had gotten a glimpse of Clinton's happy face. The pressure to peek through the curtains at him was just too risky. Besides, who wanted to see anyone happy? If she wasn't happy, then no one should be!

Before she left, she did make time to squeeze in a little heart to heart with her young 'uns.

"Don't you let that mean ol' woman boss you around, you hear? Just remember that she ain't your Mama. So you don't have to do anything she asks you to do. Now, there is a chance that she might try to lure you into her wicked web, just like a spider would. She'll play calm and cool. And when you least expect it, she'll grab you up and suck all the blood right out of ya!"

Both Earl and Earlene sat fixed to their mother while she filled their heads with horrifying tales. By the time she was finished, they were so frightened that they had no desire to see Clinton or that devil he had married. Which would explain why they both shivered like frozen popsicles while they were with him.

"Is something the matter?" he would ask them over and over.

Neither children uttered a word. They just made certain to stay very close to each other. Who knew when Julia might decide to use her evil powers and turn them into toads or something?

"I can't figure out what's wrong with them," Clinton said.

"Well, it's me, silly. Isn't it obvious? They're used to you being married to their mother. And now, this strange new lady has entered their lives. They're just feeling awkward right now. Give them time. They'll get used to it."

But they never did get used to it.

When Clinton and Julia finally had a child of their own, Earl and Earlene distanced themselves even more, no matter how loving Clinton was. Julia continued to keep an open mind. Unfortunately, they had permanently made up their minds that she couldn't be trusted. And what was worse was their opinion of Clinton for having anything to do with her. They were, in fact, brainwashed by the teachings of their insecure mother.

Did it change Clinton's feelings for them? Not even slightly. For as long as he was under the impression that they were his flesh and blood, he loved them regardless of how they felt toward him.

As the years grew by, Clinton did manage to find a great deal of contentment in the small family that he'd built with Julia and his daughter Darryl. Darryl, was short for Daralynn, after Julia's deceased mother. Her birth somewhat closed the gap in his once incomplete family life.

Darryl was a chip off the old female block. She was the same delightful, talented girl that her mother was, but a bit more headstrong. She took no bull from anyone at any time. Especially not from her supposed stepbrother and stepsister. They did try very diligently to make life impossible for her when they were around. How dare she be privileged enough to get to live in a fine house! They couldn't. How dare she be attractive, gifted, and smart! They weren't. She generally held her own quite well, though.

Without question, Earl and Earlene grew up to have the same distorted mentality as their mother did.

Over time, the friction between the children grew, and at a certain point Earl and Earlene stopped coming around almost altogether. They did make the rare exception, however, when they wanted something. Usually Clinton gave them what they asked for, because he felt that they'd been dealt an unfair hand. But it was the things that he didn't know that would one day greet him with a big slap in the face.

One Sunday afternoon, Darryl was outside frolicking near the waterfall when she heard the sound of a clunker speeding up the driveway. She tiptoed around to the side of the house to get a peek at who it might be. There, idling in the driveway, was a half-rusted automobile that junk yards are made of.

"Who is that?" she said, disgusted. She dove into the nearby camellia bush so she could do her inquiring without being seen.

The windshield was covered in a year's supply of sap, so it was hard to see who or what was seated behind the steering wheel. For a while there was no movement inside. But when Clinton walked out of the house, the car door finally opened. The squeaky hinges on the door made about as much noise as its lack of a muffler. Out hopped Earl Lee. He had just turned sixteen and looked as conceited as ever, now that he was able to drive. Of course, "drive" wouldn't have been the best description of someone behind the wheel of that car. It was more like a slug being fired from a shotgun with a crooked barrel. Nothing but backfire.

Nonetheless, he was proud as ever. His hair was slicked back with so much grease that just about anything floating in the air stuck to it. Darryl could even see the specks from yards away. He looked more like a chicken going through puberty than an adolescent teen. The outfit that he had thrown together was mismatched to the point of looking comical.

"Hey, Daddy," he said. "What you up to? Got me my driver's license just the other day."

"Well, that's great, son. I'm proud of you. I see you got yourself a car to drive. I wish I'd known. I might have been able to help you. The bank has repossessed a few cars in the past year or so. Could've found you one at a halfway decent price."

"That's kinda why I'm here, Daddy. I was wonderin' if maybe you could give me some money to help fix up my ride here."

Clinton stared at the car, noting its obvious need of repair.

"Hmmm. Let's take a look at her. We'll see what she needs." He walked up to the car and carefully inspected it from the inside out. He looked under the hood, then slammed it down.

"This little jewel's gonna need some work. It'll cost a few dollars to fix, too. You got a job or anything?"

"Naa. I ain't got no job. Didn't figure I'd need one."

"Well, son, how do you expect to maintain a car if you don't have a job?"

"Aren't you s'posed to pay me allowance or something? I mean, that's what Mama told me."

"Earl, you know I'm gonna give you an allowance, but you can't survive forever on it. You're sixteen now, and you're at an age where you need to start practicing a little responsibility. What are you gonna do when you're eighteen?"

"I don't know. I reckon I'll be doin' somethin'. Maybe I'll join the Army. They'll take care of me, won't they?"

"They'll take care of you, all right. They'll take care of all the things you didn't take care of yourself. Like giving you a crash course in responsibility."

"It won't be hard, will it?"

Clinton began to get flustered at his son's abnormal lack of common sense.

"Hard? No. It'll be like a weekend at the lake."

"Really? Huh. And you get paid too, right?"

"Never mind. How much money do you need for your car?"

"Well, I don't know."

"How much do you have?"

"I ain't got none. I done spent everything you gave me last time on my ride."

"How 'bout I give you a hundred dollars," he said, pulling out his wallet.

"That'll work." Earl's face lit up at the sight of the crisp Ben Franklin being handed out to him.

"Spend it wisely."

"Oh, I will, Daddy. I promise. I'll get this car to purrin' like a kitten. Thanks, Daddy. Listen, I need to go. I got me a lot o' things I have to do."

Clinton watched as Earl drove away with a grin across his face. In the back of his mind, he couldn't believe what he had done. He knew that it hadn't taught Earl a thing about responsibility. And he knew that the hundred dollar bill would be squandered just about as fast as it had been handed out.

Staring angrily through the bush, Darryl finally crawled out and stomped back off to the waterfall.

"It's not fair," she griped. "How can he treat Daddy like that? He doesn't even love him. And he's not my brother!"

Darryl spouted off all her terrible opinions, completely unaware that Clinton had roamed around to where she was.

"Do my ears deceive me, or is my sweet and innocent little girl letting foul words come out of her mouth?"

She screamed. "Daddy, why do you have to sneak up on me like that?"

"Answer my question. Are you talking badly about your brother?"

"He's not my brother. All he does is come around here when he wants something from you, Daddy. Why do you let him do that? He's not a good person. He's not a good person at all." Crying, Darryl ran away from her father and into the woods, where she would remain until evening. She had sat on the same rock for hours, dreaming of the day when she wouldn't have to acknowledge the fact that there were people in the world named Earl and Earlene Lee. For awhile, she was able to find a little peace of mind. That's what usually happened when she went into her fantasy world.

When the sun started to sink she scampered back to the house, wondering what her father would say to her next.

But he wasn't there. It seemed as though he too had retreated to his own hiding place to do some soul searching. Darryl walked into the dining room and saw her mother setting the table.

"Where's Daddy?"

"He said he had to go out for awhile, Sugar Plum."

"Why, is he angry with me?"

Julia stopped what she was doing, and squatted down beside her.

"Your father isn't angry with you. He's just a little confused right now. But you don't need to worry about anything. Just know that he loves you very much."

"He does?"

"Are you kidding me? You're the apple of his eye. Every time someone even mentions your name, his eyes light up. Every single time. You're special to him, and you always will be. And you know what else?"

"What?"

"You're special to me, too!" Julia tickled Darryl on the sides of her ribs while she broke into a fit of laughter.

The rest of the day flew by so quickly that before Darryl knew it, it was time for bed. Julia came and tucked her in tightly, then said a bedtime prayer. Soon, she was asleep. She began dreaming about happy things, such as fun times she had spent with her parents. She dreamed about going swimming at the lake, going on pony rides, and playing hide and go-seek. Throughout it all, she wore a grin on her face, looking like the most peaceful child in the world.

Later, Clinton returned and headed straight to her room. He gently pushed the door open, so as not to wake her. Then he reached down to take his shoes off, walking in sock feet across the floor. He sat in the rocking chair next to her bed, hoping that somewhere in her dreams she would realize how much he loved her. But, for some reason, once he entered the room, her dreams gradually merged from that of happy ones to unexpected nightmares.

They didn't happen all at once. The dreams would begin perfectly normal, then fright, or even terror, would take over. It was as if she were subconsciously aware that Clinton was sitting beside her. There was no explanation as to why her father was sending such negative vibes, but the faint grin on her face had long gone and had now been taken over by a frown. She began tossing her head from side to side and clinched her fists together.

Realizing that she was experiencing nightmares, her father got up to grab onto her shoulders and nudge her awake.

"Darryl, wake up. Come on, honey, wake up."

CHAPTER THIRTEEN

As absorbed in the nightmares as she was, it was hard for Clinton to wake her, but he shook her until her eyes finally popped open. A scream so piercing that it echoed clear into the woods belted out. The first sight of her father frightened her, then she was able to comprehend that the man in front of her was not the man in her dreams.

The scream had awakened Julia, who immediately rushed to her room.

"What's going on here?" she asked.

"Awful dream, I think."

Darryl lay still, as she was very confused. She looked at Clinton as if she knew something wasn't right. She couldn't figure out what.

"Are you all right, Sugar Plum?" asked Julia.

Darryl nodded yes, though she really wasn't.

"Do you want me or your daddy to stay in here with you for awhile?"

"No. I just want Nigel."

Nigel was her mohair teddy bear. It was almost as big as she was. She always felt safe when she slept with it. Nigel would protect her from any monster that came creeping out at night. So that would be all she needed for now.

Julia brought over the bear and put it under the cover next to her, then she and Clinton tiptoed out. They left the door partially open, just in case there was another bad dream. But there wouldn't be. Not for that night, anyway.

Darryl stayed awake for the next hour, holding tightly onto her bear. The dream itself had become fuzzy, but the symbolism remained more than clear. She'd never had a bad dream before. Trying to understand it only overwhelmed her to the point that she fell back asleep.

The next morning, she woke to the sound of birds tweeting outside. She stretched and yawned, then forced her eyes open with her fists. Lying alongside Nigel, she watched them flutter about as they landed on her windowsill.

The scared little girl had disappeared along with the night. She was now back to her same curious self. That also meant having the same perpetually empty belly.

She could smell the pancakes cooking from down in the kitchen. The smell always made her stomach growl. So she jumped out of bed, thanked Nigel for being her lookout, and quickly scrambled down the stairs.

"Pancakes!"

"Your favorite," said Julia. "What do you want with them? Honey or maple syrup?"

"I want molasses!"

"All right, then. Go on and sit down at the table. I already put your milk out."

Darryl walked over to the table and noticed that there were only two place settings.

"Where's Daddy's plate?"

"Oh, he had to leave early. It's just gonna be you and me. I was thinking that you might enjoy going over to your Uncle Martin's today. One of his mares just had a colt. Do you think you might like to go see it?"

"I would love to!"

"Well then, I'll take you over there after breakfast. I know he'll be glad to see his favorite niece."

"You're not s'posed to pick favorites."

"I know. But sometimes people just can't help themselves. Especially when they have a niece as special as you. Now, what I'll do is drop you off at the farm and I'll come to pick you up a little later. I have to go and rehearse with the musicians today. But I'm sure you'll find plenty to do to entertain yourself. You know, your Uncle Martin did mention something about taking you for a ride on his tractor, too. That is, if you still want to. Didn't you mention something about that once before?"

"Uh-huh."

By midmorning, the two were off to the Chandler farm. To say that Darryl was eager to see the new colt was an understatement. Julia hadn't even stopped the car before Darryl threw open the door and raced toward the stables. She had already made herself at home in a nest of hay beside the newborn colt by the time her mother was able to catch up with her.

"Sorry about my impatient daughter," she said to Martin.

"It's all right. I was the same way when I was her age. Probably worse. So, what do you think about our new little prize here, Darryl?"

"I think he's beautiful. Does he have a name?"

"Not yet. I thought I'd give you the honors."

"Really?"

"Why not? It's about time you give a name to something other than your toys, wouldn't you say?"

Darryl gazed into its young eyes, smitten by the colt's fragile innocence. "There's only one name that's good enough for him."

"What's that?"

"Beautiful."

Martin squatted down in front of the colt.

"Never had me a horse named Beautiful." He looked up at Julia and winked. "I thing it's love at first sight here. Next thing I know, she'll be begging me to let her take him home."

She looked up at Julia with wishful eyes.

"Oh, no! Don't you be planting any ideas, now Martin! I think he belongs right here with all the other horses. Well listen, you two. I've got to run before I'm late. Darryl, you be good for your Uncle Martin, understand? I'll be back this afternoon."

"We'll have us a fine time. Don't you worry."

Darryl was so mesmerized by the colt that she'd completely blocked the fact that her mother was leaving.

Martin kept an eye on her occasionally, but he more or less left her to herself. He could tell that she was perfectly happy without the hindrance of some adult. He never even bothered to ask if she had an interest in taking the once anticipated tractor ride.

By mid-afternoon, she was completely attached to the colt. She watched every single move he made. Beautiful's mother didn't even seem to mind her presence by the side of her newborn.

In Darryl's eyes, she had made a new best friend. Which was a good. Because she would need a friend a little more than she knew.

After awhile, Martin decided that it was time to interrupt.

"Aren't you hungry?"

"Huh?"

"You know, food? I figured you'd be barging through the kitchen by now, trying to find something to eat."

"I hadn't really thought about it."

"Well, tell you what. Let's let Beautiful here be with his mother so he can get a little something in his belly."

Darryl watched as Martin led Beautiful over to his mother to nurse.

"I believe he can handle it from here. Come on. Let's you and I go find somethin' to eat. You like vegetables, don't you? Got all kinds o' squash and corn and tomatoes. Picked some cucumbers this mornin' too. What d'ya say I teach you how to whip up some of your uncle's famous buttermilk cornbread? That would go good with the vegetables."

Walking back to the house, Martin began to tease Darryl about any and everything. Since he was a single man with no children of his own, he enjoyed having her around. She always seemed to be interested in the farming life. And that made him feel good. Because most of his other nieces and nephews didn't seem interested in anything other than being as far away from the rigorous farm life as possible.

That afternoon, he gave Darryl her very first cooking lesson, or experiment, as it would turn out. By the time everything was cooked, there was a tower of dirty pots and pans in the sink and a scattering of cornmeal on every surface in the kitchen. But it was a fine meal. The best Darryl ever tasted. Or so she said.

"You sure do make one fine cook," he said, patting his belly. "But I won't bother to comment on your housekeepin'."

"Stop teasing!"

"Oh, did I say cook? I meant chef extrordinaire."

"Stop it!"

"Okay, okay. Some fun you are! Well, Half Pint, I don't know where your mother is. It's gettin' 'bout dark-thirty. Why don't we call up your daddy and see if he's heard from her?"

He walked over to the phone.

"Whatcha know, good brother?"

"Hey there, Martin. Not much. You?"

"Oh, I'm just messin' around here with that little half pint of yours. I don't s'pose you've heard from your other half, have you?"

"No, I haven't," he said, dropping his pen down on his desk.

"That's strange. I figured she would've shown up by now."

"Me, too."

Clinton turned his wrist around to look at his watch. "Do I need to come get Darryl?"

"No, no. She's fine. I was just callin' to see if somethin' was wrong. With Julia, I mean."

"I don't know. Let me do some checking around. Maybe she had some car trouble, or something. You never know. I'll get back with you when I find out something."

"Sounds good. You be easy, now."

"Is there something wrong with Mommy?" Darryl asked as Martin hung up the phone.

"I don't know what's going on with your mother. She probably got tied up a little longer than she expected. You know how musicians are. Once they play one song, they wanna to play the whole songbook."

"You're teasin' again."

"All right. No more. I promise." Martin looked at Darryl with a serious expression. Little did she know that he had his fingers crossed behind his back.

At nearly bedtime, Clinton came driving up. Martin saw the headlights and walked outside to greet him.

"Still no word?"

"Not one. I've already called everybody I could think of. I just don't know what to think. I know something's gotta be wrong. She went down to Carlton, which is about an hour drive. Guess I'm gonna head that way myself. Do you mind keeping Darryl here? I brought some clothes for her. Brought Happy with me, too. Is that all right?"

Clinton whistled to the dog, still sitting in his vehicle.

"Come on, boy."

"Well, listen, I'll be in touch. But right now, I need to get outta here."

"Everything's gonna be all right, bro."

"I'm sure your you're right." He half-heartedly grinned, then cowered toward his truck. The 1950 model Ford truck he still drove had been somewhat of a gem for him throughout the years. But as he walked toward it to get inside, he no longer looked at it as priceless. It seemed that superficial things no longer mattered. Loved ones now took his priority.

111

CHAPTER FOURTEEN

All kinds of morbid thoughts raced through his mind. For some reason he knew that this was more than car trouble. Something was really wrong. He hadn't felt this jitterish since his divorce trial. As he drove up the road with his eyes peeled, his hands trembled to the point that he could barely hold the steering wheel.

"Get a grip on yourself, Clint."

He drove further and further, but didn't notice anything out of the ordinary. Just the usual things that a person sees driving at night, such as glowing eyes of animals near the road and headlights of passers by.

"Where in the hell is she?"

He began to cry. He, for one, rarely cried. Only on the direst of occasions did he, and even that could be summed up on the fingers of one hand.

A part of him dreaded finding out what had happened. The other part welcomed the idea of getting down to the bottom of things.

At one point, he stopped focusing so hard on the road. And it was at this time– when he stopped looking so hard– that he was able to notice things more clearly.

He was about fifteen miles from the Carlton city limits when, out of the corner of his eye he noticed a few mangled bushes. They were located near a sharp curve in the road, heading downhill. It would have been easy for a person to miss the turn and drive straight through them, only to crash at the bottom of the fifty foot embankment just beyond.

He pulled up beside them and got out, leaving his door wide open. He hoped this wouldn't be the place he found her. He hoped that he would find nothing more than a few broken limbs brought on by natural causes, and that Julia would be somewhere up the road trying to replace a flat tire.

Walking up to the spot in question, he bent down to pick up one of the broken branches. He could barely see anything, since the moon was nothing more than a sliver, so he decided to go and turn his headlights on. Though they did help some, he knew he'd have to rely on more than just his sight for the investigation.

Again he walked over to the bushes. There was a certain smell tingling his nostrils, but he wasn't quite sure what to make of it. It was a cross between motor oil and the way an iron poker smells right when it cools off.

There was an open space to the right of the row of bushes. The ground there was covered in fallen leaves from nearby trees. As he approached the spot, he felt one of his feet give a little, so he immediately backed up.

"What's goin' on here? Is this some sort of a drop off?"

Backing up further, he paid close attention to the way the ground moved. He kicked a boot full of leaves and watched them land. Nothing seemed odd about it, so he looked around for something a little heavier to toss.

Not able to find anything, he took off one of his boots. He tossed it in front of him with an average amount of force. The ground did give some, but not enough to scare him away from it. He slowly walked forward, tapping each foot on the ground as a means to test its sturdiness. As he approached the boot he had tossed, he got a little over confident that the ground was sound.

"Come to Papa," he said, picking it up.

One of his feet slipped on a soggy leaf, then the ground caved in. The pressure from it made him trip, sliding down the embankment.

The blackness of the night allowed him no sight to identify his whereabouts. He began grabbing onto any- and everything that his hands came in contact with. Finally he managed to clinch a stray tree root, which was flimsy at that. He dug his fingernails into it to get a better grip, but even that didn't offer too much help. His fingers began to slip, so he tried pulling himself up. Though he wasn't able to see, he could clearly tell that there was an enormous drop off.

The smell that he had noticed before had now become stronger. Then there was a noise like a breeze blowing against a hollow metal object. It was all too evident to him that there was something down below him that Mother Nature didn't have in mind. Something he feared would put an end to the mystery of what brought him there to begin with.

Exhausted from hanging onto the root, he decided to let go. He tumbled down over forty feet, until he reached the bottom. Somewhat disoriented, he lay there at first. Leaves from the fall had gathered inside the neck of his shirt. He began to itch. That, along with the dirt in his eyes and the bruises on his limbs, irritated him to the point of yelling. He didn't yell any particular word or phrase, just a plain, simple, one syllable, all vowel, prehistoric yell.

Rolling over on his stomach, he pushed himself up into a squatting position. He pulled off his jacket and flung it on the ground. Out of sheer aggravation, he jerked his shirt out of his trousers and ripped it too. He staggered around until he finally managed to maintain his balance.

And there he stood, slightly lopsided and with only one boot on, trying for the life of him to figure out what in the hell to do.

It took him a moment but he realized that even though he didn't have his sight, he did have a workable set of arms and legs.

"If a blind man can do it, so can I."

He decided to feel around first for a sizable stick or limb to use as for walking. Once he found a suitable one, he began to maneuver it around in front of him. For awhile, he found himself coming in contact only with a few trees and oversized rocks. And most of what he was able to hear was the sound of his own feet crunching through the leaves.

He walked aimlessly around for the next half hour, then heard the sound of a car driving on the road above him.

As it happened, he was near a small city where people were naturally nosey.

The car stopped after noticing the headlights on his truck and the wide open door. A man stepped out.

"Hello? Is there some sort of trouble? Hello?"

From down below, Clinton stood still so that he could hear. From where he was standing, any voices would have been faint, but he remained still and continued to listen.

The man wandered all around the truck and, not seeing one soul, concluded that it had been abandoned. Anxious to be some sort of help, in the event there might've been someone up the road on foot, he hurried back to his car.

Clinton heard the door slam. Then he heard the engine start.

"Wait!" he yelled. "Come back! Hey!"

He began running through the blackness toward the sound of the car, stick still in hand and yelling at the top of his lungs. It was no use. The driver had already gone. Clinton was hostile. For awhile all he did was stare angrily in the dark. Then he would walk around, halfheartedly swinging his stick through the air.

"It's either perfect or perfect shit!"

He sat down to take a rest. In doing so, he leaned back, propping up his elbows.

"Ouch! What in the world? Oh, no. Don't tell me I'm bleeding. What was that?"

Sure enough, Clinton had sliced a big chunk out of his elbow. When he had leaned back, he had landed right on top of a piece of broken glass. He reached around, poking his fingers on the spot where his elbow had pounded. And, after picking up the chiseled fragment, he immediately knew what it was.

"Glass. Why would there be a piece o' . . . ?"

He jumped to his feet and tossed it back on the ground. He began walking around again, but this time with a more eager approach. He knew he was coming close to something. There was the smell of oil again.

He began to feel an ache tugging inside. No question there had been some sort of crash. He also knew that once the sun broke, he'd find his dear, sweet Julia somewhere trapped beneath the remains of a car that had somehow lost control.

He followed his nose toward the source.

For some reason, the clock must have slowed down, because he started counting the seconds. The next couple of hours took an eternity to go by.

He was tired and weak when his pupils began adjusting to the first shimmer of daybreak. He couldn't believe that he'd held out for so long.

He looked around, surprised at what he saw. During the course of the night, he had conjured up his own idea of what his surroundings must have looked like. Now that he was able to see, he found that things were slightly different. The glass he had cut his elbow on was one of many pieces of the automobile that were scattered about. Everywhere he looked there were pieces. Clearly, the crash had been so severe that the car had literally become disassembled during the course of the fall.

Looking down at what appeared to be part of a car door, he instantly put his hand across his mouth. The sheer fact that he recognized the color of paint made him feel nauseated.

It was pale blue. The same color of an automobile that once had a home under his own carport. Shaking, his eyes filled up with tears.

"It can't be. Not her."

But where was she? He hadn't seen a body. Maybe she was alive. Maybe she was lost somewhere in the woods. But, then again, how could anybody be so fortunate to survive such an incident as this?

On the road above him, traffic had once again begun to surface. At least when he climbed his way out, he would be able to flag down some help now.

He looked up to the edge of the drop-off, trying to figure out the easiest route to the top. No way seemed less complicated than the next, so he just took the first course he saw.

Struggling through filth, roots, and the occasional briar cluster, he managed to make it. Out of breath, he stopped for a moment before trying to signal any cars.

Most drivers whirled right past him, as if in a hurry to get someplace that they were already late for. A few drivers slowed down and pulled the rubber-neck stunt, trying to figure out why he was standing on the side of the road. But no one bothered to stop.

Somehow, he had forgotten that his presentation had gone grossly downhill since he'd initially started out on his venture. He had a combination of sweat, blood, and dirt covering his clothes. Not to mention the fact that he wasn't wearing anything up top and was missing one shoe.

"What's the matter with you people? Doesn't anyone care to help a ..." It was then that he looked down and finally realized how utterly unapproachable he was. Even a physically endowed gentleman would know better than to stop to help the likes of him. Forget about any ladies traveling along.

It was also then, though, that he was spotted by one ill-natured police officer who was out looking for anyone he could justify writing a ticket to. The officer turned his siren on. Clinton, overwhelmed with delight, walked toward the squad car.

"Finally!"

The officer got out of his car and started patting his clipboard against his chest.

"Well, looky what we got here."

"Oh, officer, am I glad to see you!"

As though it were someone he actually knew, Clinton didn't hesitate to walk right up in his face.

"Sir, you'd better keep your distance."

"But, listen. I really need your help."

"Sir, if you come one step closer, I'll have to cuff you."

"But you don't understand..."

"Oh, I understand all right. I've seen your type before. What, did you stay out all night drinkin'? Look at ya! You've probably been drunk for days. You even got a shoe missin'."

Equally as uptight that the officer had pre-judged him based on his appearance as he was for the fact that his wife was presumably dead, he began ranting, trying to explain himself.

"That's it. I'm gonna have to place you under arrest."

"Arrest? For what?"

"Failure to comply to the orders of a police officer, for one thing."

"What? Why, that's the most ridiculous thing I've ever heard!"

"Ridiculous or not, I think you'd better turn around before things get worse."

Outraged, but desperate to avoid getting himself into a deeper mess, he turned around to get cuffed, then found himself being shoved into the back seat of the squad car. He sat with his eyes closed, trying to think of anything pleasant to take his mind off of the things at hand. Anything, just as long as it wasn't related to embankments in the middle of nowhere, car crashes, missing shoes, or jerks who had the gall to wear a police officer's badge. So, while he was busy trying to focus on more pleasant things, the officer began fidgeting with his radio, trying to pick up a signal.

Squrrr.zrrr

"What's wrong with this dad-blamed thing?"

"Bam!" went his fist on the side of it.

"This is squad car seventeen. I've got one white male that I'm gonna bring in. Looks to be some sort of trouble maker. Might possibly be dangerous. He abandoned his truck on Route 13, just outside Carlton City. What was that? Yep, it was a Ford. His name? Didn't get a name. Had to cuff him before I could get any name out of him. From the looks of him, he ain't got no identification, anyway. We'll be by shortly."

As they neared Carlton, Clinton remained with his eyes closed. The officer couldn't help but notice.

"What is it that you're doin' back there? Goin' through some Voodoo ritual or somethin'? Hello? Mister, when an officer of the law says somethin' to you, I think you might outta consider respondin'!"

Clinton opened his eyes.

"Gee, officer, is there something that I'm doing that offends you? Perhaps it isn't enough that you've managed to hold me prisoner in the back seat of your car for....some reason that I can't possibly explain! So, whatever it is that you think you need to know about what it is that I'm doing.....well, to put it as bluntly as I can....is none of your damn concern!"

The officer quickly looked away. There was something about Clinton's outrageous outburst that made him uneasy. And for all he knew, Clinton really was sitting there in the back seat chanting some Voodoo spell.

CHAPTER FIFTEEN

The nonexistent voodoo spell managed to get Clinton to the Carlton Police Station without any more hindrances from the officer. Even when they got out of the car, the officer kept his distance.

Refusing to touch him, he walked behind Clinton, motioning him toward the door. Once inside he was led to a holding cell where he would remain for the next two hours.

His temperament declined even more. Maybe it was the chalk-white paint on the block walls fenced in by iron bars that made him feel the way he did. Maybe it was the fact that his cellmate smelled worse than him. Or maybe it was because the past sixteen hours closely resembled a trip to hell. But, whatever the case, he was clearly a victim of lawless judgment.

Leaned up against the wall, he began to drift off when a different, slightly more pleasant lawman came to release him from his cell.

"Hey, mister, wake up."

His eyes opened.

"Welcome back. So, I suppose you have a name?"

"Yeah. Clinton Lee. My name is Clinton Lee."

"Well, Mr. Lee, why don't you step out of the cell and follow me down the hall? Sorry, but I'm gonna have to cuff you. Just routine."

"Yep," He noticed the name on the officer's badge. It read "Right," for

Detective Right. How classic that was, considering most of the officers he'd ever met were convinced that somewhere on their birth certificate was the very same name.

"So what is it that you're in here for? I've read the paperwork, and it don't look to me there was much reason to slap you in this joint."

"Thank you."

"Thank you?"

"Yes, thank you...for being the only person that I've come across in the last eighteen hours that has had a shred of consideration."

"Common sense, you mean?"

"That too."

"Well, why don't you tell me what you were doin' wandering around, lookin' the way you do. I mean, let's be honest here. You look worse than some things my cat's dragged up."

"Well, if Officer what's his face' had've taken the time to listen to what I had to say, you guys wouldn't have needed to go to such trouble of preparing the hospitality suite back there. I know it must've put you out."

The officer laughed. "I like you. You've got a savvy spirit, there."

"Just the aftershock comin' out. So, where are we goin'?"

"In this room, here. First, we're gonna get what really happened on paper, then I'm gonna let you make a phone call."

Clinton explained everything from top to bottom, but before he was through, Detective Right interrupted him so that he could put a search team on Julia.

"Mr. Lee, I'll try to hurry this thing along as quickly as possible so we can get you out of here. At this point, I'm gonna give you a choice. You can either call someone to come and get you, or you can ride with me over to the accident scene."

"Clinton's heart sank as he heard the words "accident scene" become official. The way he felt must've matched the expression on his face.

"I'm sorry you're having to go though all this. I guess it's times like these that make me wonder why I would even want a job like this. Just doesn't seem right. But, then I have to remind myself of all the positive things I've done for the community while wearing this uniform. You gotta take the good with the bad. So, do you wanna ride with me or make that phone call?"

"Let's go."

Clinton refused to look out the window during the trip. He didn't want to know how close or how far he was from the infamous curve in the road. He just wanted to wait until the car got there before dealing with the reality of the situation.

Ironically, he didn't get to have that luxury. He couldn't help but look, once his peripheral vision got a glimpse of the mess that was up ahead. There was a jam of vehicles, backed up nearly two hundred yards from the curve. Not to mention half a dozen officers parading around an ambulance.

"I shoulda expected this. Looks like we're gonna have to park it here." He patted Clinton on the shoulder. "Just hop on out whenever you feel ready. I'm gonna go on, though."

Clinton chewed the side of his lip as he stared out the window.

"Oh, for pity's sake. Sittin' here ain't gonna change a damn thing!"

He kicked the door open with such force that it ricocheted, sending it right back to smash his toe.

"Shit! Curses! That hurts!"

Whimpering, he opened it again, less aggressively.

Scooting out, he placed his injured foot on the ground, making one more awful facial expression. But, being the rugged individual that he was, he limped right along, not stopping until he got to the ambulance.

"Uh-oh." The officer who initially arrested was there and saw him. "I best not let him see me. I'm sure he'd like to hang me up to dry."

Clinton saw him, though. He walked up to one of the officers to inquire about him.

"Could you tell me the name of that poor excuse for a cop over there making a beeline for the bushes?"

"Sir, you need to go back to your car."

"I'm not going anywhere. I'm the poor bastard whose wife you're trying to find."

The officer gulped. "I'm sorry, Mr. Lee. I didn't realize..."

"Could you answer my question?"

"Question?"

"I asked you who that wise-ass cop was over there." Clinton pointed his finger, but by that time the cowardly officer had made his successful getaway.

"Which officer are you referring to?"

"Never mind. That rat bastard!"

"Sir, I was informed just before you got here that they did find a body."

"A body?"

"I, uhm...your wife...uhm, Mrs. Lee, I mean. Gee, is there ever a time that's convenient to stick your foot in your mouth?"

Ignoring the officer's attempt at humility, Clinton shouted, "Where is she? Where's my wife?"

"Mr. Lee, they're putting her on a stretcher. I'm sure they'll be bringing her up any minute now."

"Oh, forget this. I'm going down myself!"

"Sir, I wouldn't recommend doing that."

"You gonna stop me?"

He hobbled down the side of the embankment, where he met Detective Right guiding a crew of men carrying a covered stretcher. They had found her body buried underneath a large fragment of the car. All Clinton had to do was to make eye contact with Right, and he knew everything was over. The life he had made with the love of his life was all over.

He turned and walked back up the embankment, warding off the tears that wanted so badly to stream down his cheeks. It was almost as if half of him had died. He felt numb all over. His mind even went blank. And, as the crew made it to the top with Julia's body, he stood, watching as he waited for the other half of him to fade away.

No one wanted to approach him. Not the police officers or the ambulance crew. There was just too much of an awkwardness in confronting a person who looked as hollow as Clinton did.

Detective Right looked around, hoping that someone would make the attempt. And though he would've liked to walk away himself, he didn't have it in him.

CHAPTER SIXTEEN

It took several years before Clinton fully recuperated from her death. The funny thing was, no one really knew why the accident happened in the first place. There were a few theories that floated around, but never anything concrete. Whatever the facts were, the impact that it had on Clinton was equally as devastating to Darryl.

In the beginning, she isolated herself from the rest of the world. Clinton, not being any stronger about the situation himself, followed right behind her. Other than the social issues he was unable to avoid, it didn't appear as though he had a life at all. In a matter of speaking, he had become a recluse. So there they were a father and daughter couple of hermits.

The act of being alive, but not really living, went on for about six months. This was an especially bad thing for Darryl since she wasn't even ten years old yet. She was still at an age when everything was supposed to be uplifting and meaningful, the time of her life that dreams were supposed to be born.

Everyone in the immediate family had given some sort of effort to break through their shell, but without a whole lot of success. Finally, it was unanimously decided that Father Time would be the only one able to help. But, as it turned out, someone else managed to beat even him to the punch.

Good ol' Mattie Arthur came around in just the nick of time.

She, being the loyal confidant that she was, got wind of his retreat into hibernation and decided to come and remedy the situation.

When she arrived to town, she came without invitation. Not that she needed one, but her plan was to stay as long as she wanted until she felt like inviting herself to leave.

She walked around the place, acting as though she still lived there.

"Just look at the dust in my great room, "she said, or, "Can you believe the clutter in my dressing room?"

Comments such as those seemed to fly freely from her lips at any given moment, and after a while, they began to annoy Clinton. That was okay, though. At least it took some of the focus away from feeling sorry for himself.

Mattie stayed on, day after day. She made sure that food was on the table, clean linens were on the beds, and everyone was up and out of the house when it was time for work and school. That was about all, though. As far as being congenial, it was out of the question. She didn't try to nurture anyone's lowly spirits, or try to put a smile on anyone's face. With the exception of acting like queen of the castle, she was about as somber in attitude as Clinton and Darryl.

Days turned into weeks, and weeks into a month. It didn't take a genius either to figure out that Clinton and Darryl began to act slightly different.

Clinton began tiptoing around the place as though he were the uninvited guest, instead of Mattie. He felt awkward for some reason, as though he might say or do something to displease her.

Darryl just gave her the evil eye. She didn't know what to make of this inattentive woman who had taken it upon herself to move in without asking. How dare she walk around like she owned the place! And how dare she not be in the least bit concerned about tending to her emotional needs! Didn't she know that she was supposed to be like everybody else and feel sorry for her? So she decided right then and there that if no one else was going to stand up for her rights, she would!

Darryl noticed that Mattie had taken the authority to have the drapes in the sitting room changed. Had she no shame?

"So, when are you planning on leaving?"

"I rather like these drapes. They do brighten the room up. And they're a huge improvement from the old ones."

"I like the old ones better!" Darryl stood, looking disgusted. "Are you gonna live here forever?"

"Why do you ask, Missy?"

"Well, I just don't like..."

"Do you not want me to stay?"

"You're just not..."

"Not...what?"

"You're not nice. All right?"

Mattie looked at Darryl as though she were hurt.

"I see. I suppose I have outworn my welcome. I'll leave, if you want me to."

This, of course, put Darryl on a major guilt trip.

"I just don't understand why you haven't been payin' attention to me and Daddy."

"Well, my dear, it's because I can't. You see, the two of you have been paying so much attention to yourselves that there's not a whole lot of room left to let anyone else."

"Huh?"

"That's right. I've watched the two of you walk around like zombies the whole time I've been here. You know, it amazes me to know that you've managed to ignore everyone around you. You're not the only people in the world. And I really hate to break the news to you, Missy, but you're also not the only one in the world who has ever lost someone. So, if you ask me, you and your father are acting like two of the most selfish people I've ever seen. Frankly, I've about had enough. I do think it's ironic that you asked if I planned to stay. To be honest with you, I have been humoring the idea of leaving. Was just waiting for the right time, and I think you've just helped me mark the calendar date. Now, if you'll excuse me, I believe there's a suitcase upstairs waiting to get packed."

Darryl was shocked. Almost humiliated. How could she have been so blind? If Mattie Arthur had witnessed how self-centered she was, just imagine what everyone else must've thought. Mattie was the only one who'd had the courage to tell her like it was. And for that, she was thankful. But now she had a few sour deeds to undo, and several apologies to pass out.

She tiptoed upstairs to where Mattie was. Ashamed of her actions, she was determined to make up for them the best way she could. Standing near the edge of the doorway, she peeked in and saw Mattie packing her suitcase, one garment at a time.

"I don't want you to go."

Mattie turned to her. She had an ivory lace handkerchief in her hand. Holding it, she motioned for her to come inside.

"Do you see this? It was given to me by my mother when I was almost your age."

"It's pretty," Darryl said, taking a seat on the bed.

"Would you like to have it?"

"Me?"

"Why sure."

"I'd love to have it."

Mattie grinned.

"I've always wondered what it would be like to have a daughter. But I suppose that's all a person can do sometimes. Wonder. You know, Mother Nature is a wise one. Even though sometimes we don't think so. Missy, I don't know why your Mother died, but she did. And as sorry as I am for you and your father, there's nothing I can do to change it. But I do know one thing."

"What's that?"

"All this mess? This mess you've had to go through? It's going to make you stronger. You see, life gives you tests, and in a way I look at your situation as one of those dreaded many. The way you decide to handle them determines what kind of person you'll grow into."

"How many more tests will I have?"

"I don't know the answer to that, Missy. But I can tell you that if you don't choose to make the best of them, they'll get the best of you."

Darryl imagined what it would be like to ever have to go through the same kind of agony that she went through when she first learned of her mother's death. It was also near to impossible to try and imagine being able to be strong in a situation like that. But she did know that Mattie was wise and her words were true. She did have a choice. And knowing that gave her an immense amount of encouragement.

Finally able to allow herself to feel relief for the first time in over six months, she smiled. Not a smirk or a grin, but a genuine, full-fledged smile that was so big nearly all her teeth were showing.

"Well, would you look at that! And I was convinced that you didn't know how."

Darryl reached over to hold Mattie's hand. "I really don't want you to leave."

"I know. But I think it's time to. I think my work here is done. I did have a reason for coming here. And it wasn't to visit the old manor. Whether you realized it or not, you needed someone here to take care of you and help to get things back on track. Now, I don't suppose I have to leave this very moment. I'll stay another day or so. But I want you to make one promise to me. Promise me that you'll be there for your father after I leave."

"I will. I promise."

"Good. Now, what sort of things do you suppose we can get into while I am here? You know, dear, I have been roaming around this place for a month or more without taking in any social activities."

Darryl's eyes lit up. "Do you like horses?"

"Horses?"

"I've got a horse. He's the most beautiful horse in the world!"

"A horse, you say? Well, what's his name?"

"Beautiful."

"That certainly seems like a straight-forward name. I do hope he's as sharp looking as you say he is. Otherwise, a name like that would be in vain."

"Don't worry. He is!"

"And all this time I was under the impression that your only pet was that poor, poor dog you have outside on the porch. He seems terribly starved for a certain young lady's attention."

"Oh, my gosh! He probably thinks I don't love him anymore. Poor Happy."

"See. You did need me. Dogs have feelings just like people do."

"So, do you want to go see my horse? He's at my Uncle Martin's farm across town. We can take Happy with us."

Mattie wasn't exactly thrilled about taking Happy for a ride in her new Cadillac, because where she came from animals were considered outside only. Of course, she would make an exception this time, for it meant seeing a young girl who was in desperate need of joy in her life smile once again.

Mattie, Darryl, and Happy rode across town to the Chandler farm. When they arrived, Darryl was so giddy that she couldn't wait for the car to stop before flinging the door open.

"Come on, Happy," she said, luring him out.

Martin was standing at the foot of his pumpkin patch, taking inventory of his crop. Unfamiliar with the car, he stopped what he was doing.

"Come on, Mattie," Darryl said, pulling on her hand. "I want you to come meet my Uncle Martin."

"All right. All right. I'm coming. There's no need to hurry, though."

"Darryl, is that you?" Martin smiled when he realized who it was walking out. "Who is that you have there with ya?"

"This is Mattie."

Martin tipped the edge of his hat. "I'm Martin Chandler. How do you do, Madame?"

"Very well, thank you."

"So you're the famous Mattie Arthur. I've heard so much about you."

"Well, it's nice to know that I'm not completely forgotten about in this town."

"I wouldn't think that a person such as yourself would be. Why, I have heard mention of the Arthur name several times. Just never have had the honor of meeting any of you folks. So, I see you've performed some kind of charm on our young 'un, here. Thought we'd never see our little fireball again."

"She just needed some persuading."

"Well, whatever it was, it seemed to have worked. Glad to have you back in the swing of things, Half Pint."

"When are you gonna stop callin' me that?"

"Oh, I guess when you get about quart size."

"He always teases me, Mattie!"

"So, Darryl informs me that she has a horse."

"She does indeed. I'll lead the way. Be careful where you step, now."

Making their way down to the pasture, they would spend the next hour focusing on a horse named Beautiful.

"It's getting dark, Little One," said Martin. "Don't you think we outta call it a day?"

"I can come back on Saturday and ride, can't I?"

"You bet you can. But right now, I'm sure that Ms. Arthur is probably wantin' to get back. Ms. Arthur, if you need to go, it won't hurt my feelings a'tall."

"Well, we probably should be leaving."

She grabbed Darryl's hand, called out for Happy, and walked up the hill to where her car was parked.

"Wonder what your father is doing?"

Clinton was back at the Shangri-la estate cooling his heels after a hard day's work. He was also taking notice of the fact that there were a couple of people missing from the homestead. He too, like Darryl, had been so caught up in his own world of self-absorption that he hadn't bothered to pay much attention to anything outside his work schedule. And again too, he began to realize how foolish he had been. Fortunately, he believed that it was far more favorable to show up late for the game than to miss it altogether.

His family had grown apart for way too long, and he was determined to do everything he could to put it back together.

When the two finally arrived back, Mattie held the door open for Darryl and whispered to her, "Why don't you go find your father and give him a hug?"

She didn't have to find him, though. He was standing right down the hall, past the foyer. As she walked in, she saw him standing there ready to greet her. It was the first time she'd ever noticed his modesty. Before, he was merely a figure of strength and manliness. But now, she was able to see clearer who her father really was. She ran into his arms.

"Are you crying, Daddy?"

"Yes, your daddy's crying. Grown men do break down and cry every once in awhile."

"But, why are you, Daddy?"

He put her down, and held her face in his hands.

"Because when I saw you come through that door, I knew that there wasn't anything in this whole wide world more special to me than you. Honey, I can't even begin to tell you how sorry I am for not being here for you. Your daddy's been a foolish man. But no more. We are going to start being a family again."

Mattie stood in the doorway watching, as it was confirmed that her trip back to Shangri-la was one that wasn't wasted. Not wanting to interrupt their bond, she tiptoed around them, trying not to be noticed.

"Hello, Mattie," said Clinton.

"I'm going to leave you two alone."

"Don't be silly. I have the two most wonderful women in the world, right in front of me. Why don't we all sit down and have a nice meal together? It's been a really long time since I've eaten in good company. What d'ya say? The two of you?"

"I've got an idea, Daddy. Why don't all of us cook?"

"That, Sugar Plum, is a great idea."

Darryl stood there smiling. The idea of her father calling her Sugar Plum was all she needed to hear. After all, it was the name her mother used to call her.

CHAPTER SEVENTEEN

Mattie would leave the next morning. Their last evening together turned out to be one they would all remember. After Darryl had gone to bed, Mattie and Clinton stayed up half the night catching up on old times. Naturally, she had to put her two cents in about the ever popular Earl and Earlene. Why hadn't she seen them come around? Did he still claim them as his own flesh and blood? Even if he did, it couldn't hurt to double check.

It all made Clinton wonder. Why hadn't he seen them in six months? Why was it that they didn't hesitate to cash their monthly allowance checks, but absolutely went out of their way to be as obscure as possible when visitation dates came rolling around? There was only one way to find out. Confront them. Any normal parent would.

After a few days, he got up the courage to go to Margene's. When he got there, it didn't appear as if anyone was home, but he knocked on the door anyway. No one answered, so he left a short note in the mailbox: "Hey, kids. Hope everything's going all right. I haven't heard from you in a really long time. Why don't you come and visit me this month? I miss you. Love, Daddy."

He was actually a bit relieved that no one was home to answer the door.

The whole idea of being there was risky to begin with, because until the day came that Earl and Earlene reached eighteen, he wasn't necessarily allowed to visit them at any moment he felt inclined to. Only on visitation day. And that day wasn't visitation day.

He was wrong about one thing, though. The part about no one being home. Someone was there, all right. She just went out of her way to pretend otherwise.

Earlene was in her room listening to the radio when she saw Clinton pull in the driveway. Disturbed by the mere thought of having to kiss up to the person responsible for allowing her to afford that radio, she turned it off and made a dive under her bed.

It wasn't that she hated him, she had just been properly trained to tune him out of her life. But that applied only to him. Not his wallet. Where she came from, it was proper to receive, but flat out criminal to offer anything in return.

She stayed buried underneath the twin box springs until she heard the sound of his truck crank. Slithering out, she crawled on all fours until she got to the window. She inched up very slowly till she could see, then waited for him drive off.

"Thank God I saw him drive up. That's the last thing I need right now. Having to hang out with Daddy! 'How've you been doin'?' 'How's school?' 'You found a boyfriend or anything?' God! I hate that crap!"

She was curious as to whether he might've left something behind, so she went out and located the note in the mailbox. "Don't you have anything more important to do?" She wadded it up.

Earlene was a girl with a fair amount of intelligence. How she got it, nobody knows. Her mother was more Bitch than Brains, and though she was well on her way to becoming one herself, it was also obvious that she stole a brain cell or two from somewhere. Earl was left so void in that department that it was entirely possible she collected what he had left behind in the womb. Her biggest fear was that she'd have to babysit him for the rest of her life.

Earl simply wasn't the type who could make it on his own. He needed to ride somebody's coat tails. As a matter of fact, a year and a half later when he enlisted in the Army, he was dishonorably discharged after less than two months.

After his discharge, he arrived back in Stoweville with his tail between his legs.

Last Will and Testament

"What in the hell is the matter with you!" shouted Margene. "As if I don't get an earful already about what a moron you are! Do we really need this to top it all off?"

"Mama, I don't know why the drill master didn't like me. He just didn't. I did everything I was s'posed to. I guess he just got it in his head that he was gonna give me a hard time from the very git-go."

"Spare me the horse shit, Earl. I ain't in the mood. What I wanna know is what you're plannin' on doin' now that you're back in the real world. You're gonna have to find you some work or somethin'. Doin' what? I ain't got the slightest. But you gonna have to find somethin. Cause keep in mind, you have seen the last of your Daddy's checks."

"Huh?"

"Don't 'huh', me, boy. You know what I'm talkin' about. You're eighteen now, and the child support days are over. With you, anyway. Your sister'll still get 'em for another year. But let me tell you one thing. Don't think for a minute that you're gonna sponge off me for the rest of your life!"

It had never really occurred to Earl that he'd ever have to actually earn money. What was he going to do without the aid of his "father"? Maybe he could devise some sort of way to continue mooching. But it had been two years since he'd given Clinton the time of day, so he was a wee bit bashful about barging back into his life again. But perhaps just tacky enough to ease his way back in it.

He waited for a Sunday afternoon to make his surprise visit. He figured that a Sunday would be the best chance to catch him at home. He also figured that Sundays were the days when everyone felt wholesome and Godly. The most generous, too.

Clinton was still in his Sunday best, getting ready to prepare lunch. He always cooked a big spread after church, even though there were only two mouths to feed. It was more or less a tradition.

Darryl was out on the front porch doing her best to soil her spotless Sunday clothes. That too was tradition.

She rolled around, wrestling with Happy, when Earl drove up. Because he had never gotten the muffler replaced, she was quick to recognize the sound of his car.

At first, she was so shocked that she simply ignored the fact that he had pulled up, hoping that maybe he would turn around and leave. After she heard his door slam, though, she knew she'd have to face the fact that he was going to make some sort of appearance.

"Why does he have to be here?" She sat up and held Happy as close to her as possible. For some reason, she felt like she could use all the protection she could get, at that moment. She tried to look away when he hopped up on the porch steps, but her eyes peered back at him anyway. All she could do was try and duck behind Happy as best she could.

"Wha'cha know good, Darryl?" he said.

She didn't say anything.

"You folks must o' got yo'rselves a cat. Did you git a cat? 'Cause he clean got ahold o' yo'r tongue!"

He grabbed the door handle and invited himself in, all the while chuckling, thinking he was some sort of comedian.

"Daddy? Daddy, where are you?"

Clinton dropped the knife he was holding onto the floor when he heard Earl's voice. *Uh-oh,* he thought, *this scene feels a little too familiar.* "I'm in the kitchen," he called out.

Clinton, like the rest of Stoweville, had been duly informed of the infamous dishonorable discharge, so the sound of Earl's voice brought him a variety of feelings. The father in him was elated to get the opportunity to bond with his long lost son again. Another part of him wanted to take Earl across his knee for getting himself thrown out of the Army. Yet, there was still another side of him who wondered what his son must've been up to, to be crawling back into his life.

"Did you hear me? I'm in the kitchen."

"I heard you, Daddy." Earl was in one of the rooms down the hall admiring some of the costly antiques that had been added to the place since he'd last been there.

"Dang! Daddy sure must be rakin' it in!" He wondered why he'd strayed from Clinton for as long as he had. How could he have been so foolish as to let all these highfaluting things get so far out of reach?

"You cookin' up some grub, there?" he said, walking into the kitchen.

Clinton reached out to give him a hug.

"It's good to see you, Earl. Why don't you have some lunch with us?"

"Oh, I don't want to intrude or anything."

"Don't be silly. I'll put out an extra plate."

Surprised by his father's generosity, Earl gladly accepted.

They didn't talk much during their reunion. Just enough to get away with.

And because she was feeling utterly begrudging of the fact that Earl was even there, Darryl was none too thrilled to share her Sunday lunch with him.

She reacted by saying nothing at all. The only thing on her mind was gulping her lunch down as fast as she could, so she could excuse herself from the presence of her stepbrother.

"I'm finished. Can I be excused?"

Clinton looked at her empty plate in disbelief. He knew that Darryl was generally a slow poke when it came to eating. She always finished her plate, but it took her an eternity to get there.

"Good grief, Darryl. You must have been starving today. Yes, you may be excused."

She rushed away from the table without any thought as to how obvious it was that she didn't want to be there.

Earl, being no genius, even knew why she wanted away. It didn't bother him, though. He actually took some sort of enjoyment in knowing that he had the ability to make her uncomfortable.

They did all manage to survive that Sunday afternoon, but there would be more Sundays and other days like them. And they would come more frequently than not.

CHAPTER EIGHTEEN

Over the course of the next ten years, Earl seemed to be a constant fixture of neediness around Shangri-la.

"Daddy, could you help me with this?" "Daddy, I need you to do that."

Darryl never understood why her father fell for his act. Earl was clearly a con man, and a rather good one at that. So why couldn't he make a living as a hustler? Why did he choose instead to take on a dozen or more minimum wage jobs a year, only to get fired after a few weeks and end up on Daddy's porch step?

The truth was, Earl could have done better for himself than he did. He just didn't want to. And why would he, when he had a father with means?

Clinton was of the opinion that it was normal for parents to want to help their children. So, for his sake, there was nothing wrong with what he was doing. The question was, where was Earl when his birthday came? Where was he on Father's Day, Thanksgiving, or any other holiday where he wasn't the sole focus of attention?

Earlene was the opposite of her brother. After all the support checks came to a halt, she put a barrier between herself and Clinton. But not before she informed him of it face to face, smack in the middle of the Bank of Stoweville.

"Daddy, I want to tell you something," she said, after stopping him in the lobby in front of a room full of patrons. "From this day forward I want you to know that I don't have a damn bit o' use for you. Don't need you to be a part o' my life in any way, shape, form, or fashion. You ain't never been much of a daddy, anyway. Just thought I'd come here and make it official."

Clinton couldn't move.

"That's all I came to say," she said. She walked away, noticing several people staring at her. "What are you people lookin' at?"

Humiliated and hurt, Clinton turned to confront the individuals insulted by her rudeness. "I apologize for the outburst. I believe you folks need some assistance, don't you? Let's see if I can find someone for you."

For the remainder of the day, Clinton tried to wipe Earlene's words from his mind. What had he done to make her hate him so much? Maybe he could have fought harder to obtain more custody of her and her brother. Maybe those checks just weren't enough. Whatever the case, though, he couldn't stomach the idea of any of his children despising him. Somehow in his mind, he figured that once Earl and Earlene had reached legal age, they would all be close again. But he was beginning to realize that there were certain things he wouldn't be able to control.

Still, he wouldn't stop treating all three of his children with equal respect and love. Nothing could change the fact that he was their father.

He had sent Darryl off to college, and desperately wished he could have done the same for the other two.

Earlene was more interested in landing herself a husband than going to college, though without much success.

Earl was a different story. There wasn't enough money in the town of Stoweville to lure him into a college classroom. He had actually dropped out of high school, but his mother did manage to see that he got a high school diploma. She certainly wasn't going to walk around having school dropouts for children. Besides, without a high school diploma, she could never have sent him off to the military and gotten him out of her hair.

Though the military was a short-lived experience for Earl, at least when he did come back home he spent more time at Clinton's home than hers! In a way, she liked the fact that he was spending so much time with him, not because it got him out of her hair, but because he was actually successful at conning money from him. She never imagined that Earl would ever have any talents, but to have one with so many advantages was just too good to be true. Instead of spending all those years keeping her children away from Clinton, why couldn't she have been using them to swindle extra cash from him all along?

Last Will and Testament

She was sitting in her living room one evening when Earl came staggering through the door. "Where you been? I been awaitin' for you for the past two hours!"

"Aw, I just been ridin' around killin' time," he said, crushing the empty beer can in his hand. "You wanna beer? I got another six pack out in the car."

"No, I don't wanna beer! I do wanna have a little chat with ya, though. Are ya sober, or should I just wait 'til mornin'?"

"I-I-I'm sober, but Mama, you know I ain't one to set down an' talk. What is it?"

"Earl, don't think for a minute that I haven't taken notice that you have all this spendin' money. I mean, you ain't gettin' your beer money from me. You been hangin' round your daddy, gettin' it from him, I know. So, I guess what I was thinkin' was that you let me in on some o' the action."

"Oh, Mama, he don't give me that much. Just a little bit here and there."

"Boy, don't you be lyin' to me. I've seen through more lies in my courtroom than St. Peter on Judgement Day, so don't even think that you're gonna pull one over on me. You may have your daddy fooled, but you ain't ever gonna fool me. Now, as I was sayin', I've noticed that you've had all kinds of extra money to blow lately. So, I'll tell you what, Earl, you can either share this good fortune of yours, or I'm just gonna have to start chargin' you for rent."

"Rent!"

"Rent. You been livin' here for thirty years, and I don't see any signs of you ever movin' out. Now, I ain't had no reason to charge you before now, seein' that you can't keep a job or anything, but from the looks of it, what you been rakin' in is sufficient to classify you as someone with a job!"

"Aw, damn it." For awhile, Earl was under the impression that he had it made. But leave it to his mother to put an end to that. "Aw'right. How much do you want?"

"Hmm, well, if you calculate all the years that I've put up with your sorry ass, I'd say fifty-fifty might be a fair percentage."

"Fifty-fifty!" Earl's chin dropped.

"Watch it, or I'll make it sixty-forty. So, how much you got left?"

"I don't have any left, Mama."

"Earl, I'm gonna tell you one last time, and that's all. No lyin'. Now, I'm gonna ask you again. How much you got left?"

Earl slapped two tens on the table. "There. That's all I got." He watched as she picked one of them up. "Why ain't you houndin' Earlene like you are me?"

141

"If you haven't noticed, your sister's done gone out, gotten herself a job, and her own apartment. That's why. Besides, she won't have nothin' to do with Clint. So, I guess that just leaves you, now don't it? Besides, I know you got a talent for hustlin'. And what a gem that is! Do you know the world revolves around people like you?"

"It does?"

"Son, with my brains and your gift, the world is our oyster. Or, in this case, Clinton's world." Both burst out laughing.

"I see what you're getting' at, Mama."

"Now, the small wad o' bills you been gettin' from him, up until now, which is what I consider to be pocket change, ain't gonna work. You're gonna have to go bigger than that. You're gonna have to dig deeper. Are you with me, Earl? What we need to do is find out what Clinton's weak spot is, and move in on him when he least expects it."

"What do you mean 'we'? It's me that's gonna be...."

"Earl, we are a team. When I say 'we,' that means while I'm doin' the thinkin', you'll be doin' the leg work. We. Get it?"

"We." Earl's face lit up. It wasn't every day that he got to be a part of a team. He was especially intrigued at the idea of doing some highflown scheming. Because all that petty stuff he'd been focusing on before was for peons. And he wasn't no peon! He was ready to plunge right into the big time. Now, he wasn't exactly sure how he'd go about getting there, but with his mother masterminding the whole thing, he was sure to make all the right moves.

CHAPTER NINETEEN

With Darryl away at school, Earl had every opportunity to hover over Clinton and make it his business to find out as much information as he could about him; his work habits, hobbies, favorite snacks, anything to get deeper inside of the head of the man he called Daddy.

Now, Clinton wasn't really a person who could be described as a closed book, so it wouldn't be very hard for Earl to gather the information he needed, nor would it take an eternity to get it. Why, in no time at all, he was able to get Clinton's daily routine down to a T. And since that went so successfully, he decided to move on to the next task of polishing up his buddy routine so that he could get to know the more intimate side of Clinton.

Clinton had begun sharing his business ethics with Earl, hoping that he might learn a few important aspects about the real world. Much of it flew straight over his head, but he did manage to grasp a thing or two. Enough to report back to his mother, anyway.

That wasn't all, though. He had also begun sharing things with Earl that, with a few exceptions, would normally be things that he kept to himself. One of those things involved a certain coin that he had been holding onto for awhile, and a certain bit of information he'd recently learned about it.

It was the coin that he had come across during his first few days working at the Bank of Stoweville. The one that had stood out to him so much while he was busy taking on that ridiculous task of sorting the ungodly amount of coins. The information on it had miraculously fallen into his lap about a week prior, while he was strolling around town.

It was his lunch hour, and rather than being cooped up in his office to contract an even bigger headache than he already had, he decided to go stretch his legs and take in a few sights. He noticed that a new bookstore had opened next to the bakery, so he figured that he could kill two birds with one stone– clear his head browsing around the store, then grab a fresh pastry on his way back to the office.

When he walked in, the first thing he noticed was that everything was perfectly categorized. One shelf would be labeled "Classical Fiction," another "Eighteenth Century Poetry." There was even a section labeled "Signed First Editions." None of the labels really reached out and grabbed him.

He had made his way to the end of one aisle, turning around to walk back out, when he felt one of his shoes gaping loose. Sure enough, he looked down and saw that his shoelace had come untied. He looked over at the salesgirl and blushed, then squatted down to tie his shoe. It was then that he came eye to eye with a short row of books on the bottom shelf. They were all about valuable coins.

"Well, what a surprise," he said, pulling one of them out. He flipped through a few pages, then grabbed another one doing the same. "Excuse me, Miss, but how much for this entire row of books here?"

The sales girl hurried over. "The price is listed inside the front flap. See?" She opened one of the books and pointed it out. "You want to buy all of them?"

"Sure."

"You must really like coins."

"What can I say? It's my livelihood."

"You must work at the bank, then."

"Something like that."

She laid them out on the counter, noticing that there were about a dozen of them. "Sir, why don't I go ask the owner if we can't give you some sort of discount. I mean, the average customer isn't going to come in and buy this many books." She turned around and knocked on the door behind her, that had a sign spelling "Private." She walked inside and mumbled a few words to the person inside. A few seconds later, a gentleman stepped out.

"You're interested in buying all my books on coins, eh?"

"Yes, sir."

"I believe we can give you a little bit of a discount." The man scribbled a figure down on a note pad, handed it to the girl, then went back to his "private" quarters.

The girl began flipping open the front covers of each of the books, then punching figures into the vintage cash register. "Congratulations. You must have caught him in a really good mood." She made out the sales receipt and handed it to him. Even with her remark, he looked at the figure somewhat surprised. It was a little more than he expected to spend, but then he thought, "How often does a person come across a book collection about coin collections?"

She bagged them up for him then watched him walk toward the door.

"Sir," she said, "your shoe is untied again."

And that was how it happened. An innocent break away from his office started a new turn of events that couldn't have come at a more unexpected time.

He thought the books would turn out to be a mediocre source of entertainment. Just something he could amuse himself with when he wanted to learn a few facts about certain coins. Though that may have very well have been the case, it didn't change the fact that he had something in his possession far more valuable than coin truths alone.

When he finished up his day at work, he hurried home to relax over a nice glass of tea, a pile of coins, and one of those books. Luckily, Earl didn't surface that particular evening.

He started by emptying his coin sack out onto the dining room table. He'd kept all his coins in that sack for as long as he could remember. It had grown on him, just about as much as what was inside it.

He ran his fingers through the pile as if it were a mound of gold, then he picked one of them up. He studied it, even though he already knew every single detail. He knew every detail of every coin he had.

Then he picked up another and studied it. Then another. There were so many, he didn't really know which one to start the research on first. Squeezing his eyes shut, he randomly picked one up and rubbed it in between his thumb and index finger. It had a familiar feel to it. He opened his eyes and looked down at the coin.

"This one. I should have known it." He began to laugh, thinking back at the ludicrous manner in which he found it.

"I can't believe Rutherford actually expected me to do that job. What a nightmare!"

The bunkmate from back in his military days who held an identical coin had told him that it was worth something. Now, he could see in published print if there was any truth to the matter.

"Let's see now. I wonder what I should look under. German or 1914? Ahh, I guess it won't hurt to look under both."

He began looking under dates. "Nineteen-O-six, seven..." He flipped through the pages, moving his way toward the coin's year.

"All right. Here we are. Nineteen fourteen." His eyes grazed down one page. As he neared the bottom, that's when he discovered it. There, in bold print were the words "*Die Irrtümliche Münze.*" Next to it, in parenthesis was "The Mistaken Coin."

"Could this be it?"

He quickly turned the page and read out loud the rest of the description. "This German coin, minted in 1914, was discontinued after a mistake was realized on the tail side..." Reading further, he soon concluded that his buddy hadn't been exaggerating about its history. On the right page, there was a small photograph of the infamous coin of error, which quickly drew his attention. He stared at it with an almost disturbed look on his face. His eyes revolved around every nook and cranny of the photograph about a dozen times, all the while rubbing his own coin between his fingers.

He knew without looking that the coin he'd found at the bank was one of the few remaining of this "Mistaken Coin." He read on and learned that a mere two hundred coins had been manufactured, and only two had surfaced since their termination. Did he and his army buddy carry the only other two in existence? Whether they did or not remained to be seen, but Clinton knew one thing– the book lying on his dining room table was a book about valuable coins. And whatever the case, the coin he had in his possession must have been worth something, otherwise it wouldn't have been listed. Right?

The question was, how much was it worth? He immediately buried his head in the book again. He skimmed over the words so fast that he was unable to comprehend anything he was reading.

"Okay, slow down, Clint. Get a grasp on yourself." A part of him was so anxious to find out what it was worth that he couldn't sit still. Was it worth thousands, or only a couple of hundred? He didn't know. He didn't really care. He was just thrilled that it belonged to him. He began reading again, this time more slowly. He made it through one sentence after another, until he finally got to the part he was looking for.

"Estimated value not determined." With that, he slammed the book shut. "I can't believe it– all that for nothing." He stopped for a moment. "Wait a minute. What does it say about the other coins in here?"

He opened the book back up and browsed through a few pages. "Well, this one here says it's worth....Oh, my Lord. Ten thousand dollars."

Surprised by that information, he began to look for the price tags of a few more coins. Their values weren't much shabbier.

So why didn't the book have a value for his coin? Was it because one really hadn't been determined, or was it because it was too outlandish to print? All he knew was that his curiosity wasn't going to let him rest until he got some concrete answers.

Clinton didn't make a big scene about his famous coin in Stoweville. He knew better. He decided to do all his inquiring out of town instead.

But, given the fact that coin shops weren't exactly a dime a dozen, he felt that his best bet would be to start at a well-respected antique dealership. So one afternoon, he walked into one and asked to speak with the owner.

"Is there something I can help you with, sir?" asked the salesman when he walked in.

"I just need to speak with the person in charge."

"I'm sorry, Mister..."

"Lee. The name's Lee."

"Mr. Lee, I'm sorry, but Mrs. Browning won't be back until tomorrow. Out shopping for antiques, you know."

"I understand. Well, could I leave her a message?"

"Sure." The salesman handed him a small notepad and a pen.

"It's very urgent," he said, handing the paper over.

"Sure. I'll see to it she gets it first thing."

"I appreciate it." He walked out feeling somewhat hopeful. Maybe Mrs. Browning could give him the information he needed, or at least direct him on the right path.

The very next day, he received her phone call.

"Hello?"

"Hello, Mr. Lee, I presume?"

"Yes, it is."

"I'm Evelynn Browning, from The Browning Company."

"Good. You got my message."

"Yes, I did. Mr. Lee, do you actually have *Die Irrtümliche Münze*, or are you simply inquiring about it?"

"I have the coin. It's actually right here on the table beside me."

"Mr. Lee, I'm going to suggest that you put it somewhere safe for the time being. Perhaps in a safety deposit box."

Clinton trembled. "Maam, do you really think that's necessary?"

"I'm going to put it to you this way; the coin you have sitting there on the table beside you is something you don't want to let out of your sight until you get it in a secure place. A piece like that would give a burglar a reason to retire."

"All right. You've got my attention."

"Good. Now, I have a acquaintance who owns a coin dealership up north. I'm going to give him a call and tell him what you have. Mr. Lee, the coin is valuable. As far as finding out how much, you'll have to give me time."

"I don't have a problem with waiting."

"Can I reach you here later on today?"

"Sure."

"It may be tomorrow, but hopefully not. So, until then, put that thing somewhere more appropriate."

"Yes, Maam."

"Mr. Lee, you did a good thing by coming in here. I will be in touch."

Clinton hung the phone up. He reached on the table beside him to pick up his little, round treasure. "Looks like you might be worth something after all." He slipped it into his pocket, then took off for the bank to put it in a lockbox.

Afterwards, he hurried back in the event she called again. The call never came, though. Not that day. Or even the next. Eventually, six days rolled by before he heard from Mrs. Browning again.

Over the course of his wait, he began to get more and more anxious. He could barely concentrate at work. He was literally worried. And for what? A tiny piece of stamped metal? It all seemed a wee bit trite. Of course, when his phone call came, it all seemed worthwhile.

"Mr. Lee, I do apologize for not calling sooner, but I didn't have any information to give you before now. The acquaintance who I told you about? I think you need to talk to him. Mr. Lee, are you aware of the rarity of that particular coin?"

"Yes, I am, actually."

"As it turns out, my acquaintance has a client interested in it. He'd like to buy it from you. Of course, he'll need to see it first."

"I don't necessarily want to sell it. I was just interested in finding out what its value was."

"Mr. Lee, if this is the coin that you say it is, the man I'm speaking of is willing to offer you three and a half million for it."

Clinton was numb.

"Mr. Lee, are you there?"

"Yes, I'm here."

"Why don't you take some time and think about it?"

"I suppose I could do that."

"I'll be here at the dealership every day for the next week. Why don't you come by? Even if you decide that you don't want to sell, I wouldn't mind seeing the coin for myself."

"Sure. Listen. Thank you for your help, Mrs. Browning. You've uh ... definitely clued me in on a few things."

Clinton spent the rest of the day trying to absorb the fact that he actually owned something worth three and a half million dollars. There was one question boggling his mind, though. Did he actually have the right to call it his? Though he had asked Rutherford way back then to keep the coin, if it's worth had been known, it certainly wouldn't have gone home with him.

He also had to figure out which was more important, keeping it for sentimental reasons, or selling if for monetary ones. He figured that he could allow himself the luxury of sleeping on it for a few nights anyway, before making any permanent decisions.

But, speaking of decisions, he must have been out of his mind when he made the decision to break down and tell his ever-loving son Earl about it!

CHAPTER TWENTY

He found himself asking the same question over and over again. "What was I thinking?"

Earl had done nothing but interrogate him, and it did absolutely nothing but hinder him from making any sort of practical decisions as to whether he wanted to keep it or not. And since he was unable to make such a decision, he figured that hanging onto *Die Irrtumliche Munze* would be the best choice for the time being.

Earl, on the other hand, was adamant in his opinion of what to do with it. "Sell it, Daddy. Sell it. What's the matter with you? Are you crazy? It's just a coin. What are you ever gonna do with it other than look at it? But now, three million dollars? That you can do something with!"

Clearly Earl wasn't able to comprehend the concept of "sentimental." The thing of it was, Clinton tolerated his constant nagging. What really shook him up was the sheer greed that Earl displayed. He knew that Earl had more or less drawn the short straw his whole life, and had reason to be a little on the stingy side, but his mannerisms went way beyond that.

For the first time ever, Clinton was finally able to step aside from his role as a father and see what the rest of the world did when they looked at Earl Lee. It seemed almost as if he were looking at Margene. He had her looks, for certain. He also had her self-centeredness and tackiness. But worst of all, he had her intentions.

Earl acted as though that coin belonged solely to him, and that the three and a half million would go directly into the pocket of his trousers.

As Clinton observed all this, it made him doubt that his son was someone to confide in.

A few days later, Earl stopped by to visit. It was then that Clinton noticed yet another disturbing quality about him. As he plopped down on the living room sofa looking for a gadget to tinker with, Clinton stared at him from the next room over. Too occupied with the gadget, he was unaware that he was being watched. Clinton didn't know why he was driven to look so hard. It was just that something finally clicked inside his head. He stared at Earl long and hard, searching for one single physical feature that held an iota of resemblance to him. There wasn't one. Not the arch of his eyebrow, or even the square of his chin.

Sure, Margene had some pretty powerful traits that could all but devour every gene, but why couldn't he find anything that could be traced back to him?

A week later, Clinton woke up, went down to the kitchen, and made himself some breakfast. As he sat with his breakfast of overcooked toast and a cup of heavily creamed coffee, he looked up at the calendar on the wall and noticed that it was almost time to flip over the month.

The calendar had scribbling in red ink more or less all over it. Clinton had a habit of jotting things down that way so he could remember certain events that he would otherwise forget.

Tossing his half eaten piece of toast down on his plate, he wiped the jelly off his fingers and walked up to the calendar. He flipped the page over and reviewed all the dates with red scribbles, all the while crunching on his mouthful.

The first scribbling he read was one marked "Earl," meaning Earl's birthday. "Huh. That time again. How old does that make him now? Let's see, he was born...what was it? Fifty-two? Fifty-two...March the first, Nineteen and Fifty-two. Why does that seem so strange to me?"

He'd never felt this way before. Earl's birthday never seemed to be an unusual event in the past. Why now?

As he finished up his breakfast he left for the office, the whole time trying to figure out why something seemed so wrong. When he got there, he was unable to concentrate on anything. He swivelled his chair from side to side.

"What's wrong here?" He glanced over to the calendar sitting on his desk, hoping the observance of a different one would help things make sense.

"It all started with that God forsaken coin! Ever since I told him about it...all he's done is turn into his mother. Damn her! I loathe the day that I ever had to meet her! A mere eight days before I went off to boot camp...Why? Why me?" Then, everything clicked.

He looked once more over to the calendar on his desk and pulled it over, holding it right in front of his face. His eyes turned into a couple of zeros, and an instant case of nausea settled in his stomach. At this point, the last thing he wanted to do was to flip through the calendar and count the days backward, nine months from Earl's birthday. He knew he had to, though. He knew that no matter how disturbing the truth would be, it was a far cry better than living in uncertainty.

He began with the first day of March. Placing his finger on the number for that day, he began counting backward one week at a time. When he made his way to January, he flipped the calendar back over, continuing on with December. Once he was finished, it was quite clear to him that the last thirty one years of his life revolved around one big fat one.

Then Earlene popped into his mind. Was she a fabrication as well? Drunken though he may have been back in those days, he'd always had a hard time convincing himself that he'd slept with Margene that second time. Realizing that there was only one way to know for certain, he hopped up and headed out of the bank.

"Mr. Lee, I need you to..." one young errand boy said, breaking his train of thought.

Clinton rudely ignored him. At this point he didn't want to be bothered, no matter who he may have offended along the way. After he made it outside, he got in his truck and drove straight to the County Hospital. Which, by chance, was the birthplace for both Earl and Earlene.

He walked into the lobby, looking like a nervous wreck. The receptionist got wide-eyed.

"Are you all right, sir?"

"I need to see Arthur Peterson'"

"I take it you have an appointment?"

"No. I don't have an appointment, but it's urgent that I see him now."

"Let me check my book. I'll see if we can squeeze you in."

"I don't think you understand. I'm not asking if you can squeeze me in. I'm telling you to squeeze me in. Tell the doctor that Clinton Lee is here to see him."

"I'll tell him."

A few minutes later she came back. "Mr. Lee, it may take an hour or so, but he said that he'd see you."

"Then I'll wait."

Clinton sat down in one of the bright orange cushioned chairs. The time couldn't have passed more slowly for him, either. In less than half an hour, he'd managed to check his watch a dozen times, memorize the names of every resident doctor from 1925 to 1981 listed on the plaque hanging on the wall across from him, and come to the conclusion that the purpose for having bright orange chairs was for no other reason than to add to a patient's medical bill by persuading them to get a prescription for their mysterious, new migraine.

By this time, he'd run out of things to think about. Fortunately, a hunched over gentleman in a long, white coat walked up.

"Well, if it isn't Clinton Lee."

"Doc!"

"What brings you here in such a persistent manner?"

"I need to talk to you. Privately."

"Sure."

They walked to the elevators and went to up the second floor.

"It's right here. But I guess you probably remember where my office is."

"How could I forget? I guess I've been here a hundred times."

"Take a seat. Door closed? Clinton, I could be wrong, but something tells me you ain't in here for a case of aching bones."

"No, not quite. I need to ask you something very serious in all confidentiality."

"You know everything that's said is confidential."

"Doc, I need to know if it's possible for me to be the father of a child born on March 1st if the mother supposedly conceived on May 30th."

"Let's slow down a little bit. Now, first of all, you know that's not my area of expertise."

"Damn it, Arthur. You're a doctor. This is about Earl. Earlene, too. I know you didn't deliver them, but you are their family doctor. Can you help me with this or not?'

The old man looked at him, seeing desperation on his face. "All right. Let's sit down and do the math." He first went to his file cabinet and pulled out all the records he had for them. He browsed through Earl's files, then scribbled down a few calculations. "You say that you were with their mother on May 30th? Are you certain about that date?"

Last Will and Testament

"Doc, not only am I certain that May 30th is the date I was with her, but I'm damn near sure that it's the only time I've ever been with her."

"Clinton, if you're telling me that you had intercourse with Margene on May 30th, to my calculations, Earl would've been born somewhere around February 22nd. I don't know what to say. Earl ain't your boy. Clint, why haven't you mentioned this sooner?"

"I don't know. I guess it's because I didn't figure it out 'til today, Doc!"

"Ugly news, Clint. But there is a bright side."

"I'm all ears."

"Earl is over eighteen. You can handle the situation any way you want without any legal hoopla."

"What about Earlene? I've always known that something didn't seem right about Margene being pregnant with her. I swear, Doc, when I tell you that I think I was only with her once, I really mean that."

"A blood test will give you the answer to that."

"That could be a problem. I don't know how I could convince her to come in for one. She won't have anything to do with me. Nothin' at all. Yep. She waltzed right into the bank and officially disowned me. In front of some fairly important patrons, at that. The single most embarrassing situation I've dealt with so far."

"Clint, you know I'm not just your doctor, I'm your friend, too. I'll help you out any way I can. But first, you need to promise me that you're not going to do anything irrational. We'll figure out something to get her in here. I promise."

He began rummaging through Earlene's files. "Um, hmm. Clint, what's your blood type?"

"O positive, why?"

"Do you know Margene's?"

"Funny, I don't guess I do. I should. But I don't. Shoulda' paid more attention when we got our blood tests before we got married. You can check the file, though, can't you?"

"Officially? No. Legally? No. Children are one thing, but ex-spouses are entirely another."

"Look, I respect this confidentiality thing, but under the circumstances, don't you think you could make an exception? I mean, I'm not trying to invade anybody's privacy here. I just want to know if mine has been."

Peterson rubbed the hair on his chin. "Tell you what. I'll look up Margene's chart, for, let's just say, medical reasons. If I come up with any substantial news, why we'll just have to label it a life or death crisis." He winked. "Life or death, you understand. But I'll tell you what. Why don't you get outta here for awhile? Go take a breather. Clear your head for a little bit."

"Impossible, Doc. Just can't do it. I don't think a lobotomy could clear out all the crap I have in my head right now. Humor me for awhile, alright? If you don't find anything after looking through the Hussy's chart, I'll leave and deal with this later. Right now, I'm stayin'."

"Suit yourself." Peterson walked to his file cabinet once again and pulled out Margene's records. He hunched over them at his desk and skimmed through as much information as he could, until he came upon one section offering blood information. Glued to the page, he finally came across the answer he was looking for. He remained hunched over, not wanting to make eye contact with Clinton.

"What? What is it, Doc? You must've found something. You've had your head buried in that one corner long enough for me to know that you found something."

Peterson pursed his lips. "You know, I believe it might be a good idea for Earlene to come in and give a pint of blood."

"What?"

"She needs to, as rare as her blood type is. If anything ever happened to her, it would be good to know that there would be an ample supply on reserve."

"What are you talking about? Why are you saying this?"

"Remember what I said about life or death."

"I still don't understand" Clinton watched Peterson's facial expression, then realized what he was doing. "I get it. You're hinting without releasing information, due to doctor-patient confidentiality. I get it."

"Assuming that Margene is her real mother..."

"I think we can rule that one as a yes..."

"It appears that you and Earlene would have to have the same blood type."

"And..."

"You don't. That Earlene's got one of the rarer types. One you don't see that often. But now, assuming Margene is the mother..."

"What's Earlene's type?"

"B negative. But, now, assuming Margene is the mother..."

Clinton tried to rationalize what the doctor was suggesting. "If Earlene is B negative, then I'd have to be B negative, because Margene isn't B negative. But I'm not B negative. That means somebody else is the father. Oh, my Lord."

Last Will and Testament

Strangely, Peterson was able to feel the same shock as Clinton. Not only because he held a great deal of empathy for him, but because he somehow felt responsible for the whole mess. As his doctor, and Margene, Earl and Earlene's, he couldn't help but think that he should've paid more attention to genetic details. "I'm sorry."

Clinton walked out of the room. He had been betrayed to the most extreme degree, and was enraged with an anger that was borderline sinful. He was ready to kill someone. Driving home, he squealed his tires every chance he got, and was even tempted to run off the road in an attempt to injure himself.

After he got home, he stomped through the front door and went straight for his gun cabinet, pulling a pistol out from one of the bottom drawers. He caressed it in his hands like a lover. At nearly the same time that his head began rehashing dreadful memories of Margene and her exploitations, he fantasized about how simple it would be to put her out of her misery. It was only a fantasy, though. A lifetime in prison for murder wouldn't do him any good. It would only be yet one more reminder of everything she'd gotten away with. And even though he knew that he wouldn't use it, he continued to hold the gun in his hands, because it gave him the fulfillment he needed at that moment. And even though the fulfillment didn't relinquish any craving he may have had for vengeance, it did calm him enough to conjure up a legal, and much more hurtful way in which to achieve it.

CHAPTER TWENTY-ONE

That night he slept with his pistol by his side. It was the first time he'd ever had the inclination to. Somehow he felt as though it would lure peaceful dreams to his sleep. And it may very well have, because the next morning he woke as solid as ever.

As he prepared for the day, he stayed focused on only one thing. The thing that would successfully allow him to cut the cord from the things that had been burdening him since as long as he could remember. He wanted to do it, too. He'd made up his mind. He was going to make certain that no one ever imposed on his well-being again. And cutting two-thirds of his heirs from his will would be the ideal thing to start with.

Now, Clinton didn't know whether Earl or Earlene even knew the truth about their family ties, but to him, it was beside the point. Earlene had dismissed the whole thought of him, so there really wasn't anything to question, as far as she was concerned. And Earl, well, Earl had more than proven himself over the years.

The bottom line was that Clinton didn't care how it would affect the two of them. He may have raised them on a partial basis, but he had more than paid the price for it. So, as far as he was concerned, when it came to them, his job was done.

What he needed to focus mainly on was a bigger issue. Their mother.

Though his will didn't contain her name in any shape, form, or fashion, she, too, would be as affected by their omission as they would, because he had no intention of keeping the matter private. As soon as he was finished with what he had in mind, the embarrassment alone would be all it would take to make her fall from grace.

Imagine what would happen to Margene once she jumped, head first, into the sea of reality, acknowledging that she no longer had Clinton's chain to pull. She'd drown so fast, it wouldn't even be clockable.

Clinton grinned as he thought about it. Was it possible that she could be out of his life for good? He seemed to think so, anyway.

And with that, he was off to his lawyer's office.

Aaron Prouty, who had long since replaced the infamous Burtus O'Kelley as his legal advisor, was an older man who had built his reputation on drive and experience. There wasn't a case too big for him to handle or win. Clinton found him invaluable. Prouty held the same amount of regard for him too, especially since he'd basically made a mint off him.

As his client, Clinton made certain to clue Prouty in on all the new and less than charming facts that had surfaced. Based on Margene's past performances, Prouty was none too surprised to find out about it.

"I don't know whether to boo or applaud," he said. "All I can say is she's one hell of a stunt woman. Mmm..mmm..mmm. Clinton, your life never ceases to amaze me. It's like one bad drama after another. But I'll tell you what, that woman's looking at her final heyday. She'll be a thing o' the past, after I get done with her. She'll know what the poor house is really all about. Do you know, we've got at least a half dozen lawsuits to nail her for, based on what you've just told me this afternoon?"

Prouty propped his feet up on his desk and crossed his hands behind his head. "You know what the best part about all this is, don't you? She's going to lose that upscale title of hers. I don't guess I've ever disrobed a judge before," he said, laughing. "Those two kids of hers? They won't ever have any idea how much money they missed out on! Too bad. Well, Clinton, congratulations, I guess."

"Huh. I guess. So, what do I need to do now?"

"Now you need to take a copy of the adjustments we've made on your will home with you, and make sure there isn't anything else you want to add or change. If you can bring it back in sometime in the next couple of days, we can go ahead and have it notarized. You know about the witnesses, too."

"I'll do it."

Last Will and Testament

Those next couple of days seemed to change Clinton into a new man with tireless enthusiasm. Not that he didn't richly deserve to have it, but somehow conceit began to ease in right behind. And what goes hand in hand with conceit? Carelessness. It's what happens to a person once they have it in their head that they are invincible. They begin to slack off. They get sloppy. And that's more or less what happened to Clinton, which led to his first mistake.

In all the hubbub of dealing with his near freedom from Stoweville's Finest, he had quietly cut his ties from Earl and Earlene. Earl was the only one of the two who noticed. All in all, doing this wasn't necessarily the wisest move on Clinton's part, considering his will hadn't been formally notarized yet. Ending his relationship so hastily and without any explanation as to why made Earl a bit on the curious side. Which leads to the second of Clinton's mistakes. The unsigned will in which he had so proudly made the changes had been openly placed on top of his bedroom bureau.

The thought of anyone seeing it didn't really cross his mind, because the only people who he was under the impression had free access to his home was Darryl and himself. He'd never even bothered to have a door key made for the housekeeper since she only came once a week, and she'd already made her rounds that week. What was the risk in leaving it out for a couple of measly days?

The fact was, there may have been one more individual with access to the Shangri-la mansion.

Not that Earl could have been tagged with a sign of ingenuity for pulling the old sneak the key and make a copy of it before anyone finds out trick, but he had come up with less brilliant ideas in his day. This stunt, which he'd pulled some six months earlier, had given him the freedom to snoop his way through Shangri-la whenever he took a notion to. The thing was, he'd never stolen anything more than a little cash that might have been lying around. The main reason he wanted a key to begin with was because he simply felt entitled to have one. And knowing within reason that Clinton would never offer such a thing, he did what he had to do.

Usually, he would hang out there, pretending that it was his mansion. And he always felt the need to nose through just about everything. It's one of the ways he managed to learn so many of the nit-picky details about Clinton. He knew how categorized Clinton kept his sock drawer, that he always coiled up his tube of toothpaste, and that no matter what, had a freshly made pitcher of tea in the refrigerator waiting for him when he came home from work. These were the types of particulars that he reported to his mother from time to time.

There was one thing that he didn't share with her, though. And that was the fact that he owned an entrance key. It was something that Earl had chosen to keep to himself, because for some reason it made him feel powerful.

When he came across the document laying on Clinton's bureau entitled "Last Will and Testament," it didn't take long for him to realize that having this so-called power was something he wasn't quite ready to handle. Not by himself, anyway.

"What's this thang? It wudn't here before." He reached across and grabbed hold of it. "Last Will and Testament...Last Will.... Oh. This must be a Will. Wonder what Daddy's got a Will in here for?"

He began reading through it, trying his best to comprehend as much of it as he could. Much of it was easy for him to understand, even though it was flooded with legal terminology. Chalk that up to living under his mother's roof. Somehow that had prepared him at least mildly, when it came to formal documents such as this. In other words, he knew to skip over the legalities and get straight to the good stuff.

The first page seemed a little too mundane to read through. So he flipped over to the second page, which contained more than a few surprises.

The first thing he noticed was that Clinton referred to Daralynn Lee as his sole heir.

"Why does he keep sayin' sole heir?" Earl stopped reading through what he knew didn't pertain to him and started searching for anything that had his name attached. He looked and looked as hard as he could. There was nothing there. Not one sentence, paragraph, or phrase contained the name Earl Lee. What was more, he didn't find one single reference to his sister either.

"I don't understand," he said, fumbling through to the very last page. "Is that all of it?" Noticing that the last page contained all the signature spaces, he knew right then that there weren't any missing pages. "Now wait. What about that damn coin? Who's s'posed to get it?"

He sat on the edge of the bed, glancing once again over everything, beginning from page one.

"Darryl gets this, and she gets this," he said as he went down the list. Suddenly, he stopped reading, fixing his eyes on two words in particular. He couldn't pronounce those two words, but he knew exactly what they referred to. "No! She ain't gettin' that!"

He began to shout, and throw one awful temper tantrum. For about twenty minutes he was so unable to contain himself that it was only by sheer miracle that nothing in that bedroom got broken or damaged.

With fire literally streaming through his veins, he could barely hold his hands still. And it took all the control he had to gather the pages of the will and place them back on top of the bureau exactly like he'd found them. Realizing that power was only something he thought he had, he walked away angry, but more humbled than ever. And having just enough common sense to know that he was completely clueless as to how to handle the situation, he did what he always did and went crying to his mother.

Nearly wrecking his car about a dozen times, he somehow managed to make it to Margene's stately office in one piece. Angry and huffing for breath, he stormed in the building and went straight to her quarters, where he found her robing for an afternoon hearing.

"Mama," he said, trying to catch his breath, "I gotta tell you somethin'!"

Having no expectations of experiencing a run-in with her son at that time, she was a little taken back to see him standing there. "Earl, go and shut the door, would you?"

"Mama, I gotta tell you somethin!"

"Shut the door, first!"

"All right, already. But why are you whisperin'?" Earl shook his head, as he walked back and closed the door. "Mama..."

"Earl, let's take a walk down memory lane for a minute. Now, do you remember back when you were, oh, ten or eleven?"

"Yeah...I guess I do."

"That's good. So, do you remember any conversations we might have had, oh, say pertaining to you callin' or droppin' by my office?"

"Whuh, yeah. You told me not to."

"I believe there was a little more to it than that. What did I always tell you? Under..."

"Under no circumstances was I to bother you at work, unless tornado, hurricane, flood, or fire."

"So, let me ask you something, Earl. Do you think anything has changed since then?"

Earl stood blankly, all but forgetting what brought him there to begin with. "No, Mama. I don't guess anything's changed."

"Well, then. What in the hell are you doin' comin' into my office like this? Take a look at me. Can t you see I'm robing up for court?"

"How was I s'posed to know? But that don't matter, anyway. I got some news to tell you, and I don't think it can wait."

"Spit it out, then."

"Daddy's got a will. I saw it. And I ain't in it. Earlene ain't neither."

Suddenly interested in what her son had to say, but realizing that court was only a few short moments away, she looked down at her watch. "Hold on a minute, Earl." She thought for a moment, trying to figure out what her options were. No, this wasn't a tornado, hurricane, flood, or fire. It was much worse. Her link to the Clinton Lee fortune was in jeopardy. She couldn't just stand by and let everything she'd worked so hard for go flying out the window.

She had to take action. And quickly. Looking over at Earl, she held up her index finger, then grabbed the telephone receiver. "Nancy," she said to her secretary, "call the D.A.'s office and tell them that an emergency has come up. I'm gonna have to issue a postponement of court 'til tomorrow."

Looking curiously over at her son, she hung up the phone. "All right, Earl. Why don't you take a seat here and tell me everything you know."

CHAPTER TWENTY-TWO

nxious to get out all the facts that he knew in the least amount of time as possible, his words came across as more of a load of gibberish than information.

"Earl, you're not makin' a bit o' sense. Slow down, already."

So he did. He told her everything he knew, down to the bit about Darryl being the sole heir, and that long, funny spelled word he saw.

"What do you mean, funny spelled word?"

"I couldn't even read the thing, much less pronounce it. But I know, just by the way it was described, that it was that million dollar nickel."

"You sure about that?"

"Mama, it was obvious. I ain't no brain surgeon, I know. But anybody who took a look at that will and read what I did would know. Trust me."

"And you say Clinton's leaving it to Darryl?"

"He's leaving every damn thing to her!"

"Okay now, you say that there weren't any signatures, right?"

"Nope. Ain't nobody signed the thing."

"And you just saw it today?"

"Yep."

Margene took a minute to think. "Ain't today your birthday?"

"Well, yeah, Mama. It's my birthday. Don't you know that? Daddy ain't

165

had a thing to do with me either. And to top it all off, I find this will. Somethin's happened. I don't know what, but somethin's happened. Daddy ain't never acted like this before."

Margene leaned her head back. Though she did appear somewhat distressed, the look of concern was more on her behalf than it was Earl's. "Now, hold on a minute. I believe there's one part you've left out."

"What's that?"

"Where is it that you came across this will?"

Earl's cheeks flushed. "Uhm. Hey! I, uh, sorta saw it layin' in his bedroom."

"You lost me. I thought you said you just saw it today."

"I did just see it today."

"Now you said that he hasn't had a thing to do with you."

"He ain't!"

"Well, how is it that you managed to be inside his house? I mean, did you break in or somethin'?"

"Heh. Mmm-aybe, kinda?"

"Earl, there ain't no 'kinda' about it. Either you did or you didn't."

"I sorta have a key that you didn't know anything about, okay?"

"What? Do you mean to tell me..."

"Mama, don't get mad. I've only had it for a couple o' days."

Earl was lying through his teeth, but it did salvage him from getting any further tongue lashings.

"This changes everything."

Earl watched as a transformation took place in his mother's face. One minute she was a shaken up woman who couldn't figure out whether to be angry or desperate. The next, she looked like the cat who swallowed the canary.

"Why don't you just hand over that key you have? I think I can take over from here."

Earl didn't question her. He did what she said. "Do you want me to..."

Margene closed her eyes and nodded. "Just let me handle it from here."

It was almost as though Earl was relieved to be getting rid of the key. Somehow he knew that once it went from his hands to his mother's, everything would get handled the way it was supposed to.

Margene had more than a few plans up her sleeve.

Throughout her many years reigning Stoweville's legitimate and not so legitimate, she had always made certain to stay in cahoots with the "not sos" who had the talent of being immune to the legal system. In short, the Dixie Mafia. And though this particular group didn't hold the weight that their northern relatives did, they were not to be looked upon lightly.

Some ten years earlier, Margene had tried a case involving the leader of one of its top families, Jackson "Grampus" Healy.

Clocking in at about seventy-one years old, he no longer participated in the mafia legwork. Instead, he sat on his throne making decisions that no one else had earned the right to.

Margene knew of his secret authority those ten years earlier, which basically explains why she ruled in his favor.

"It never hurts to do a favor for someone you might want one from in return," she always said. The thing was, she didn't want to cash in this alleged favor too quickly. First, she needed to make sure she was good for it, and second, if it were granted, she wanted to use it on something big. Up until this point, nothing had ever been too outlandish for her to handle on her own. But now, she knew that in order to get exactly what she wanted, she would have to keep her hands as clean as possible and let someone else tackle the dirty work.

She waited until everyone in the building had gone home, then she went through the old files on Jackson Healy. After locating his telephone number, she locked up and headed straight for the most inconspicuous pay phone she could find. Making absolutely sure that no one saw her, she got out of her car and creeped toward the booth. She kept one hand held near her face to shield her identity and used the other to dial the number.

By the third ring, there was an answer.

"Hello."

"I'm looking for a Mister Jackson Healy. Would this be him?"

"Well, now, that depends. Who's doin' the lookin'?"

"This is Margene Lee."

Suddenly, all she heard was a dial tone. "What was that about?" She looked around to see if anyone had noticed her yet, but to her knowledge she was still the only living soul in sight. Reaching for another dime, she wondered if her second attempt would turn out the same.

Again, the phone rang, and again there was an answer.

"Hello."

"I'm gonna ask that you don't hang up. I've taken off my robe. Right now, I'm just a civilian same as you. Mr. Healy? It's you, isn't it?"

"What do you want?"

"Just to talk. That's all." Margene was used to manipulating people. But she knew that this wasn't someone to use her one and only skill with.

"Talk?"

"That's all. I swear." And she actually meant it.

"Well, then, talk away."

At first she didn't know what she wanted to say, or better yet, how to conduct a business call with a mobster. "Grampus? Can I call you Grampus?"

"No."

"I'm sorry. Uhm, I need......something done."

"What makes you think I can help you?"

"Well, you know, about ten years ago...."

"Let's get something straight right away here. Jackson Healy doesn't work that way."

"Just hear me out."

"No. You hear me out. I believe you are the one soliciting me. First of all, I don't conduct any kind of business over the telephone. And as far as ten years ago is concerned, I don't remember twisting your arm for that verdict. You see, Margene, I don't swap favors. The way I work is, I take your back whenever I feel enough respect for you to do it. Otherwise, you may as well be a stranger on the street."

Margene's high hopes quickly faded into modest intentions, yet she still felt determined to give it everything she had.

"We're talking about a lot of money here. I'll let you handle it anyway you want. I'll stay completely out of it. Will you at least meet with me?"

There was a long silence.

"Tomorrow morning. The old railroad salvage. Five o'clock. Don't be late."

The next morning at four o'clock, Margene was up with bells on. She was so eager to have her face to face that she showed up well before Healy and the two thugs who would accompany him.

It was pitch black outside, so she didn't really get a good look at their faces. The little bit that she could distinguish was their outline created by the flow of Healy's headlights.

One was short, with a bushy head of hair. The other was slightly thin and wreaked of cloves. Healy stood between them.

"So, tell me what this business of yours is all about," he said.

"In a nutshell, it's about a will. I want you to get rid of it."

"Boys, let's pack it up."

"You're not giving me a chance. I told you there was some money involved, didn't I? All right. A lot of money."

"How does this will relate to you?"

"It's my ex-husband's."

"Lady, not only are you barkin' up the wrong tree, but you're livin' in some sordid fantasy world." As Healy walked back to his car, the thugs took guard in the event that Margene tried to pull something dirty. "Boys, what is it that I do to people who pull me outta bed at five o'clock in the morning for a false alarm?"

Margene felt her blood turn cold. The thought of two faceless men dislocating her kneecaps or something even worse literally left her trembling.

"Mr. Healy, you have children, don't you?" she yelled in desperation.

Healy stopped. Almost in the car, he pulled himself out and walked toward Margene. "What did you just say?"

"No, no, no. I, I didn't mean it like that."

"You've got about ten seconds to explain yourself."

"How would you feel if the mother of your children purposely left them out of her will? Not that she would, but you'd do everything you could to make sure they got everything they deserved, wouldn't you? You'd want to make sure of it, right? Well, that's all I'm trying to do here. My ex-husband... No, the father of my children has excluded them from his will."

"How is it that you know about this, if he's your ex?"

"You have your secrets. I have mine. Mr. Healy, my children have been deprived of their father's wealth their whole lives, and I'm not about to sit back and let him rub their faces in it anymore. It's gone on for long enough."

"And you know the whereabouts of this will?"

"I do. Right now, it's in his home. He actually has it sittin' out in plain sight."

"You have an insider feeding you all this information, I suppose?"

"Like I said, I have my secrets."

"Margene, I'm suspicious of you."

"That's all right. I'm suspicious of you, too."

"Umm-hmm. So, what's this truck load of money you were talking about?"

"That's fairly obvious to anyone who knows of Clinton Lee. I take it you're not too familiar with that name?"

"Lady, I know who he is. But my question is, how you intend on getting your hands on his will? Let's say, I do get this will to disappear for you. How are you gonna keep ol' Clinty from scratchin' up a new one?"

"He won't be scratchin' up a new one."

"How do you figure?"

"Because I want you to kill him." She then went on to suggest ways in which to do it.

Healy was stunned. He knew she was corrupt, but up until now he hadn't known exactly how much. "You can't afford it," he said.

"Try me. I'll pay you fifty grand to do it. I'll give you ten now. The rest I can give you after the estate is settled."

"A hundred, or I won't touch it. And I want another ten grand by noon today."

Margene cringed at the thought of having to dish out more money, even though there was more than enough to go around. But what other choice did she have?

"A hundred. But I can't give you another ten today. It's out of the question. It was all I could do to scrape up this amount in such a short time without being obvious." She handed a large, brown folder over to Healy. "You're going to have to trust me on the rest."

"Margene, you already know that I don't trust you. But I am positively certain that you won't pull a fast one. 'Cause you know that I know where to find you. I think you'll be good for it. Now, is there anything else I need to know about this will?"

"It was unsigned. Make sure that hasn't changed. I guess you need to do that first, before anything else."

"I think my boys are bright enough to figure that out."

"I guess that's it, then. But one more question. How am I supposed to get in touch with you?"

"We'll find you."

Margene waited in her car until they drove off. Rather pleased with the way things had turned out, she decided to go home and celebrate for awhile. Besides, she had to get the pent-up giddiness out of her system before going to work. She couldn't chance anyone getting suspicious of her unexpected mood shift.

So, as she got on with things, so did the two individuals who had accompanied Healy earlier that morning.

Healy was not only their mentor. He was, in some ways, their god. When he said to do something, that meant do it. No questioning, no infusing common sense into the equation, and no complaining. So, if he said to jump, it wasn't a question of how high. It was a matter of off which bridge? In this case, he didn't exactly ask them to commit their own suicide but merely to get a job done in the means of raking in a little extra cash.

"Boys, I don't want this one to look like cold-blooded murder, now. I want you to give it a little more subtle effect. A death-by- natural-causes feel. Heart failure. That would work. I do remember, some twenty-five years ago that ol' Clinty up and had himself a heart attack. It was during his divorce from that bitch. Do you know that I was actually sittin' in the courtroom when it happened? I guess that had to have been the single most spectacle I'd ever seen up until that time. Huh. Oh, well. Just make it look natural. I'll deal with the coroner. The will? Bring it to me. I think I'll hang onto it for good measure until Lady Lee hands over the other ninety. Other than that, I guess you two still know how to break into a house, don't you?"

Healy's sidekicks were about as mysterious as the cure for cancer. To everyone but Healy.

No one really knew anything about them, or even where they came from. The only thing anyone knew was that they existed and they spent an awful lot of time around Jackson Healy. What people didn't know was that Healy had plucked them straight off vagabond row. He found them in a city out west when they were a couple of homeless teens, headed for nowhere other than a meeting with their maker.

Healy decided that they would be better off if he became their maker. So, there they were. Two new eyes and ears for the Healy crime family.

Though earlier that morning Margene was unable to make out any distinguishing facial characteristics, she got the pertinent things down pat. For one, it wasn't too often she'd ever seen a fluff of hair like the one she had seen on the little one. Which, by circumstances, happened to be his nickname. The other thing she had noticed was the smell of cloves on the tall, lanky one. She couldn't quite figure that one out. What, had he just come from a mincemeat pie bake-off?

Later that morning, Little One and Shakey, the other one, drove a majority of the way to where Cinton lived. After hitting Old Jordan Road, they looked for a somewhat secluded area to park their vehicle in. When Little One opened his door, he immediately got slapped in the face with a branch full of thorns. "Damn it, Shakey. Do you think we could've found a spot just a little bit more briary?"

Shakey wasn't the talkative type. He only said what was necessary. So he never bothered to back-talk Little One when he nagged. He hopped out of the car, avoided the whole splinter in the face bit, and began investigating the area for the best trail that led to the Shangri-la estate.

"What d'ya think," said Little One. "This way?"

Shakey shook his head, then pointed in a different direction.

"Yeah, I guess you're right. That does look a little better than this way over here. Hey. Did you bring something to pick the lock?"

Shakey patted the pocket on his trousers.

"Good. 'Cause I didn't bring a thing."

The two traveled onward, reaching a dense thicket just outside Shangri-la. Shakey once again stopped to investigate his surroundings. Little One began to mutter something, until Shakey interrupted. "Let me go first," he said, slipping on a pair of kidskin gloves. He crept through a row of trees until he was right on the edge of the estate grounds, then looked carefully right and left for any sign of people lurking around. When he was absolutely sure the coast was clear, he made a dash through the yard and up the porch steps to the front door. Letting his peripheral vision do most of the seeing for him, he reached for his lock-picking tools and successfully cracked open the door. He stood there for a split second, long enough to signal Little One that it was safe to make a run for it, then walked inside.

As soon as Little One was inside too, he reached to push the door shut. He wasn't wearing any gloves. Shakey felt the need to make up for his partner's shortcomings by wiping the knob clean.

"Oh. Sorry. They're in my pocket here."

Shakey didn't wait around. He headed straight for the staircase.

"Where you goin'?"

"To find the will."

He nosed through a few bedrooms until he found one that was masculine enough to justify being Clinton's. He remembered what Margene had said about the will being out in plain sight, so he looked for any signs of a document that fit the description. And as easily as Margene said it would be to find, that's exactly how easy it was.

He flipped through it to make sure there weren't any signatures, then rolled it up to slip it into his jacket.

"Where you at?" whispered Little One, just making his way upstairs.

Shakey poked his head out the door, so his partner could find him.

"Had any luck?"

Shakey pulled his jacket open, exposing the rolled up will.

"Well, that was quick. Now what?"

"I'm still thinking."

What he was thinking about were the suggestions Margene had given as to possible ways in which to pull off the murder. Though she'd never actually been part of a deviant act such as murder, the ideas that popped out of her head could've proven to any jury that she was a pro at it.

There was one particular suggestion that seemed to stand out more than the others. Given the fact that he was prepared to carry that one out, he felt as though it would be the most convenient way to handle the task.

Little One followed him around and watched as he went to work. Being the half-tuned one of the two, it was about all he could do. His purpose was mainly for moral support, and taking care of nitpicky legwork.

"I think it's time to split," said Shakey.

"Is that all you're gonna do?"

"For now."

They left the house and headed back to their car. When they got there, Shakey leaned up next to the door and pulled a pack of cigarettes from his shirt pocket. They were clove, and had a red tip on them.

"I'll never understand how you can smoke those things."

He lit it and took a big drag. "Why don't you take the car and get out of here. I'm going to wait around until the deed is done."

"How are you gonna get back?"

"You're going to meet me at midnight about a mile down the road. Right now, you need to get word to Grampus that things are still underway, but the job will be done by the end of the day. Give him the will, too. Don't lose it."

"All right. Well, you be careful out here."

Little One backed out of the briar patch, leaving Shakey there to finish his cigarette and wait.

Back in town, Clinton was in his office at the Bank of Stoweville putting some finishing touches on a business document. When he laid his pen down, he began thinking about the will he'd left at home. Wishing that he'd brought it with him so he could take it to Prouty's office and make it a done deal, he decided that it could wait one more day. He also hadn't decided who he wanted to use as a witness since the whole thing was so touchy and personal. There were a couple of names that crossed his mind, all of which were bank personnel, but he'd have one more night to think on it.

Then something else crossed his mind. He hadn't told Darryl a thing.

Granted, it would be something disturbing for her ears to hear, but he knew she needed to know the truth. He knew that it was something he should tell her in person, too.

Unfortunately, given the fact that she was away at college, he would have to wait until the weekend before he might have a chance of seeing her. He reached for the phone to give her a call, dialing the number and waiting for it to ring. Surprisingly, she was there to answer.

"Hello? Hey, Daddy, I was just thinking about you. Dinner on Saturday? You bet. You pick the place, Daddy. Ha ha ha. You know the West Country Steak House is one of my favorite places to eat with you. It's about the only place in town to get a decent piece o' meat. Six-thirty? Sounds fine to me. See you then. 'Bye, Daddy."

CHAPTER TWENTY-THREE

Darryl was working on her fourth year at college, with only half a semester left to graduate. She had chosen to follow in her mother's footsteps and study music. Only her gift was vocal rather than instrumental.

As a child, she remembered standing alongside her mother at the piano and singing to entertain her father. He couldn't have been a more devoted fan, either. That's why, as a surprise to him, she had written a special song. Her plan was to perform it at her graduation party, since everyone, including the family, would be there. The hard part would be to do it without getting misty-eyed.

Sitting there in her worn-out lounge chair, she looked through an old photo album. It was one she hadn't pulled out in awhile. It had all the pictures from her early childhood, all the way to her awkward teenage years. She had gotten as far as the post-toddler section when her father had phoned and interrupted her.

"I must be psychic," she said after getting off the phone with him. "Every time I think about Daddy, it seems like he's thinking about me. I can't wait to see him. I bet he'll wear that God-awful shirt I bought him when I was in the eighth grade. He wears it every single time he hasn't seen me for awhile."

The shirt, indeed, made the list of fashion's biggest no-no's. It was a shade of peach with red and dark purple squiggles all over it. Obviously, it wouldn't have been Clinton's shirt of choice if he were out shopping for himself, but at the time he'd originally opened it as a Christmas gift from Darryl, he felt obligated to appreciate it. Back then, he wore it to please her. Now, he did it just to humiliate her.

About that time her dorm-mate skattered through the door. "Hey, Darryl."

"Hi, Jodie. You know, if you got a jacket one size bigger, you could actually fit two people in there."

"What, do you think it's too big?"

"Just a hair."

"Well, it does a good job covering up all the extra weight I put on this winter, don't you think? Hey, listen, can I borrow your car Saturday night? I've got a date with you know who. Plus, it's not like you'll need it or anything. You haven't gone on a date the entire year! I don't know why, either. I've watched half the guys in Trembly Hall trip over each other trying to get the desk next to you."

"First of all, you're exaggerating. But, secondly, that isn't the case. They're just after an easy grade. For some reason, I find myself unintentionally letting them cheat off my paper. Oh, and last but not least, no, you can't borrow my car Saturday night. As it turns out, I do have a date."

"Details, honey, details!"

"With my father. So there!"

"Oh," she said, disappointed. "Well, have a great time. If you can."

"You know, just because you have a rotten relationship with your parents doesn't mean everybody does. I happen to like my father."

"Well, consider yourself one of the fortunate few."

"Believe me, I do."

"So, uh, if you're going out with your dad, does that mean you'll be gone for the rest of the weekend?"

"Yeah, I thought I'd take off early afternoon on Saturday and come back sometime Monday morning."

"So, the place is all mine?"

"The place is all yours."

"Cool!"

Saturday morning Darryl got busy packing for her trip. She was looking forward to being back at Shangri-la, since she hadn't been in over two months. Besides, Shangri-la always made her feel like a kid again. Though there were a few things different from that of her childhood, like the absence of Happy and Beautiful, the feeling was almost still the same.

Last Will and Testament

She slammed her suitcase shut, inadvertently waking Jodie up from her usual oversleeping. "What time is it?" she asked, yawning.

"Time to get up, lazybones."

"Some of us need more rest than others."

" 'More rest' meaning four hours over the average?"

"Shut up. Hey, what was wrong with you last night, anyway?"

"Huh?"

"You don't know?"

"What are you talking about, Jodie?"

"Darryl, you were talking in your sleep last night. I thought maybe you were having a bad dream or something. You woke me up two times. You'd roll around, talkin' to yourself, then you'd kind of quiet down and fall back asleep again."

For the life of her, Darryl couldn't remember a thing. "Did I yell or anything?"

"No, you didn't go that far. Don't worry 'bout it too much. You were probably just having a nightmare."

Driving back home to Stoweville, she kept thinking about what Jodie had told her. How could she not have remembered a dream that intense? After thinking about it for nearly an hour, she decided to put it out of her mind, because it clearly wasn't going to come to her. So, to draw her attention elsewhere, she pulled onto the next exit ramp to put a little gas in her car.

Driving up to the pump, she noticed a bright blue Trans Am parked right in front of the door of the station. *Nice car*, she thought, halfway expecting it to belong to some young male hot shot.

Admiring it while she pumped, she waited in anticipation for the mysterious hot shot to come waltzing out with a wide grin and a pack of cigarettes. After her pump clicked off, she walked toward the station door, hoping to catch a glimpse of him.

Who was he? Was he a young hot shot like she thought?

She stopped to shuffle through her purse for some dollars. Then, as quickly as she could look up, a teenaged girl rushed out of the store and hopped into the car. It was then that she looked down and saw the license plate, reading "Julia."

It hit her that the name she saw was that of her mother. It hit her that the nightmare she'd had the night before was starting to come back to her. And it hit her that the last time she'd had a nightmare so horrific was when she was

177

just eight years old. The same time that her mother was presumably on her way to meet her maker. Was it deja vu, or did she have a talent of foreseeing the future?

"This is ridiculous. You're not physic. You were just having a nightmare last night. Besides, Mommy's death way back then didn't have anything to do with the bad dream you'd had. You were eight years old, for pete's sake! It was just a coincidence. Yeah. That's all it was."

CHAPTER TWENTY-FOUR

She drove into the Stoweville city limits in the late afternoon, thinking she would spend a couple of hours with her father before they headed off for dinner.

"It's good to be back in this town," she said, admiring the spring flowers that decorated the downtown area. "Only in Stoweville do they celebrate spring so perfectly."

Perfect it was, too. There were urns, wreaths, and hanging baskets smothered in colorful flowers everywhere she looked. Even the train station looked less like a home for railcars and more like a florist shop.

The country didn't have any less appeal. Though it wasn't purposely decorated the same way that the town was, it had been touched by the hand of mother nature, making it equally enticing. The birds were chirping, the trees were budding, and the air was fresher than she'd ever remembered.

For her, there couldn't have been a more perfect day. She was far away from her school curriculum, with nothing else to focus on except what was around her and spending time with her father.

Nearing Old Jordan Road, a squad car passed her speeding like a bat out of hell. She was puzzled for a moment, but soon forgot about it. Then another one passed, going seemingly faster than the first.

Puzzled again, she became nervous and clinched the steering wheel.

When she made her turn onto Old Jordan Road, nothing appeared to be unusual. There were no wrecked cars in the road or houses on fire. But after several more yards, she spotted a third car way up the road, near the edge of the Shangri-la grounds.

The fresh spring air seemed to turn into a stagnant fog, making it hard for her to breathe. As her foot was no longer pressing the gas, she sat idle in the middle of the road. She felt scared. Scared that something terrible had happened, and scared that her dream last night had something to do with it.

She got out of her car and walked toward the drive of Shangrila. The police car she'd spotted was empty, so she continued down the driveway. At first there was a sort of silence, but as she got closer to the house, she began to hear the chatter of voices. Those voices became louder every step she took forward. Louder to the point that she was able to recognize one. It was one that was so familiar that she had learned to hate it. The voice of Earl Lee seemed to resonate above every other that she could hear.

"What's happened to my daddy?" he cried. "What are you gonna do with my daddy?"

Earl was making a spectacle of himself, all right. He was causing such a scene that literally no one present would be able to leave the premises without having thoughts of him at the edge of their brain.

"Miss, I don't think you ought to be here," a voice whispered from behind her.

She turned around to find a gentleman in uniform a few feet away. "This is my house. Or, it's.....it's my father's house."

"So, you don't live here anymore?"

"I'm in college right now."

"I see. Did you just get here then?"

"Uh-huh."

"Then you've heard the news."

"News? What news?"

"Clinton Lee, your father, was found dead just this morning."

Darryl fell instantly to her knees.

"I'm so sorry. You didn't know."

There was a long pause. "How did he die?"

"According to our reports, he died of a heart attack."

"Heart attack? He's only forty-eight."

"It's what's been reported."

"Where's Sheriff Slack?"

"He was here a couple hours ago. You need to speak with him?"

"He was one of Daddy's good friends."

"Well, I'll be. I know who you are now. I just didn't recognize you. You might've been five or six the last time I saw you. Yep, I remember your daddy bringin' you along one time when he came out to see the sheriff. You'd pitched a fit 'cause your daddy was gonna make you go with the both of 'em fishin'."

It was then that she finally cried.

"I'm sorry. I didn't mean to upset you."

"Where's his body?"

"Hon, his body's been taken to the funeral home to be embalmed."

"What? I don't understand. Nobody called me. Nothing."

"Why don't I take you to see Sheriff Slack?"

"No. I can do it myself. It looks as though I'm on my own here. I was on my own as far as finding out about all this. I guess I can be on my own for the rest of it."

"Hon, don't think I'm tryin' to be impersonal here."

"Don't call me Hon." Darryl started to walk away, but stopped. "Who reported him– his death?"

"Earl Lee. He related to you?"

"Huh. I wouldn't go that far."

"He's supposedly around here causing a scene, I've been told. We're trying to keep the place blocked off from everybody except the law. That wouldn't be him up on the porch there, would it?"

"That's your man."

"Listen, I'm..."

Darryl held her hand up to stop him. She didn't feel like talking anymore. As she walked away from Shangri-la, she didn't bother to look back. In an instant it stopped feeling like home. The sight of yellow tape stretched across everything didn't help matters, either. And Earl. Who did he think he was hanging out on the porch like that?

"That bastard."

Suddenly, she felt utterly alone. She'd been alone, plenty. But she'd never felt alone. She didn't quite know how to handle it, either. It was almost as though the whole world was closing in on her, and she didn't know whether to lay down and get suffocated or run.

"I've gotta get out of here. But where am I supposed to go?" She got back in her car. She looked around, but everything was a blur. Her head was filled with so much anxiety that she began to shake.

"I'll go to Uncle Martin's," she said, crying. "Yeah. I'll go to Uncle

Martin's." She stepped on the gas and began to drive, looking through a sea of tears.

She drove halfway to her uncle's farm before she changed her mind and headed back toward the Sheriff's office. Eddy. He'll be able to help me. He can tell me what's really going on."

Darryl's expectation of her father's old friend Eddy Slack might have been set a bit too high. As it turned out, he was about as informative as a blank sheet of paper.

"Darryl, honey, I'm so sorry about your daddy. Is there anything I can do for you?" he asked her.

"I've got a million questions to ask you."

"I know you do, and I'll try to help you, but you know how busy I am trying to handle things."

"Of course. I wouldn't want to hinder you from your work on account of my petty questions."

"Darryl. It ain't like that and you know it."

"Isn't it? It looks as though I'm irrelevant here. Earl's the one that matters, right? He's the one who called and reported that Clinton Lee was dead. He's the one who's hangin' out on the porch at Shangrila while everyone else has been asked to leave."

"Take it easy, now. Don't get too riled up. You're upset, I know. I understand what you're going through, though."

"No, you don't understand what I'm going through. How could you? 'Cause I don't even know what I'm goin' through!"

"Sit down. I'll tell you everything I know. But just calm down. That's all I ask."

Slack went through everything he knew about the case, challenging as that might have been. The Darryl he was dealing with wasn't exactly the bundle of innocence he'd remembered her being. In fact, the moment she had arrived at his office she'd become a different person entirely. Though she was showing signs of grief over the loss of her father, she still seemed to have a sort of vengeful side, aware that something foul had taken place.

Clinton had been dead for nearly two days before his body was found. No autopsy had been performed, either. The mysterious new coroner in town had labeled the incident as a heart attack and had sent him on his way to the embalming headquarters. That was only one of many happenings that didn't make sense to Darryl. She went along with the show, though, saving up her true retaliation until after the funeral.

CHAPTER TWENTY-FIVE

Jodie, I'm gonna be out of school for awhile."

"Why, what's going on?"

"My father died."

"Oh my gosh. I'm sorry. But I don't understand. When did he die?"

"It appears that he died a few days before I got here."

"But you just talked to him a few days ago."

"I know, Jodie."

"I guess I just don't understand."

"It doesn't matter. Just listen. I need you to talk to my professors for me. Can you do that?"

"Of course! Where are you right now?"

"I'm staying at my uncle's. I'll be here for a few days anyway."

"What about your father's house?"

"I'm not goin' back there till after the funeral."

"Well, when is that? I mean, do you need me to be there? Darryl, I'll come if you need me."

"No, you don't...no, it's okay. It's just a mess here. I need somebody on the outside to be sane, okay? I'll call you after it's over. Funeral's tomorrow. I'll be okay. My uncle's been real nice. He knows I'm upset, and he's stayin' out of my hair."

"Just call me if you need me."

Darryl spent that Saturday night at her uncle Martin's. He had been informed of his brother's death by a visit from one of the deputies only minutes before Darryl had arrived. The both of them went through the shock of it together, then went their own separate ways to sort their feelings. Martin was much like Darryl in the fact that he needed his alone time to stay sane. They agreed to take turns informing family and friends, since neither were good at delivering bad news.

Most people were surprised to hear of his death, given the fact that he was relatively young. Some blamed it on a weakened heart from his heart attack some twenty-five years prior. But, all in all, it was an unexpected notion to literately everyone.

Once the word was out, Darryl felt the need to brush off the outpour of affection she got. It seemed that everyone wanted to smother her in condolences, even though sympathy wasn't what she wanted.

"They're all just worried about you," said Martin.

"I know. It's just so overwhelming, though."

"You think it's overwhelming now? Wait till tomorrow!"

Darryl didn't want to think about the funeral. She didn't want to know what it was like to look at her father's corpse lying in a casket.

"Uncle Martin?"

"Yeah, hon?"

"I don't know if I can do this. You know. Say goodbye to Daddy. I don't know how I'm gonna act in front of all those people. And Earl. I can't even imagine being in the same room with that son of a bitch. Do you know he had the audacity to authorize what Daddy's gonna be wearing? He had the funeral home pick out a casket, too! Probably the cheapest one, knowing him! He supposedly made the decisions on everything! And all before I even found out! I don't even know how he has the intelligence to make any decisions. It's like a nightmare, Uncle Martin." She began to cry.

"Come here." He walked up and grabbed her, giving her the biggest hug she'd gotten since the last one she'd gotten from her father.

"Be patient. You'll get through this. And I'm going to be here to make sure you do. You understand me? I'm not gonna let that punk run over you. I don't care if he is Clinton's kid. He's a loser, and he has been from the start. Just hold on till tomorrow is over. Then you can bump heads with him all you want to."

"Bump heads? I want to do more than that!"

"Go get some rest. You've been through enough today."

Darryl took her uncle's advice, and hoped that a good night's rest would help her to forget about Earl and the hostility she felt toward him.

The next morning she no longer felt animosity. All she could feel was pain. Her heart ached so badly that it felt like the only organ in her body. She walked around in slow motion, acting as though there were no tomorrow. Her uncle Martin was able to feel her pain, just by being near her. But he knew there was nothing he could do to make it go away. It was one of those burdens that could only be lifted by the hands of time. They rode to the funeral home together without uttering a word.

Once they got there, the funeral director separated them by asking Darryl to attend a short conference. He led her down a corridor, explaining that there were a few last minute details to go over.

She had somehow expected a private meeting that would consist of the two of them and perhaps a dozen papers. Instead, he opened a door, leading her into a room where two pairs of eyes would burn straight through her. For a moment she felt awkward, to the point of being frightened. Then she remembered who she was, in comparison to who they were, and calmly took her seat.

"Darryl, there's a few matters we need to go over, that you haven't been included in on yet."

"I don't see what it matters now," blurted Earl, seated next to Earlene.

Darryl looked at him glaringly. Just long enough to make him squirm.

"You were saying?"

"Well, let me interrupt for a moment. Earl, I know you and Earlene have given the okay on most everything involved, but we're going to need to get your sister Darryl's signature too, in order to make everything official."

Darryl looked at the funeral director, stunned. Sure, the concept was always there, but never in her life had she heard the likes of Earl or Earlene being referred to as her siblings. She opened her mouth as if to respond with a gesture that was less than appropriate, but nothing came out. Her mind was too blank to think of a response as equally insulting as the one she had just heard.

The director proceeded to hand over papers, explaining what each one meant. Nothing included in the details was what she would have chosen for her father. The problem was that it was too late to consider any alternatives. Everything whirled by so fast that there wasn't any time to plan things out.

The fact that her father had been dead for almost two days before his body was discovered was the main reason.

"Daddy was military. Shouldn't he be having a proper burial to support that fact? Was the VFW informed so that perhaps there could be a twenty-one gun salute?" Tears began to flood her eyes again.

"Earl suggested that we adorn the casket with an American flag as opposed to a floral spray."

Darryl thought for a moment. She wondered if he'd made the decision out of respect or frugality. Whatever the case, though, it seemed to be the only thing she had the time to approve of.

"Do you have a pen?" Darryl signed the papers. All but one. "What is this?"

"This one deals with the headstone."

"Headstone?"

"Yes. Earl and Earlene opted to go with one by our own supplier. There's a few options to choose from, but as you can see, all of them are basically standard."

"Standard."

"Well, with all due respect, it's much less expensive than ordering from a different source. You're better off ordering through us."

She looked over to Earl. "I didn't realize this was a money situation. My father was anything but standard. What I wanna know is when you had the time to make all these decisions. When did you have the time, being glued to Daddy's porch step all day yesterday? And you, Earlene! Where did you come from? You blew Daddy off years ago. Why would you even care to take the effort to make decisions about anything pertaining to him?"

"Darryl, it's customary to round up all the children to make these decisions."

"Are you sure they qualify?"

"You hold on for a second, now!" said Earl. He jumped up from his chair and hovered over her.

The director promptly put a stop to what he thought might turn into a brawl. "There's no need for this. This isn't a time to bicker and fight."

"You're right," said Darryl. "I do have one question for you, though. How is it that they have already completed this paperwork, and I wasn't even contacted about it?"

"Darryl, it was Earl who found Clinton. He was the first to know anything, and he was the first to have an opportunity to do any decision making.

Obviously he contacted Earlene once he knew. I don't know why you weren't informed, but I think that's a matter for you and Earl to sort out."

She nodded. "I apologize. It is between me and ... them. So, um, this tombstone? I can t go along with it. I won't sign this paper!"

"That's fine. We can deal with that later."

"Well, me and Earlene both signed it. It's two against one, here."

"Earl, it doesn't quite work that way. If she doesn't want to sign the paper, then we can't legally proceed with ordering the tombstone. You all three need to agree."

"What if we can't?"

"Then there'll be no stone."

"What are you tryin' to do, cause trouble? All you gotta do is sign the paper and it'll be done."

"I won't. Daddy deserves better. Don't you think that Daddy deserves better, Earl?"

Earl turned his head. It was bad enough knowing that Clinton's true intentions were to drop him and his sister from the will. Now he had to deal with Darryl, whom he knew hated him. He was afraid that she might cause some serious trouble, not just over a tombstone, but over all the money that he wanted so much to get his hands on. And though he saw Darryl as a potential threat, he knew that he had two of the grandest bitches in Stoweville on his side. His mother and his sister.

"Is there a copy of Daddy's death certificate I can look at?"she asked. "I presume Earl provided the details of that, as well."

"It's right here. I'm sorry. I didn't realize you hadn't seen it."

She took the article and read it.

"Heart attack. That's what the deputy told me yesterday too. I only wish I could understand how anybody could so easily slap down the words 'heart attack' without an autopsy. Are we finished here? I think I'd like to go see my father now."

Darryl was aggravated. She was also nervous. She was unsure how she would react to seeing her father's corpse. The idea of going through the experience in the company of two people she had such contempt for was too excruciating to fathom. She only wished that Martin could accompany her to soften the blow.

"Can my uncle come with me to do this? He's waiting right out in the entrance."

"The first view is limited to spouses and children."

She heard Earl chuckle. It was almost as though he were a second grader trapped in the body of a man. He had no tact. No class. But mostly, no conscience.

She tried very hard to contain herself as they approached the curtain dividing them and what would be the last she would ever physically see of her father. She'd passed through those same curtains at least twenty times before, each time to give a final farewell to a loved one who had greeted death. It was never like this, though. Never so close or dear. Never so heartbreaking. As she walked in, she forced her vision out of focus, because an obscured view was the only one she felt like she could trust.

Only five or six feet away from the open casket, she stopped. Earl and Earlene walked up directly to it. They both took a good look, then whispered something to one another. After that, they walked out in single file.

Now it was just her and her father, with the funeral director standing reverently at the rear. She wanted to say something to her father, but she realized that there was no longer a soul inside that could acknowledge her. She blinked her eyes several times to regain her focus, seeing if that would inspire her. When she did, she felt oddly at peace.

It was as though her father wasn't dead, but merely sleeping. She didn't feel sad or alone. Her father's presence seemed strong and very much inside her. So she spoke. Without hesitation, sorrow, or concern as to what the director might think. "Daddy? You went away too soon. I had a surprise for you. It was one I think you would have liked. Daddy, I just want you to know how much I do love you. You'll always be right here." Darryl put her hand over her heart. "Tell Mommy hello for me. I miss you, Daddy." She turned to walk away, then nodded to the director. "I'm ready."

The funeral lasted all morning and well into the afternoon. What a funeral it was, too. Half the town, it seemed, gathered to pay their respects. Unfortunately, that was the only factor that gave Darryl any comfort, because Earl had managed to make a rigmarole of it.

He sobbed with more volume and insincerity through as much of the inside ceremony as most people could stomach.

All but two of the pallbearers were utter strangers to Darryl. And since Earl had provided the list of men to carry out the task, the unfamiliarity was again no surprise.

Even after all that, the thing that ate at her the most was the gentleman who stood all the way across the cemetery during the gravesite service.

He was yet another stranger. But it wasn't that fact or even his choice of locations from which to watch the service that disturbed her. It was the fact that she had seen him in the funeral home parking lot, right before the procession to the gravesite, talking to Margene who, in fact, never made an official appearance. Who was he, and why was he talking to Margene?

Once the service was over, Darryl and Martin were the last ones to leave.

"You know everybody's waitin' back at the farm, don't you?"

"Yeah. Funny. There'll be tons of food, but I don't think I could eat if I tried. I never understood all that, anyway. The food."

"I try to look at the food as nourishment for the soul. It's always starving after the loss of someone you love."

She hugged her uncle, as he always seemed to know exactly what to say.

After a few days to allow for the dust to settle, she began taking steps toward discussing her father's will. She knew how he was adamant about keeping his valuables locked away in his lock box, and ever since she'd heard her father mention anything relating to his death, he made it clear that there were two things she should do: go to Rutherford, who was Executor of his will, and look in his lock box for any further instructions. The key was kept in a place that only he and Darryl were aware of. The clay pitcher that sat on top of the piano once played by Julia was the perfect hiding place, according to Clinton. "Nobody would ever think to look here," he always said.

She drove to Shangri-la late that morning and walked up to the porch, plopping down in the middle just like she did as a child. With her father's spirit dwelling in her, she didn't feel the loneliness that she'd somehow expected. There was a voice inside that told her to be strong and everything would work out fine.

When she got up to go in, she spotted something odd out of the corner of her eye. It was a slender, brown, red-tipped cigar butt lying near the edge of the porch railing. She knew how her father hated the smell of cigars. When she went to take a closer look, it became obvious that it wasn't a cigar butt at all. She reached down to pick it up, while a grimace formed on her face. It smelled of cloves. "Yuck," she said, dropping it. Quickly she sent inside to go wash her hands.

The house was quiet. Almost haunted. But that didn't stop her from wanting to be there. She walked through the dimly lit corridor to what her mother always called the parlor. It was where the piano was, along with the clay pitcher sitting on top. Climbing onto the bench, she reached over to stick her arm down the mouth of it. Her elbow barely poked out of the top as she pawed around the bottom. Once the key was in her hand, she knew it was time to leave, because the old house would now be off limits until the will was read and the estate was settled.

CHAPTER TWENTY-SIX

She arrived at the bank sometime before noon, where the employees couldn't have been more gracious to her.

"I'll tell Mr. Rutherford you're here, Miss Darryl," his secretary said. "He'll be eager to see you, I'm sure."

She barely had time to sit down before he hurried out to greet her.

"Darryl. It's good to see you. Come. Come to my office. Can I get you anything? Soda?"

"I'm fine."

He closed the door behind them.

"I don't know what to say to you. It was a shock to everybody. I just don't understand it. He was perfectly fine when he left here Thursday."

"That's one of the things I want to talk to you about. Daddy told me to come to you if anything ever happened to him. He said that you were Executor of his will."

"That's right. I tried to talk him out of it. I'm almost twenty years his senior. I told him that he'd outlive me by a long shot. He wouldn't listen, though. Said that if something happened and I wasn't able to take the role, he'd cross that bridge when the time came. It's almost as though he knew."

"Are we talking confidentially?"

"Yes ma'am, we are."

Darryl hesitated before saying what was really on her mind. "I just have to say this to someone other than family."

"Talk to me."

"I don't think Daddy died of a heart attack. I'm not convinced, anyway. You know there wasn't an autopsy, don't you?"

"I wasn't aware of that. Are you sure?"

"Positive. I mean, forgive me if I'm wrong, but something just doesn't seem right about the coroner calling it a heart attack without a proper autopsy. I mean, from what I was told, he was found sitting straight up in his lounge chair with a plate of cookies in his lap. That was two days after he supposedly died. Somehow that doesn't seem like a heart attack situation. Not enough of a struggle."

"Have you told anyone else what you're telling me?"

"No. I know it sounds like I'm being paranoid, but I've gotta follow my instinct, and it says that something ain't right. I don't know why I'm telling you this. I guess it's because Daddy did trust you so much. I guess I thought maybe you could help me figure it out."

Rutherford seemed taken back by her assumption. It was one thing to take on the task of distributing Clinton's assets to three individuals who literally hated one another while keeping an unbiased frame of mind. But to delve into the possibility of homicide seemed more than he was ready to deal with. "I don't want to seem dismissive here, but don't you think you're jumping the gun a little?"

"Like I said, it sounds paranoid, but I need to find some solid answers, with or without your help or the confidence I've placed in you by sharing this."

"Darryl, if this is truly how you feel, then rest assured, you can count on me to help. I don't know how much good I'll be, though. But I'll do anything I can. First though, little lady, we need to get Clinton's estate settled and squared away. Sound fair?"

"Uh huh."

"I don't guess I need to tell you that we need to have everyone here in order to proceed, so why don't I contact the others and we'll set up a date to meet officially."

"You'll do the honors?"

"I'll be glad to."

"Good. Somehow, I didn't feel comfortable with the idea of contacting them."

Last Will and Testament

"I understand. Wish I could say that I knew what it felt like to be in your shoes, but I can't. My brothers, sisters, and I all get along."

"So, do you want to call me when everything is set?"

"That would be best. While you're here, I should ask if there's any particular time you'd prefer to take this thing on."

"It doesn't matter. Anytime. I'm gonna go back to school tonight to make arrangements for an extended absence, but I'll be back tomorrow afternoon. You can call me at Uncle Martin's."

"Darryl, first before you leave, I want to say something to you. You were Clinton's pride and joy. And I know this may sound unprofessional of me, but the others? It's a shame for them to be treated as your equal."

"I know that. But Daddy was fair. That's what made him who he was." She smiled and walked out, leaving Rutherford feeling more uneasy about being the one in charge of evenly distributing Clinton's wealth.

It was the way Clinton had legally left things before everything exploded in his face. His first Last Will and Testament provided all three of his children with an exact one-third of his estate. It was the only way he knew to divide things without anyone rebutting. His second one, that was never properly revised, left everything to Darryl. But not only had it been legally un-officiated, it was now in the hands of Margene. There was no proof that it even existed, other than the knowledge that she, her culprits, and Clinton's lawyer, Aaron Prouty, had of it.

Prouty was one of the vast many who attended Clinton's funeral. And though he held only a slight familiarity to Darryl, she was someone who was highly familiar to him. Clinton never brought business home with him. Home was a resting place, as far as he was concerned, so other than the fact that Prouty was his lawyer, Darryl knew nothing more of him than that.

He was very gracious to her at the funeral, but held his tongue for the most part. Like her, he ignored Earl and Earlene throughout it, but instinctively knew that something fishy had taken place. The idea of jeopardizing his career by spilling the beans had crossed his mind about a thousand times, but he was too attached to his career to actually go through with it. He did want to do something, though. He just didn't know what.

Over the course of the next twenty-four hours, things in Stoweville began to move in a direction that was anything but straight and narrow. Darryl, being on the road during this time, would be unaware of such things until she returned.

"Darryl, we have a slight problem," Rutherford explained over the phone that next afternoon. "I've contacted the other two. I had anticipated that we would set up a meeting where everyone would come together for the reading of the will."

"That's not the case?"

"I don't know how to say this. Darryl, there's another will."

"Another will? What?"

"Darryl, I talked to Earlene, and I suppose she was speaking on behalf of Earl, too. I suggested to her that we set up a time to all get together, and she asked me, 'What for?' I explained to her that I was the Executor of Clinton's estate."

"And?"

"And, at first, she acted about as puzzled as you are right now. She told me that she wasn't aware that another will existed, other than the one that had recently been read to Earl and herself."

"Wait a minute. Another will has already been read?"

"According to her, Clinton s estate is already being divided."

"That can't be."

"I informed her to stop any action that was currently taking place, then she made a few remarks. She asked me if the will I had possession of was dated before March 2, 1980."

"And is it?"

"Yes. It's dated 1970. I told her that."

"What did she say then?"

"She said that if I or anyone else had something to say, that it would be best to take it up with their lawyer. Darryl, I'm going to tell you right now, you need to get an attorney. And do it quickly. I don't know what's going on exactly on the other end, but it doesn't sound very good. In the meantime, I'm going to hang on to the will that I've got. But let tell you one other thing. As Executor of this will, I'm supposed to remain unbiased. But between you and me, I don't see it happening. Only out of respect I have for you and the friendship I had with your father am I telling you this. Now, you do have an attorney you can talk to, don't you?"

"Yeah. I have someone in mind."

She hung up the phone and searched around for a phone book. "Uncle Martin," she yelled, panicking, "I can't find the phone book. Where's the phone book, damn it!"

"There's no need for a foul mouth," he said, walking in. "Here's your phone book, right here."

She jerked it from his hands, hers shaking so badly that she was barely able to hold it.

"What's the matter with you, hon?"

She tried to explain what she'd just heard, but all that came out was stutter.

"Darryl, you need to sit down or something. You look like you're hyperventilating. Holy Mackerel! You *are* hyperventilating!"

"I gotta call Prouty."

"No, you need to calm down."

"I gotta call him now, before it's too late." She resisted her uncle's pleas to relax, leaving him to look on in shock as she frantically dialed Prouty's number.

"Mr. Prouty, this .... this is .... Darryl Lee. I n...need to talk to you. N..now."

"Darryl, you don't sound good. Why don't we forget about conversing over the phone? Tell me where you are. I'll come to you."

"U...Uncle....Martin's."

"I know where he lives. You just sit tight. I'll be over as quickly as I can."

It was no surprise to Prouty that she had summoned him. The surprise was that she hadn't contacted him sooner. There was still one tiny problem he was dealing with, though. He had absolutely no idea how he would address the subject of Clinton with Darryl without letting certain confidential information slip. It was already hard enough to simply have knowledge of the certain things he did. But he was determined to find some way to expose Margene in all her corruption without exposing himself as the source from which it came. The question still remaining was how. Information he knew about the birth records of Earl and Earlene was a recorded fact that had somehow never gotten past the file cabinet of Doc Arthur Peterson.

The murder was yet another of his concerns. First of all, his belief that it was a murder was exactly that. His belief. He had little to nothing to point the arrows in that direction without first exposing Earl and Earlene Doe. Unlike Rutherford, he had no visual foresight of playing an unbiased role. So he'd have to bow out of the spotlight and acquaint young Darryl with the finest attorney he knew of, next to himself.

His name was Charles Wiley. He'd known Prouty since their arrogant wanna-be days back in law school. Neither had changed much since, with the exception that they were no longer wanna-be's. And while Prouty had made a home for himself in Stoweville, Wiley had planted his roots in Groverton, coincidentally, Clinton's stomping ground once upon a time.

Prouty rushed to aid Darryl in whatever had made her sound so devastated during their brief phone encounter. When he got there, the last thing he expected to hear was that another will had surfaced. Another one besides the one he had very recently drafted for Clinton, that is.

"Who told you that a will had already been read?"

"Mr. Rutherford," she said. "He was supposedly the Executor of Daddy's will."

"All right. You're going to have to elaborate for me a little bit, Darryl. Which will does Rutherford have, and which will has been read? What are the dates, I mean?"

"Mr. Rutherford has a will that dates 1970. Daddy made arrangements with him back then to take care of everything. But now, a new will is in the picture. Mr. Rutherford didn't even know it existed."

"Obviously, it is dated after the one Rutherford has?"

"It's one that, according to Earlene, was drawn up a year ago."

"Wait. Earlene? Don't tell me you talked to her."

"No, Mr. Rutherford did. She told him and he told me."

"Do you know anything about this new will?"

"Only that I'm clearly not in it."

Prouty didn't say anything. He walked out on the porch to try and piece things together. The fact that a will dated 1980 had even surfaced didn't make sense to him. He knew that if such a will existed, Clinton would have told him. He also knew that the one he had drawn up only a week prior contradicted having any part of Earl or Earlene.

There was only one logical explanation. It was a hoax. That, or a forgery. And with all the circumstances that had come from Margene's direction already, he had no doubt who was behind it.

"Mr. Prouty," Darryl said, "what are we gonna do?"

He wanted badly to tell her everything. For that matter, he wanted to tell the world. But all he could do was camouflage his knowledge with a wavering attitude, because that was the price he had paid for becoming a lawyer.

"Here's what you're going to do." He reached inside his blazer and pulled out a card. "His name is Charles Wiley. He's the best attorney I know."

"What do you mean? I ... I don't quite follow."

"Just call him. Tell him who you are, and tell him you know me. He's a good lawyer, Darryl."

She took a step back. "You're not gonna be my lawyer? Has the whole world gone crazy? Don't you hear what I'm telling you, Mr. Prouty? I don't guess you did. So maybe I can spell it out for you this time. I'm being robbed. Robbed! I don't know how they've pulled it off, but they have. I know as the sun comes up every morning that Daddy would've never left everything to them. I just know it!"

"Darryl, I just need you to listen to me. I know you feel like hating me right now. And I wouldn't blame you if you did. But you've got to trust me on one thing. I've got a very good reason for not backing you on this. I can't really say anymore about it. But I do have my reasons. I know your father would want me to do what's best for you. That's why I want you to call Charles Wiley. He's a friend of mine. As a matter of fact, I'll call him first."

He looked at her for a reaction. "Darryl, will you please say something?"

"Please leave."

He nodded. He placed the card that Darryl had yet to take from his hand down on the porch railing, looking at her. The disgust that covered her face was something that would remain on his mind for the rest of that day and many more after that.

It was one of the very few moments in his life that he felt utterly ashamed. But the fact was he knew too much. Too much to give Darryl the representation she so rightfully deserved. And though he hoped Darryl's recent hatred for him would somehow soften the guilt he had for abandoning her, it didn't. Not then, and not ever.

Darryl waited for him to leave before she completely broke down. The tears were already streaming down.

Martin, who had been watching from inside, left her alone. He knew something unpleasing had taken place, but he knew better than to ask what. In all the years that he spent watching her grow up, he had learned that she was a chip straight off the ol' block when it came to being ill at ease. It was best to give her time to get the craziness out of her system. And considering the state of mind she was in, he'd need to give her plenty of it. He didn't even give her grief when she left in a rage and came back some six hours later, inebriated from head to toe.

The next morning she woke, feeling about as swift as she did the night before, just before she missed the bed and landed on the floor. It was shockingly similar to her father's experience the morning after his drunken first encounter with Margene. Same hangover. Different time and place. And again, like her father, it was in fact the doings of Margene that drove her to wind up in such a situation.

For some reason, she had all but blocked the idea of Margene Lee from her psychological encyclopedia since she was about ten years old. Beyond then, it had been Earl and Earlene who she considered to be the unnecessary evils in her life. It wasn't as though she was unaware of Margene's capability to torture nearly everyone she came in contact with, she just figured that Earl and Earlene had enough wickedness all on their own. But on this day, all that changed.

It could have been blamed on the alcohol fumes still lingering, but as sure as the room was spinning before her, she had wakened no longer thinking and believing the way she once had. For it was this very day she knew within reason that Margene was far too power hungry to be shadowed by Earl and Earlene. If anyone was guilty of stealing her father's fortune, it wasn't them. It was the woman who never managed to steal his heart.

CHAPTER TWENTY-SEVEN

argene felt like the woman of the hour. She had accomplished so many things, and without anyone being the wiser–anyone important enough to matter, that is. Earl and Earlene couldn't have been more thrilled with her accomplishments, either. The truth of the matter was that Earl and Earlene were completely unfazed by Clinton's death. It was what they could obtain from his death that mattered.

Another truth was that they had absolutely no idea what had actually taken place. They didn't know how his will had ended up in their corner, offering everything to them. They knew their Mother was behind it in someway, but as far as the specifics, they didn't care. Which was just as well, because Margene wasn't fool enough to share that information.

Another bit of information she'd failed to share was the bit about Clinton not being their birth father. They were bastards without even realizing it. But a wise Margene knew that the less truths they knew, the better. Now, all she needed to do was explain to them exactly why a majority of Clinton's estate would wind up in her pockets, rather than in theirs, as the will stated.

"Now you two – when this meeting is over, I'm going to need to explain a few extra things. There'll be a some things Saunders won't be covering today."

Neither Earl nor Earlene questioned her. They simply agreed to what she was saying and followed her into their final meeting with their lawyer, Saunders, and assumed will Executor, Emmet Sims, to cover the last phase of its execution.

"Come on in and take a seat," said Saunders. "Now that we have everyone here, we can finish this puppy off. Margene, I don't suppose anyone has come forth to rebut the will we have presented here today? No. I know better than that. You would've already told me if that was the case, wouldn't you have? So, with that said, I'm going to turn this thing over to Mr. Simms. He ll read the will, and if anyone has any questions, we can stop and discuss them along the way. Mr. Simms..."

Simms cleared his throat. He looked around the room at everyone, knowing fully that each person, himself included, was a crook. He was glad to be there, though. It wasn't every day he got to join hands with so many of his own kind.

Margene had placed a lot of trust in him to ask that he participate in such an unruly game of flat-out theft. The two were not connected whatsoever in their circle of friends. Margene knew of him only by reputation. That's why she chose him. It was a means of covering her tracks; she didn't want the forged will to be linked to her in any way. Simms did have a heavy price for taking his assumed role of Executor, however, one that he refused to disclose until all was said and done.

As he began reading, not one time did Earl or Earlene interrupt with questions. Earlene, being as crafty as she was, knew how to make sense of it. Earl did bob his head back and forth between Simms and his mother several times. He was confused throughout the duration. But Margene shook her head no each time.

When Simms made it to the end, no one really knew how to respond. It was as if each one were too fearful of getting caught before they could collect the goods to let their emotions show.

Earl sat wide-eyed and anxious. Earlene looked as if she were in deep thought. Margene looked as though she were in deeper thought. Simms was the hard one to figure. He was expressionless. For that matter, he was for the moment faceless. His head was bowed down so low that the only facial feature evident were his untamed eyebrows. Saunders, who was the only soul not a beneficiary in the matter, looked around at the huddle of personages for as long as he could stand the silence.

"Okay, so....no questions," he said. "Well, that was quick. Earlene?"

She shook her head.

"No? How 'bout you, Earl?"

"He doesn't," Margene said adamantly.

"Margene, with all due respect, I believe Earl needs to speak for himself here."

Like always, Earl did what his mother's facial gestures told him to do.

"Naw, I ain't got no questions."

"All right, then. I suppose we can adjourn ourselves." Saunders tried to keep to himself after that statement. Though he was notorious for bankrupting many an individual, he always did so in what he classified to be a legitimate manner. He wasn't actually in on the makings of the will that they had just reviewed, but that didn't stop him from using enough common sense to be aware of its lack of authenticity. He knew it was manufactured by Margene. That's what made him nervous.

"I guess you know where to send the bill," Margene said, nudging him.

When she and the other three walked out of the building, Simms pulled her aside. "I'll be in touch with you later," he said.

Margene didn't exactly know what that entailed, but for the moment, she felt it to be the least of her concerns. She now had the task of rushing to Clinton's estate and rummaging for any quick valuables to pawn.

"Fine," she said, then waited for him to leave.

"Let's get down to Clinton's," she said to Earl and Earlene. "What I have in mind is to take as many tangible items as we can."

"Mama, what's the point in hurrying? All his stuff is legally ours," said Earlene.

"True. But remember I told you that there were a few things I have to explain? I guess there's no time like the present, huh? But let me do it in the car on the way."

"Yeah. I knew it. I knew it wasn't as cut and dried as you made it out to be," said Earlene. "But, Mama, I think at this point you no longer have a say-so in the matter. If you remember, everything belongs to me and Earl. Fifty-fifty."

"Hate to tell you, Miss Snotty Pants, but if you want one red cent of Clinton's fortune, you'll do as I say. It was me who conjured up your phoney inheritance. And as easily as I conjured it, I can also make it go away. You got it?"

"Yeah, I got it."

As they drove away, Margene began explaining her plans for dividing the estate.

"All right. First things first. I've got a rather large sum of money to pay off. Nothing, and I mean, nothing, comes before that."

"So, you plan to pay your bills off first," said Earlene.

"Not exactly. They're more like our bills. But now, I don't want to hear it. No sarcasm. Like I said, I'm the reason you got anything at all. It cost me a large sum to pull this off. Once that's paid, anything left over will get divided between the three of us. The way I figure it, forty-thirty-thirty sounds like a fair amount."

"I suppose the forty percent is yours," said Earlene.

"That's correct. Relax. It's still a good chunk o'change."

After making it to Shangri-la, they made no bones about their presence there. There was no tiptoeing or whispering. They were actually louder than they usually were on their own turf.

"What a house," said Margene, walking up the porch steps. "Do you know I have been in this house before?"

"When?" asked Earl.

"Long time ago. Before you were born. I went out with the fella that lived here."

"You mean, that rich woman's son?"

"Yep. But that was a long time ago. The Arthurs didn't much like me."

"I wonder why?" mumbled Earlene.

"I heard that! What? Do you think yore Mama ain't good enough?"

"Never mind. Can we just get inside already?"

"Yes, if I can ever find the door key."

Margene barely got the door open before Earl barged in front of her, racing inside. Out of all the times he'd been there, it was the first time that he actually felt like a kid in a toy store.

"You gotta come in this room, Mama. This is where Daddy kept all the good stuff."

Margene stopped for a moment. The sound of Earl referring to Clinton as Daddy made her wonder if she shouldn't break down and tell him and his sister the truth. But what was the purpose of telling them? They didn't like the man past his wallet, anyway. Plus, telling them would only make things more suspicious if they were ever questioned about it. She didn't trust either of them to put on a quality 'poker face.

"Where'd you go, Earl? I hear ya, but I can't see ya."

"In here! You gotta see this room!"

"Earlene, why don't you search the house for that coin while I go in here to see what he's bein' so fussy over."

"What makes you think the coin would be here? Don't you think it would be in his lock box?"

"More than likely. But you can never be too sure. If Clinton did have it lyin' around here, at least we'd be the first ones to find it."

"What d'you mean, the first ones? Who else would be lookin' for it?"

"Earlene, stop askin' questions and just look for the damn thing."

"Fine, Mama!"

"Oh, and while you're at it, pick up any crystal figurines and that sort o' thing you run across. We can pawn off them small things for quick cash."

Earlene walked away backmouthing.

The few hours that passed after their arrival flew by quickly. They had done a fine job of disarranging what was once a well organized house. They each ran out with an armful of what-nots they felt were of significant value, each time loading them in Margene's car. But no sign of the *Irrtümliche Münze*.

By the time the car had gotten too full for passengers to fit, Margene put a halt to things.

"You two, I think we need to take some of this suff out. I don't know how in the world anybody's gonna be able to get back inside. You know what? Why don't we haul some o' this stuff in that ol' rinky dink truck o' Clinton's. Earl, do you know where the keys are?"

"I can hot wire it."

"You ain't hot wirin' nothin'! Find the keys!"

He went back inside to look around, during which time a vehicle appeared unexpectedly in the driveway. It was Emmett Simms. Completely caught off guard by his arrival, Margene advised Earlene to go inside with her brother.

"Hey there. Somehow when you said you'd be in touch, I didn't think it'd be today."

"You didn't ask."

"So, what are you doin' here, anyway? I thought we'd continue our business somewhere more appropriate."

"See there again, you didn't ask."

"All right, then. Give it to me. What's goin' on?"

"Just thought I'd come by. Chat a little bit. Give you the low-down on my piece o' the action."

Back at her uncle Martin's farm, Darryl was doing her best to recuperate from her hangover. Martin had fixed a big breakfast, hoping that once she had a little food in her stomach, the day would improve some for her.

"Is that all you're gonna eat, hon?"

"It's all I can eat. Maybe after awhile, I'll have a bigger appetite. I think I just need some air. I'm gonna go sit on the porch awhile."

She walked out and plopped down in the big rocking chair. Directly in front of her was the scene in which Aaron Prouty had the day before denied her of his legal expertise. She replayed the scene in her head, trying to understand why he would do such a thing. She didn't find an answer. But what she did find was the business card he'd left behind on the railing. With little to nothing other than curiosity driving her to pick it up, she managed to coerce herself into doing so. It had the name Charles Wiley printed in bold, cursive letters.

"How typically snobby! Only a lawyer would have a business card in cursive."

She scraped the card back and forth against the inside of her wrist. For the moment she didn't quite know what to do.

On the one hand, the last thing she felt like doing was talking business with a hangover under her belt. But, on the other hand, hangover or not, the longer she waited around doing nothing, the more her father's estate would dwindle away.

"All right, Charles Wiley. Let's see if Aaron Prouty was right about you." She moped back inside to the telephone. Before she began dialing, it was perfectly set in her mind that she would do no pleading of any sort to squeeze a meeting out of him.

"Charles Wiley's office," his secretary answered.

"Yes, this is Darryl Lee. I'm calling for Mr. Wiley."

"Yes, Miss Lee. I see here that he's expecting your call. I'll punch you right through."

She was shocked. When Prouty mentioned that he'd make introductory arrangements, she didn't expect that he actually meant it.

"Miss Lee?" he said in greeting.

"Yeah. I, uh suppose Aaron has already done the honors of the pre-introduction, right?"

"A little. Why don't you talk to me, though. Tell me the story in your own words. And you don't need to worry about being formal. Fair enough?"

"Well, it's like this. My father died. Other than myself, he also had two children from a former marriage. Now, I know you don't know my father. Well, I guess you don't. His name was Clinton Lee. But, anyway, it seems as though those two other children have one will that states everything should be left to them, and I have access to another that states his assets and so forth are to be divided equally among the three of us. Supposedly their will is dated ten years later than mine. But that's the thing. *Supposedly* it is. I don't know for sure, 'cause I haven't seen it. For that matter, I don't know if anybody has. And another thing I've been told is that they're already dividing things up."

"Wait a minute. How did you know about this? Their will?"

"The Executor of my will contacted the others for a meeting, and at that time they informed him that they had a different will than what he had. Theirs is dated 1980 and mine is dated 1970. But that's just one thing I wanna deal with. The other thing is a bit more complicated. Huh. Gosh. I don't know how to say this without sounding crazy. It's about my father's death. I don't think he just died. Point blank, I think he was killed."

"You think your father was murdered?"

"Yep. I do. Look, I don't know if you're interested in taking my case, but if you're not, that's fine. There's plenty of other sharks in the sea."

"Huh. I don't guess I've ever heard it put that way. But at least I'll know how you feel about me up front when I meet you."

"Meet me? So, you are interested?"

"Come by my office this afternoon."

Darryl finished up her conversation with Wiley, then made a quick call to Rutherford. She wanted to be sure and keep him informed of everything that transpired in her pursuit to get to the bottom of things.

"Mr. Rutherford?"

"Darryl, I was about to call you. I just received a call from Margene. She, Earl, Earlene, and I'm not sure who, but somebody's on their way up here to open Clinton's lock box."

"What!"

"I tried to tell her that she needed to hold off on it, but she wouldn't listen. She threatened me with a court order."

"A court order? She can't do that!"

"Unfortunately, she can. If she had a notarized will stating that the belongings in Clinton's lock box are the rightful property of Earl and Earlene, then there's nothing I can do to stop them."

"But....I'm on my way to see a lawyer. I'm trying to stop all this. Mr. Rutherford!"

"Get crackin'. I'll stall them as long as I can, but Darryl, you know how Margene is. She thinks she owns this town. And if she thinks something belongs to her, she won't hesitate to get it."

"But..."

"Listen to me. Stop wasting time. Get to your lawyer. Protest this thing. Then everything will freeze. Just hurry. Like I said, I'll hold off whoever comes by as long as I can. After you and your lawyer talk, have him call me. We might even be able to stop this rigmarole before they get here."

"I'm out the door." Darryl knew there would be no such chance of stopping Margene in her tracks before she met up with Gordy. There was too little time and too much distance to travel to make it happen.

She was nervous the entire drive to Carlton. Her mind rambled so much that by the time she reached Wiley's office, she had to stop and wonder how she'd actually gotten there. And after talking to him, she also began to wonder if he too, like many others, had at some point been strangled by the reins of Margene Lee.

"Just let 'em take everything," he said. "Let 'em take it. They'll have to give it all back in the end, anyway."

CHAPTER TWENTY-EIGHT

arryl was frustrated for the next solid week. Frustrated, angry, worried, and every other state of mind under the sun that could be classified as negative.

She was frustrated because her lawyer who received such impeccable reviews from Prouty had done nothing to support his reputation.

She was angry because she had been told to just "let 'em take everything," because in a matter of one week's time, Margene and her clan had done exactly that.

She was worried because if Margene was responsible for her father's death, she might find herself next on the target list.

"Darryl, you've got to pull it together, hon," said Martin. "You can't keep pacing the floors day in and day out."

"What am I supposed to do? The only thing I've been advised to do is sit back and wait while it all happens. I can't even go to town without running into somebody telling me they've seen or heard about Margene doing this or that. That she's taken this or that. Do you know that two days ago, I saw Earl walking around at the salvage yard? It didn't dawn on me at the time, but when I did a double take, I saw Daddy's truck parked there with a bed full of stuff from his house. They're cartin' things off and selling 'em for peanuts! It's like nothing that Daddy had is in the least bit sacred to them. And, to ice the cake, I think I've gotten tangled up with an incompetent lawyer. Prouty said he was some sort of genius. I don't see it. After Prouty decided to dump me as a client, you'd think I'd be a little cautious trusting him, anyway. Margene, wherever you are right now, I hope you're happy with yourself. I hope you're proud that you got away with murder!"

Margene wasn't quite as proud as one would have expected her to be given the circumstances. It seemed that the more belongings she accumulated, the more she would find herself parting with. As if the split between her and her offspring wasn't enough, she had to quickly fork out the unpaid amount she owed to Grampus Healey. Then there was the ever so tiny share that Emmett Simms expected from her.

"Mama, how come we're still livin' here?" Earl asked. "Why ain't we stayin' in that big mansion?"

"Earl, I'm still sortin' things out, all right? An estate settlement does take a little bit o' time. It ain't all gonna fall in your lap at once."

"When, then?"

"Stop it with the impatient act, already. It'll happen when it happens."

At the time, Margene really didn't have a solid answer for him. She apparently didn't have one for herself, either. Emmett Simms set his price higher than she had anticipated for his affiliation in her scheme. Unlike Grampus Healey, he didn't want a dollar amount for his services. He wanted Shangri-la.

The house was practically empty, except for a few minor odds and ends. But that didn't matter to Emmett Simms. He didn't want the place for the furniture. He wanted it for the structure. A structure that so conveniently happened to be nestled in the most hidden of hideaways. He couldn't have had a more perfect base for his drug ring if he'd designed it himself.

Like Margene, he was somewhat immune to the legal system. But, unlike Margene, he generally had something to show for his criminal involvement. He had a fleet of homes and vehicles to boot. Shangri-la would simply be his newest, nicest, and most industrial.

Margene didn't want to give it to him. But at the time he asked for it, she was far too consumed with the idea of getting her hands on Clinton's coin collection than worrying about his house.

Until the priceless coin surfaced, though, she would have to busy herself with dispensing and collecting the rest of everything. She had quickly acquired the fifty thousand that she owed Healey from Clinton's bank accounts. He had a little more than eighty thousand in his savings alone. There were also his insurance policies and stock. And last, but not least, she had the the contents of his lock box. They were what she cherished the most. After searching from one end of Shangri-la to the other for his coin collection without any success, she later found them there, along with a few other miscellaneous items.

Margene had every scrap that she had collected from lockbox number 1122. "He was proud of that birthday," she said, rolling her eyes. "One-one, two-two."

Indeed, Clinton had chosen the box number in accordance with his birth date. Lucky for him, that particular number happened to be available when he went looking for it. He thought it was luck, anyway. Margene thought it typical. She couldn't quite understand why a person could be so entertained by such simple things. She never was.

In fact, it seemed as though she was never fully entertained by anything at all. Not even when she schemed her way into the highly coveted seat of Judge. All in all, she was an unsatisfied human being, not only in the things she couldn't acquire, but in the things she had.

"Well, at least I had a taste of him at one time."

Being as hollow as she was on the inside, it was only when she had recollections of Clinton that her feelings began to waver. She always knew that he was the one person she could never measure up to. And that always got to her. It wasn't every day that someone took a step back and saw her for the coward she really was.

But coward or not, she now had every last stitch inside Clinton's notorious sack of coins. And that was all the confidence she needed to overpower her hidden insecurities.

Grampus was back in his setup trying to figure out the most intimidating method to approach Margene for the rest of his fifty thousand. Even though she had successfully acquired more than that amount from Clinton's savings, she hadn't yet delivered the goods. There was something about having that much cold, hard cash in her possession that turned her on. She wanted to hang onto it for as many days as she could get away with. But Grampus wasn't typically the patient type. He was the extreme opposite. And though busting the kneecaps of a lady wasn't typically his style, threatening one's life was.

"Shakey, you and Little One need to meet over here in an hour," he said in a phone call. "We've got a little business to discuss about our lady, Margene Lee."

The two arrived less than half an hour later.

"What is it with you two and being early? I said an hour!"

"We can come back later," said Little One.

"Well, you've already hindered my schedule. May as well stay. But next time, be here when I say. Hell, for that matter, be a minute or two late. Now then, let's discuss Ms. Lee. She's holdin' out on me. It's time to give her a scare."

"Whatever you want us to do. Me and Shakey can handle her, can't we, Shakey?"

As usual, he answered with his eyes.

"I want you to follow her home from work. Make sure she sees you, though. If she pulls in someplace to throw you off, wait for her. Just make sure she sees you. Come by in the mornin' 'bout seven. Let me know if she caves."

That afternoon just before five, they drove into the courthouse parking lot to wait. They parked two rows back from Margene's usual spot; close enough to let it be known that they were there, but far enough away to appear as though they were trying to be inconspicious.

When Margene left her office, she walked over to her car and searched her purse for her car keys. Once she was situated in the driver's seat, she peeked in the rearview mirror and immediately spotted a man with an afro quite similar to the one she'd seen the morning of her meeting with Grampus. She stared for a second, then looked away. When she looked again, she noticed the tall, think physique of the man seated in the driver's seat next to him. It didn't take much brilliance for her to put two and two together. She knew that the two gentlemen were in fact the two lugs who had accompanied Grampus that morning. And unlike then, she was now actually able to distinguish their faces.

What're they doin' here? she thought to herself.

She started her car, all the while looking at them with her own manner of inconspicuousness. As she pulled away, she kept an eye out to see what they would do.

At first, they did nothing. They were, after all, trying to look inconspicious. But Margene was no fool. She knew they were going to follow her. And, sure enough, they did.

She was nervous. She knew that she was taking serious advantage of one dangerous man by holding onto the money she owed him. Had she finally come upon the one chamber with the bullet in her risky game of Russian roulette?

As Grampus had warned that she might try to stop and throw them off, that's precisely what she did. She pulled into a store parking lot hoping to get lost in the mass of vehicles. But, no matter which direction she turned, they were always two steps behind her.

Damn it. Huh. Okay, Grampus. You made your point. Money's yours.

She white-knuckled the steering wheel all the way home.

Though Shakey and Little One did tail her there, they didn't stop once she did. They just slowed down long enough to scare her even more, then skidded into high gear until they were clear out of sight.

Margene didn't waste any time after that. She rushed inside and reached into her desk drawer for the key that unlocked the cabinet containing all the money.

Wait a minute. I don't even know where he wants me to send this.

That was the one particular that they hadn't sorted out.

I guess he was leavin' it up to me all along.

Indeed, that was the name of the game. A person as powerful as Grampus didn't have to give too many instructions. Everything was a given.

Margene picked up the phone. She was nervous, even more so than when she was being followed. She dreaded hearing what Grampus might say. Because at this point, she didn't know if she had blown it and gotten all the way on his bad side.

"Well, well, well," he answered. "How you doin', Margene?"

Not too terribly convinced by the calm sincerity of his voice, she cut straight to the chase.

"Where do you want me to deliver the rest of the money?"

Darryl was still at her uncle Martin's trying to cope. She'd decided to skip the remainder of her senior year at school and make it up in the fall. Graduation was something she had been anticipating for what seemed like an eternity. But it was something she would happily put on the back burner in order to get the current mess she was in straightened out.

She had put aside her whining, and dried her last tear. She was now ready to tackle the issues that Margene had seemingly tossed her way. She was now ready for that sweet little thing called justice.

CHAPTER TWENTY NINE

Darryl knew the moment she woke up that morning what she was going to do. She was going to look at her lawyer face to face and tell him exactly where he stood.

"You're fired," she said.

"Wait. Did we have an appointment this morning? How did you get in here?"

"I told your secretary that I was your mistress."

"You did what?"

"Joke. It's a joke. Not the part about you being fired, though."

"All right. All right. Just take a seat and talk to me. What's going through your mind?"

"What's going through my mind is that you don't have the slightest idea what you're doing. It's been weeks, and all you've done is tell me to wait. 'Be patient and wait.' Well, I've done that. Now I'm done with it! 'Let 'em take everything,' you told me. Guess what? They have. At this point, I'm left with nothing. And why? Because I sat back and listened to you. Hell, I can't believe you can justify charging people for this. How much did I pay for a retainer?"

"Darryl, I think you need to re-think what you're saying."

"Miss Lee, to you."

"Miss Lee, why don't you re-think this?"

"There's nothing to re-think. You're dismissed. I just wanted to tell you to your face." She turned and walked out of his office with her nose up in the air. From this point on, she was going to take control. No longer would she sit back and listen to a lawyer, or anyone else for that matter, who gave out advice that she knew better than to follow.

The one question that did keep lingering through her mind was why didn't Wiley do more. Did Margene's connections reach as far as Carlton? It was the only thing that made any sense. Why else wouldn't he have taken some sort of action against her? The scary part of it was that Wiley hadn't even gotten the word out to Guy Saunders that Darryl wanted to contest Margene's so-called will.

Her next stop was to see Gordy Rutherford.

"Darryl, tell me, how are things going with your lawyer?"

"They're not. I fired him. Today, in fact."

"Was that a wise thing to do?"

"Under the circumstances, it wouldn't have been wise to keep him. He hasn't done a thing to get this ball rolling, and you know me. I ain't the patient type."

"Well, what can I do to help? Anything you need. Just name it."

"For one, I need a new lawyer. But one that I know isn't connected by the hip to Margene. Someone I can trust. If it's possible to trust a lawyer. Other than that, I guess I need a loan. I've already used up my savings on the moron I just fired. I hate to ask you that. I've never had to do this before. It's a little on the humiliating side."

"Done. Whatever you need. And don't worry about paying me back. It's the least I can do, since I couldn't stop Margene from coming in and taking the whole lot. But, right now, why don't I let you in on a little research that I've been up to myself?"

"Okay."

"Darryl, I've thought about this long and hard. You know and I know that if your father had changed his will, somebody other than Margene and a bunch of total strangers would know about it. And I don't mean to toot my own horn, but I would've been one of those people. In other words, Darryl, Margene's will is a fake. We've just got to prove that."

"So, how do we do that?"

"Are you ready for this? I've taken it upon myself to locate a handwriting expert. I've vaguely discussed the situation with him. I haven't so much as hired him. But I will. All I need is the go ahead from you. Under the current circumstances, before I do so, you're first going to need to nip this thing in the bud. It doesn't need to go any further."

"Since you suggested that Charles Wiley hadn't done anything for you, I'm assuming that he has not come forth to contest the will at hand?"

"Yep, that's right."

"Well then, we need to find you a new lawyer as soon as possible. Give me the day to work on it. But I'm assuming you're with me in hiring the expert?"

"Absolutely!"

"His name is George Garnet. He's good. One of the best in the nation, if not the best. He's worked with the FBI on many a case. He's bridged the gap on everything from murder to government scandals. You're not going to find a better player for your team than him."

"He sounds too good to be true. The biggest question is where we're gonna find a lawyer who isn't somehow hobnobbing with Margene. You know she has connections literally all over the place. I mean, look at Guy Saunders. Now there's one dutiful servant. I don't know what she has on him, but whatever it is, it must be good. He may as well take himself off the market and become Margene's personal lackey. He's right there beside her every move. And I can't figure it out. There's no two people on the planet who have less in common."

"That's a tough one. One that I don't even want to think about. You know, Darryl, I would suggest you using my personal lawyer. But I don't think he's what you need. I don't even think you should settle for an estate attorney. What you need is a good criminal attorney. After hashing it over I tend to be in agreement with you as to the suspicion of Clinton's death. But let's not jump into murder accusations just yet. Good Lord, Darryl. I know this must be an armful to carry. Believe me, though. When it's all been said and done, you'll be a much richer person from it all. And I don't necessarily mean in the dollar sense, either."

On the other end of the spectrum, dollars were all that Margene seemed to be able to think about. That, and figuring out how best to spend them.

The sack of coins, she'd decided, had been kept tucked away for a cry too long. In each moment of her spare time, she researched every single round, precious piece of metal that she assumed would lead to her early retirement. It wasn't something that would happen overnight, though. She had no idea what was what when it pertained to the connoisseurship of coins.

"Earl, do you remember anything that Clint said about that coin? What was it called? What'd it look like? There must be a hundred of these damn things in here. Good heavens! They all 'bout look alike. Earl, can you get off your ass for a minute and help me figure this out?"

Earl, as usual, was quietly perched on his corner of the sofa doing little more than nodding off.

"Earl! Do you hear me?"

His chin bopped down on his chest, then ricocheted up to where his eyes, finally popping open, came in contact with his mother's face. For a split second he saw her angry expression, then came the blur of her palm racing past his jaw.

"Oww! What'd you slap me for?"

"For bein' good for absolutely nothin'!"

"Whoa!"

"Earl, you can 'whoa' all day long, but that don't change the fact that your good fortune is about to run dry. Just because we're sittin' on top of Clint's estate don't mean we're sittin' high on the hog! Look around you, for cryin' out loud. Is this what you hoped to gain from all the hard work I've put out to see that you and your sister got what you rightfully deserved? Is it? I mean, are you satisfied? 'Cause I sure as hell am not. Now, will you put on what little of a thinkin' cap you have on that skull o' yours and tell me what Clint told you about that damn coin?"

"Mama, I'm tellin' ya, I never saw it."

"What was the name of it, then?"

"I don't know. I couldn't even pronounce it. Don't you remember? I told you that."

"Fine, then. But I'm gonna tell you something. The sheer fact that literally everything that gets accomplished in the dealings with this estate, due to the talent of yours truly, boils down to one thing. You wanna know what that is?"

"Mama, I ain't that dumb. I already know that you're gonna get most everything. Me and Earlene both know that."

She eyeballed him, then walked back to where she came from. He was not only somewhere in the ballpark, he was accurate. He was accurate in acknowledging the fact that she was the greediest of the three. And by God, in her opinion, that was just the way it was supposed to be.

"So, what do you think about Lady Margene?" Grampus was sitting back on his porch, hashing out the opinions of his two proteges.

"She smells. Smells fishy," said Little One. "I don't know why, but she does."

"Yep." Grampus sat up in his chair. "Don't seem right to me."

"So, why did you do business with 'er?"

He knew why he'd made a deal with her, but didn't bother saying. He didn't take a business call from Margene Lee in order to gain a few extra bucks. His business with her was purely power driven..

"Follow her," he said. "Follow her close. But follow her private, this time."

"You can count on us, boss."

They followed her, all right. They followed her to work, to the grocery store, to the dry cleaners, to the out-of-town coin shops.

"Coin shops!" yelled Grampus. "Were they high dollar or just the trinket pawn shop types?"

"They weren't pawn shops," said Little One.

"I didn't suggest that they were pawn shops. I meant the pawn shop type."

"Naw. There were up town. Fancy cars parked in front."

"Did you manage to go inside any of 'em?"

"Couldn't. Not if we were gonna keep tailin' her."

"Go investigate, then, would you? Find out what she was up to. And I don't care what you need to do to find out. Just find out."

Margene herself wasn't even sure what she was up to. She was dealing with such unfamiliar territory that she felt a bit on the foolish side. But foolish was all right, just as long as it meant being a three million dollar fool.

CHAPTER THIRTY

The day after his confrontation with Darryl, Rutherford phoned her just as he had promised.

"Darryl, how are you doing, sweetheart?"

"I'm all right. So ..."

"So, I guess you're wondering what I found. Or who, rather."

"Yeah, I guess I am."

"He's out of state, but I think you might be pleased to know that not only was he interested in your case professionally, but for personal reasons, too."

"Personal reasons? Why? One of Margene's past victims or something?"

"Close. He wasn't the victim, but his father was."

"So, does he have a name?"

"Mac Arthur."

"Mac Arthur. You found him out of state? What? Do you know him or something?"

"Or something. I know the family. And so do you, in a round about way."

"I do?"

"You haven't figured it out yet? Think back. Think of anyone you may have known with the name Arthur."

Darryl stared blankly at the wall.

"Come on, Darryl. Think."

Her face suddenly lit up. "Mattie Arthur. Is it ..."

"Mac is her grandson."

"I don't understand. How did this happen?"

"How it happened is the last thing you should be worried about. Just be happy that it did. This one is definitely on your side."

"Even though he doesn't know me?"

"Let's just say he's been waiting on an opportunity to tangle with Margene."

"So, he's not connected with her or intimidated by her?"

"I'm going to let you ask those questions directly to him. He'll be calling you before noon."

"I, uh, guess, thank you. There is one question. If he's out of state, how does this commuting thing work?"

"Got that all taken care of. He's going to temporarily relocate here to Stoweville. Found him a small office that was vacant right across from the bank."

"I don't know how to thank you. This just seems like so much."

"Don't thank me yet. But come see me after you've set something up with him. Then I want you to talk with George Garnet. Hopefully, in the meantime Margene won't have any more shenanigans up her sleeve."

Darryl's drawn out feelings of hopelessness seemed to lighten. It was as though she was already sitting in the courtroom, face to face with the woman who had taken her birthright away.

She felt a sense of strength coming on. And it felt good, for a change. It made her want to confront everyone who had done her wrong. She wanted to waltz up to every single one of them and tell them to go to hell. Even Aaron Prouty. In her opinion, he was just as bad as any of them. And to supposedly be her father's trusted attorney, he turned out to be nothing more than a dud. Perhaps even a bit of a salesman. A salesman who conned her into retaining that good for nothing, Charles Wiley. Salesmen working together. That's what it was. After all, weren't attorneys just salesmen wrapped underneath higher priced suits?

Then she began thinking about Mac Arthur, another salesman. Did he honestly have an interest in her case, or was it really about putting Margene down to size?

When the eagerly awaited phone call came, she was there ready with a mouthful of questions and other pertinent things to say.

It was as though she'd known him all her life, because in no time flat she seemed to be comfortably acquainted with him. Chalk that up to his being an offspring of Mattie Arthur.

"So, if it's all right with you, we'll just meet tomorrow," he said. "Tomorrow's Wednesday. It should give us enough time to get something properly prepared in the way of contesting their will, and on their lawyer's desk by Thursday. Then we'll still have a decent amount of time to get things rolling on the real dog and pony show. We're gonna have to work fast, though. If everything is how you say it is, then they've already gotten a major jump on us. I don't want to disappoint you by saying that, but what's fact is fact. So don't worry about the things we can't do. Concentrate full force on what we can get accomplished right now. Today, tomorrow, and the next day. Now, you know where to meet, don't you?"

"Yeah, I know."

"Tomorrow, at, say, elevenish, then?"

"I'll see you then."

Darryl's confidence grew even stronger. This time, however, she knew where to draw the line. She knew there was a limit as to how far she would allow herself to trust another lawyer. No matter how good he might've been at selling horse shit.

"Horse shit!" said Margene. "These people don't know the difference between a coin and a coaster. Earl, are you sure you know what you're talkin' about with this coin bit?"

"Yeah. I'm sure. Trust me. Daddy went on and on about it. He was proud o' that thing."

"Why is it then that I haven't had any luck with these so-called experts? They offered me a hundred dollars for one of those dad-blasted pennies. But that's it. I laughed in their face."

"So you didn't take the money?"

"Take the money! Take the money! For all I know they're trying to scam one over on me. No! I didn't take the money. I'm gonna keep everything right where it is until I get some more things figured out. Where's your sister? Have you heard from her lately? I'll see if she wants to take a few road trips with me. No offense, but she's a lot better at wheelin' and dealin' than you. I'm thinkin' I might have to spend a weekend travelin' around to some o' the bigger cities, maybe heading north a little."

"What do you need me to do?"

"Well, if you want to see about pawning off some more trinkets, you know where the rest are. Don't, and I mean don't, take less than what the list I wrote up says. Everything we took from that house is categorized on that list, and I don't want one dollar less than the amount written beside it."

"All right already! So, when you leavin'? This weekend?"

"Yep. If I can get ahold of your sister."

Margene began planning her trip, but this time around she wanted a bit more leverage while she was out trying to sell her product. She went to the library, which surprisingly was not a first. She found that the library offered substantial information on the most unlikely of subjects. Today, it would be rare and pricey coins.

She took the infamous pouch with her, keeping it safely nestled under her arm. She walked down one aisle after another until she found the section she was looking for. After pulling a few books from the shelf, she dumped them and the coins on a nearby table and began her research.

Hours went by, and not a single book was of any avail in finding out which one of those coins would be the one to set her up for life. Frustrated with her lack of findings, she packed it up and left.

The next day Darryl met with her new, and seemingly competent, attorney. He was sharp, humorous, and dangerously good looking. That was the part that scared her. She could barely carry on a conversation with him without getting jitters. Her fear was that she would develop some sort of crush on him and be unable to determine whether he was doing her case harm or good. So, she tried as best she could to remember that he was a lawyer. A salesman.

"I think I've told you everything except one thing."

"What's that?" he asked.

"It's just a theory, okay? And, for the record, I'm not the only one who holds to this theory."

He looked at her curiously while she tried her hardest not to make eye contact.

"I don't think my Daddy died of natural causes. Can't prove that, of course. No autopsy, and all."

"What are you suggesting? That he was killed?"

"Yep."

"How strongly do you believe that?"

"Fairly strong. It's just that the whole thing is so suspicious. Everything that could've and should've been explained has turned out to be the one big question mark."

"It's certainly not out of the question to look into it. But you've got to be willing to go through some messy situations. You've also got to be willing to invest a great deal of time. The detective research can be costly, too."

"I'm sure of all that. And it's okay. I'm willing to go there."

"All right. But let's start with lesser important matters first. First we'll contest their will. Then we'll pull in the expert. What's his name again? George ..."

"Garnet. I should be talking to him after our meeting."

"Give me a call after you do. Better yet, why don't you have him call me." She nodded. "So, what do I need to do now?"

"Nothing, other than answer the phone when I call you."

She finally smiled.

"I'll take care of everything. It's what I'm here for, right?"

She got up to shake his hand. "Your grandmother was a great lady."

"She was, wasn't she?"

She started for the door and without looking back at him, said, "Nice office, by the way."

He looked around, realizing she was being a smart aleck. The office was a one room get up, with a stale aroma and barely even a window. It was her way of warming up to him without losing control of any giddiness she was trying so cleverly to restrain.

After leaving, she immediately went to the bank to talk to Rutherford.

"What'd you think of our boy, Mac?"

"He seems to know what he's going. But I'm not sure I like the fact that he's so good looking."

Rutherford chuckled. "I think you'll be all right. So, no problems with contesting the will?"

"No. I mean, how much of a genius do you have to be to do that? I'm still blown away that Charles Wiley was so flippy about it. But, I'm not gonna think about that. I'm gonna focus on today. So, this George Garnet thing ..."

"I'm going to make that call right now."

Rutherford called, talking to him briefly, then handed the phone over to Darryl.

"Hello."

"Miss Lee, George Garnet. How are you doing today?"

"I'm fine."

"Let me ask you a question. Are you of complete understanding as to what it is I do?"

"You're a handwriting expert. You study forgeries."

"Something like that. I study a person's signature, and from that I'm able to determine whether someone else may have forged it. I do that by analyzing dozens of authentic signatures and other handwriting samples. I get to know that person's unique style and movements. Once I'm convinced that I know these particular qualities, I examine the questionable signature, etcetera, which has been submitted to me, and I compare it to the proven authentic ones. I do this through many different methods that I was professionally trained in. If a situation calls for me to present my findings in a court of law, I go about doing this through enlarged diagrams. That procedure is very tedious, but very accurate. In a courtroom, I make certain that everyone present knows and understands my conclusion. Now, do you have any questions?"

"Not so far."

"All right. Miss Lee, as your situation was explained to me previously by Rutherford—and forgive me for being informed by someone other than yourself—I'm going to ask that you round up as many signatures and any other writing samples you can of your father's. Of course, I'll also need to be in possession of a copy of the assumed forgery."

"I'll make sure you get those."

"The sooner you get 'em to me, the sooner we can get crackin'."

"I guess that goes with everything, right. I'll just call you when I have everything. And, before I forget, my lawyer wants to speak to you sometime today. I'm sure you expected that, right?"

She spouted out the number, then waited for some sort of friendly conclusion to their telephone meeting.

"Good enough. Miss Lee, a pleasure, and I'll look to hearing from you soon."

She hung up the phone and looked strangely over to Rutherford. "He's all business."

"Well, are you looking for the best handwriting expert money can buy, or Mister Congeniality?"

"Yeah, yeah. I didn't tell him this, but I'm gonna tell you. There might be a problem getting enough writing samples for him. You know Daddy. He wasn't exactly the writer type. Other than some cards that I saved, and maybe an old report card or two stashed in my dorm room, anything that would've had his writing on it would be here at the bank or at Shangri-la."

"Signatures, no problem. I could round up a thousand of those. Did Garnet need other samples, too?"

"It's what he said."

"We'll find something. Maybe an old calendar he may have had in his office. He used to scribble all over those things."

"Let's go look."

They made their way to Clinton's office, still untouched since his death.

"Let me ask you, did Margene go through all his things in here?"

"Didn't come in here at all," he said, flipping the light on. "All she was interested in was that lock box of his."

CHAPTER THIRTY-ONE

hen Guy Saunders walked into his office that next morning, the last thing on his mind was the possibility of getting slapped in the face with documents of rebuttal for Clinton Lee's Last Will and Testament.

"What's this?" he said. "I don't believe it." He called out to his secretary. "When did this arrive?"

"This mornin'," she said.

"It wasn't sent by Parcel. There are no markings on the envelope."

"That's because it was hand-delivered. I believe he introduced himself as Mac Arthur."

Saunders walked across the floor with his head buried in the documents. "Unbelieveable."

"What is it, Mr. Saunders?"

I don't know whether to laugh or applaud."

"What's going on?"

Saunders looked at her for a moment, realizing that his behavior was less than authoritative. "Never mind. You can go now." He closed the door behind her.

It was a shock to him that someone would have the courage to go up against his vindictive client. In a way he was tickled by the thought of it. Of course, his oversized ego was convinced that it was a vulgar waste of time. He was still the reigning champion of the legal society.

He paged his secretary again. "Get Honorable Lee on the phone."

Like Saunders, being interrupted by opposition just wasn't on Margene's mind or agenda. She was far too busy focusing on her upcoming trip of coin inquiries.

"You're shittin' me!" she said. "Are you tellin' me that little girl is contesting the will that I've already presented?"

"According to what I have here in my hands, that's exactly what I'm telling you."

"What does she intend to do? Take me to court?"

"It would appear that way."

"That's a laugh."

"That may be, but Margene, as your lawyer, I'm going to advise you to stop everything you're doing as far as collecting Clinton's belongings. You know the law."

"Fine, then. But frankly, there isn't a whole lot that hasn't been dispensed."

"What do you mean by 'dispensed'?"

"I mean it's been handed out, sold, lost, whatever."

"What about the house?"

"Sold."

"Sold?"

"Uh- huh."

"You didn't tell me that. Margene, why would you sell that house? Are you out of your mind?"

"I have my reasons."

"Margene, it's me you're talking to."

"I had a debt to pay off. We'll just leave it at that."

"Sorry I asked. Whatever the case, though, you still need to stop what you're doing till we get things cleared."

"Were you actually serious about that?"

"Darryl and her lawyer are opposing the will you presented. I'm sure after I supply them a copy of it, there won't be any questions as to whether it goes to court of not. The will you presented leaves her completely out without a scrap. You figure it out. Now, I know the three of you, meaning you, Earl, and Earlene, originally presented this. We're going to have to narrow that down a bit. What I mean by that is, you're going to have to step aside."

"What?"

"Just hang on for a minute. What I'm saying is that it's in your best interest to step aside and let Earlene step up to the plate."

"No ..."

"Listen to me. You're the ex-wife of Clinton Lee. There isn't a soul on the planet who wouldn't wonder why you're the one defending the will. It looks too suspicious. Remember, it's Earl and Earlene who are the beneficiaries."

"I don't know."

"Don't know? Well, I'm gonna put it in plain English for you. If you want to win, do what I tell you."

"I've gotta go."

"I can't believe you sold the house, Margene!"

She slammed the phone down. All her plans, it seemed, had gone straight out the window. There would be no coin selling for her. Not yet, anyway. It could wait until later. After all, no one really knew it existed. According to Earl, the coin was a big fat secret, except for the fact that Clinton had told him about it.

So, what she needed to do now was find the most covert hiding place she could to stash the collection away, and wait for the dust to settle before she went to claim her millions.

The other thing she needed to do was conjure up some sort of bill of sale for Shangri-la.

It wasn't the first lie she'd ever told to Saunders. But what else was she supposed to do? Tell him the truth? That she'd literally given the property to Emmett Sims in exchange for his phoney role of executor?

"Ah, damn it." She'd forgotten one thing. "What am I gonna do about the witnesses?" It was one thing to slap signatures down on paper, but now she had to come up with the actual people to back it up.

When she created the will, she had literally traced every signature on it. The two witnesses' names she traced were conveniently those whom she'd had past affiliations with. One was Earlene's real father, Troy LeMaster. The other was the name of one of the many men she'd slept around with after her encounter with Clinton. His name was Leonard Moss. She chose him because he was dumb as dirt. He wouldn't have the intellect to know any better than to question matters if the possibility presented itself. Troy she chose randomly.

"I coulda picked somebody other than Troy. God, why didn't I? Guess I better deal with him first. Then Emmett. Then Leonard. Naw. Coins first."

Late that evening she arrived home and quickly changed out of her work ensemble into a generic one. Her intentions were to appear as low profile as possible when she went to dispose of the coins. If that went smoothly, then she'd go try to charm Troy LeMaster.

The hiding place that kept standing out to her was an old well house near an abandoned shack that she'd spotted years earlier in some of her ramblings. Because it was in the middle of nowhere, the coins would be safe there.

She grabbed the pouch and a flashlight and headed out the door. She drove a mile or two and noticed headlights. They seemed far enough away, but not wanting to take any chances of being seen, she turned onto the next street and waited for the car to pass. After counting to thirty, she continued on her way. The radio was on, playing a tune that she found catchy. She turned up the volume and began to hum. Absorbed in the music, she didn't notice when a car, the same car, pulled back onto the road and began tailing her again. It followed closer this time, because its headlights were off.

When she reached the shack, she took off on foot to the old well house, wading through the soppy grass. Once she'd made it there, she pushed the door gently open. There were years worth of cobwebs strung from one wall to the next, shining like spun silver. Her nose wrinkled, as she was horrified at the idea of being confronted by any eight-legged prospects, but walked inside anyway. It was rank from being closed up all those years. The mouth of the well had a thin slab of lumber across it.

"I think this'll work."

The well itself was made of thickly stacked rock, which she knew would support the small pouch of coins if she could just shove them between it and the slab.

After carefully rigging it, she turned her flashlight off and made her way back in the dark. Relieved to have one thing out of the way, she was now ready for job number two.

Troy lived in a run down trailer in about as remote an area of nowhere as the old well house. Margene hadn't seen him since their last rendezvous nearly thirty years prior. Not even in town. When she showed up on his doorstep, he was less than thrilled and more than surprised.

"Good God amighty," he said. "Look what the cat done gone and dragged up!"

"How you doin'?"

"Not as bad as you, it don't look like."

Casually, she looked down at her clothes smeared with webs and dust. Her shoes were stained.

He knew she was up to no good. But then again, he wasn't exactly known for ever being up to any better. He certainly wasn't the product of a stellar background.

"You gonna invite me in, or what?"

"Or what." He held the door open for her and pointed to the living room. He walked in after her and sat down in the worn out recliner.

She stood there, looking down at what would've appeared to have been a sofa.

"Here?"

"What do you want? The Ritz? From the looks o' you, I don't see why it matters anyway."

"Fine, then."

There was silence. It was strange for both of them to be in the same room again, yet enough alone in it.

"What are you doin' here, Margene? I thought we agreed to stay clear of each other."

"Things change."

"Uh-huh. Well, let me ask you this. What is it that you want from me? I know you ain't here to be social. And I damn sure don't think you got it in ya to rouse me back to the bedroom."

"How can I put this to ya?" She paused. "Troy, how would you like to earn a little money?"

"Must not be legal, if you're comin' to me."

"How'd you like to earn five thousand dollars?"

He got up from the recliner and walked across the floor. "Five thousand dollars for what?"

"Nothin', maybe. Unless it goes to court."

"Court? Nawp. I ain't messin' with no courtrooms."

"Tell you what. If it doesn't go to court, I'll give you five just for agreeing. If it does, I'll give you ten."

"Ten? All right. Maybe you got my attention, now. But agreeing to do what?" He walked back into the room and sat down.

"It's about a will. My ex's. Clinton's. Your signature is on it as a witness."

"Wait a minute. You got me all screwed up. How did my signature wind up on his will?"

"That's beside the point. All you need to do is testify if ... if it goes to court that you were a witness and the signature on it is yours."

"For ten thousand dollars?"

"If it goes to court."

"That's it? Say that I signed a will?"

"Well, there might be a few more questions you'll have to answer."

"Won't do it. Ain't good with questions."

"What if I brief you?"

"What me?"

"Brief you. What if I tell you everything to say. What if I give you every question you could possibly be asked, and I tell you exactly what to say."

"I'll agree to do this for five. If the court thing don't happen. But if it does, and I gotta be answerin' a bunch o' questions ... I'll do it for twenty-five."

"That's highway robbery!"

"Lady, you came to me."

Her face turned red. "Twenty-five. But not a penny more. And don't you think for a minute that you won't testify if I do give you the money. I'll bury your ass in so much dirt, you'll think it's your funeral."

"So, it's a deal?"

"It's a deal." She walked to toward the door.

"Wait a minute."

She stopped.

"What about the five thousand?"

"That, you'll have to wait 'til tomorrow for."

She drove home infuriated. All she could think about was how much effort she'd put into obtaining Clinton's estate, and how she'd ended up so far without much to show for it. The money she'd hadn't yet cashed in from the insurance and stock would inevitably go towards paying people off. And burdened though she was by that, there was still that glimmer of light at the end of the tunnel, or possibly at the top of the well.

Earlene was waiting at her house when she got there.

"Where you been, Mama? Earl had me worried sick."

"Out."

"So, you're all right?"

"Yeah, I'm fine. Earl, what did you do, go and call your sister?"

"You ain't ever been out this late," he said.

"For Pete's sake, boy. You ain't got to go stir up trouble."

"Well, you wasn't home when I got here. And you're always here when I get here."

"That don't mean you gotta ..."

"Mama, he didn't call me 'til about half an hour ago."

"Both o' you are plum crazy! But seein' that the both of yuns are here, I guess now's as good a time as any to let you in on the latest."

Though Margene did appoint Earlene to be the public face representing their team, she would still be the backbone holding everything together. The tactics and even the words themselves were all products of her brainstorming. One thing in particular she emphasized over and over was that neither Earl nor Earlene were to tell a soul that the coin existed.

"Heaven forbid that little troublemaker actually succeeds in this nonsense she's tryin' to pull, but if she does, we'll still have one over her, because we've got the coin. Nobody has to know about it but us."

That could have been the case. But it wasn't. The coins were discovered the day after she'd tucked them away in the well house. Shakey and Little One were too busy following her from point A to B to investigate that same night. But when they went poking around the next day, it didn't take long for them to find the reason. They brought the pouch immediately to Grampus.

"Coins? She drove out to the middle of the sticks to hide coins? Put 'em back."

"What?" said Little One.

"I want you to put 'em back."

"Well, they must be valuable, otherwise she wouldn't have gone out of her way to hide 'em."

"They may be valuable. Or they could be a link to something entirely different. That's why I want you to put 'em back. I want you to find out why she hid 'em. Now this Troy LeMaster things got me stumped. I haven't found much of a background on him other than a few misdemeanors with the law. Your general mediocre bum. See if she goes back to see him. If she does, find out what they talk about this time."

Shakey and Little One continued to follow Margene for the next few weeks. What they found was that she had more than a few middle of the night rendezvous. But once Grampus found out that Margene was just coaching her witness in what he knew was a forged will from the get-go, he was able to relax a little. But that only pertained to Troy and Leonard. What inevitably shook him up was her meeting with Emmett Sims.

It was one puzzle he couldn't quite master. Why would Margene have gone out of her way to see that her children be included in their father's estate, if she was just going to give the mansion away? It didn't make sense. Which brought him back to the belief that the coins would somehow be the map that led the way to logic.

CHAPTER THIRTY-TWO

Mac Arthur was very good at being a lawyer. And after numerous sit downs with Darryl, she was feeling fairly confident about her case. The only problem was that she was not only fixated on resolving the case of the will, she was damn near determined to nail Margene for murder.

"Darryl, I want to see her crumble just as much as you do. But you need to hear me out on this one. First things first. We don't want to go after her, or them, for issues that shouldn't be dealt with yet. We're putting the cart before the horse here. All we need to focus on right now is slamming her for presentation of a forged will. Nothing more. Not yet. I do have some good news for you. I talked to George Garnet. From the samples you provided him with, he's found thirty-seven errors in the signature on their will."

"Thirty-seven? That's almost absurd."

"Can you believe it?"

"No. I can't believe that it would take thirty-seven botches to trace a signature."

"But that's the good news."

"Uh-oh. So that means there's bad news."

"Not exactly. That means we have an expert who can testify that their will is a fabrication. But on the other hand, it's not going to be as simple as 'Poof – their will is a fake, and they go to jail.' By the way, Earlene is representing their side. Not Margene."

"Wait a minute. Go back to the part about 'Poof, their will is a fake.'"

"Just because they presented a forged will doesn't mean that we can lock 'em up and throw away the key. They'll have something up their sleeve in terms of playing innocent. Even if their will is discredited, they're gonna play dumb. That's when we delve in deeper with the 'where it came from' scenario. Remember what I said. Cart before the horse. Now, our first hearing comes up in three weeks. We'll try and discredit their will at that time. More than likely, we'll win. If we don't, that's all right. We can always appeal. What we want is to take this to a jury trial."

"What kind of jury would vote against Margene? Or them, I mean."

"With the defendant being Earlene, you don't have anything to worry about. It'll be in Superior court, tried by a competent judge."

"You don't understand."

"I do understand. But you need to understand that though Margene may hold some clout in this town, her daughter does not. Plus, there's always the possibility of a change of venue if it goes that far."

"Yeah?"

"Relax. Let's just concern ourselves with one thing at a time. You're too excited."

"I'm a chip off the ol' block, I guess. People used to say that Daddy was that way a lot. Excited."

"I suppose I would be too if I'd been in his shoes. No matter how much I'm sure he hated it, it was inevitable that he would be affiliated with Margene for the rest of his life. But let's not go there. Let's talk witnesses. I think we should bring in the witnesses of Clinton's real will. We'll just call it that for now, anyway. We've got Rutherford and a Bill Abernathy. Do you know him?"

"Yeah. Sort of. But not really. He's an officer at the bank, one of Daddy's colleague friends. But he never came over to Thanksgiving or anything. I guess I know him. Why? Does that matter?"

"No. We need to get him in here, though."

"That should be easy enough."

"And Rutherford, well, that's pretty much a done deal."

"Will I be taking the stand?"

"No. Just those two and Garnet."

The next three weeks flew by for everyone. For Margene, especially. In no way did she enjoy playing second fiddle to Earlene. Always being the mouth of the family, it was all she could do to comprehend the notion of being invisible. Which is why she chose to ditch the courtroom scene entirely when the big day came.

Earlene arrived early that morning with Earl tagging behind. Saunders, widely known for his promptness, was not far behind the two of them. The three sat together, huddled like a band of ball players trying to come up with the best tactic to win the game. When the other two players, LeMaster and Moss, showed up, they joined in the circle. It was as if they were all comrades, even though they were all basically strangers. Each was there to get a job done, whether it was motivated by love of money or love of winning. The only issue that concerned them was the fact that there was a handwriting expert playing on the opposite team. A fact that wasn't thrown their way until a week prior.

"I'm going to do my best to discredit George Garnet as a plausible witness," said Saunders. "Besides, it's hardly justifiable to have him present today, given that I wasn't informed of his involvement till just a week ago. But I believe you two should have everything down as far as what we've gone over." Saunders looked at LeMaster and Moss, hoping to see some sort of confidence in their eyes. In fact, that's all he could hope for, considering that neither were what he thought of as being remotely intelligent.

When Darryl finally made her way through the arched double doors, she didn't do so alone. She had Arthur on one arm, her Uncle Martin on the other, with Garnet, Rutherford, and Abernathy close behind. Her players appeared more promising than those of her opponents, which immediately lifted a few brows. There was no huddling to be seen by them once they arrived, either. They had done their homework and felt no need to look concerned. Instead, they sat quietly and waited for the Honorable Dickie Waters, who had been appointed Judge of the Probate hearing.

The courtroom benches filled up in no time. Like every other court hearing in town, it was what most Stoweville-ites flocked to see. It was after all, free entertainment.

Just before Waters made his entrance, Darryl took a quick peek over to the defendant's table. Earl, it seemed, had already beaten her to the punch. He'd been gazing over in her direction for the better part of ten minutes. The look he gave was one that he thought would make her squirm. Instead, she smiled back at him until he looked away.

"Bitch," he mumbled.

About that time, the court officer introduced Waters to the court. The initial hoopla was something Darryl had never witnessed before. She was instantly drawn in, hoping to gain a little knowledge.

She trusted her attorney and the hands that paid him. She trusted the ability of Garnet to render a solid argument. And since she knew that the testimonies of both Rutherford and Abernathy would be straight forward, she felt that Earlene didn't have much of a leg to stand on. What she didn't expect was the public ridicule she would face before the day was done.

"In the matter of Darryl Lee versus Earlene Lee, the plaintiff is accusing the defendant of presenting an improper will. Is that the matter being introduced here?" asked Waters.

"Your Honor, we're here today to prove that the defendant has not only produced a forged will, but has also divvied the estate of the deceased, to whom the will in question belonged," said Arthur.

"I object. That's a blatant accusation and has no evidence to support it at this time," said Saunders.

"Mr. Arthur, I'm sure you're eager to win this case before it begins, but I'd prefer that you not cut to the chase in my courtroom. Would you care to try again?"

"Yes, Your Honor. We're here to contest the proposed will of the defendant."

"Mr. Saunders, do you have any objections?"

"No, Your Honor."

"You may begin."

"I'd like to call my first witness," said Arthur.

He began with Rutherford, then Abernathy, getting claims that they both had indeed witnessed and signed the will dated March 2, 1970. There were no questions from Saunders for their testimonies. But then Garnet took the stand.

"Mr. Garnet, could you please tell us what business you are in? Or rather, what is your occupation?"

"Yes. I am a Board Certified Questioned Document Examiner."

"For those of us who don't know what that is, could you rephrase that in plain English?"

"I am a handwriting expert."

"Now, you say that you are Board Certified."

"Actually, I'm certified by two organizations: the Independent

Association of Questioned Document Examiners, and the Association of Forensic Document Examiners."

"And could you explain to the court your purpose for being here today?"

"I'm here to share my expert findings on two documents claiming to contain the signature of Clinton Lee."

"What are those documents?"

"They're wills."

"Two different wills?"

"Yes. One is dated March 2, 1970, and the other is dated March 2, 1980."

"And in your opinion, does either document contain a signature that isn't genuine?"

"Objection," said Saunders. "This witness has claimed that he would share some sort of expert findings. I don't believe a simple 'yes' or 'no' supports anything."

"Sustained."

"Mr. Garnet, as an expert, you are able to determine whether or not a document contains a forgery."

"Yes, I am."

"How do you go about doing that?"

"Generally, I begin by making a side by side visual of what is known to be an authentic signature, and the signature in question. Then I make a microscopic comparison of the two."

"When you say 'authentic,' you mean ..."

"I mean a genuine signature by the person we're dealing with."

"And you compare it to a signature that is believed to be forged?"

"Your Honor, this is argumentative," said Saunders.

"Mr. Arthur, can we just let the witness explain his craft."

"So, you compare the two signatures."

"It's not as simple as that. I take not only one, but multiple samples ... genuine samples, that is. I study them. Then I begin comparing the questionable one. But before I share my findings with you, I want you to understand a little bit about handwriting in general."

"All right."

"In writing a signature, the person at hand has written their own signature for 'x' amount of time. In this case, the person was forty-five years old. So, let's just say that he'd been signing his name for thirty-five years."

"That's speculation, Your Honor," said Saunders.

"Overruled. Could the both of you let this witness say what he has to say. I'm actually interested in this. Continue."

"Well, just tentatively speaking, let's say that this person, Clinton Lee, had been writing his signature for thirty-five years. In a time period such as that, it becomes an automatic writing experience. You don't have to stop to think about what you're doing, do you? You don't have to stop and think, 'Well, what kind of letter goes next?' or 'What should I do with the slant?' or 'Do I connect these two letters together?' or 'Do I cross the "t" high, or do I cross it low?' You just don't think about it at all. It's a flowing, fast, easy thing to do. And along the way, you pick up your own special habits and forms for the letters. The characteristics of your handwriting are inbred into that signature."

"Other than learning these so-called characteristics and comparing them, what else do you look for in a signature?"

"There are things I look for to determine whether or not it is comparatively in favor of known genuine signatures, or if it is out of the realm of the natural variations that I would expect to find in a genuine signature."

"What would be an example of those things?"

"For one, I've found many signatures that have been exact overlays of other signatures."

"By 'overlays', you mean ..."

"I mean duplicates. And when I find those, I know that someone has traced the signature. That it's non-genuine."

"How could two signatures that are exactly alike, or identical, be a tracing?"

"Well, everyone has what is called a natural variation in their handwriting. In other words, you cannot write your signature two times exactly the same, because of these variations."

"Are you telling me that if I wrote my signature two times, the signatures would not be exactly the same?"

"Try it. You can sit down all day long writing your signature over and over, but you'll not find two that are identical. No one can even trace their own signature better than they can write it."

"I'll take your word on that. You are, after all, the expert."

"Your Honor!"

"Mr. Arthur."

"Sorry, Your Honor. Where was I? So, after examining genuine signatures of Mr. Lee..."

"Excuse me, I did examine not only signatures, but other writing samples, as well."

"And from these examinations, were you able to reach an opinion as to whether either of the wills contained the genuine signature of Clinton Lee?"

"Yes."

"And what was that opinion?"

"My opinion is that the will dated March 2, 1970 is, in fact, genuine."

"Were you able to come to an opinion of the will dated ten years from that time?"

"I was."

"Can you tell the court what that opinion was?"

"The signature purported to be that of Clinton Lee's is simulated. Meaning, non-genuine."

"I have no further questions."

"Mr. Saunders, do you wish to cross examine this witness?"

"You better believe I do." Saunders stood up and walked to the front of the courtroom. "You say that in your opinion the will dated 1980 is a non-genuine one? Or, what was it– a simulation."

"Yes."

"Now, this word, opinion. That's a pretty questionable word. I presume you have evidence, or could even perhaps demonstrate these findings to the court?"

"I'm prepared to demonstrate my findings. Yes. Someone has obviously tried to sit down and practice writing in the style and formation of Mr. Lee's signature. But they failed miserably."

"All right. Let's go back a bit. Who asked you to take part in this case?"

"Are you asking me who I"m working for?"

"I think everyone here knows the answer to that. No. I'm asking you who initially contacted you about this case."

Darryl gazed over to where Rutherford had taken his seat. Rutherford shook his head.

"I'm sorry. Didn't you hear the question? Who hired you?"

"I was initially contacted by Gordy Rutherford."

"Gordy Rutherford. Now, is he the one who is actually paying for your services?"

"Objection. Irrelevant," said Arthur.

"Your Honor, I'd like to get an answer from this witness. I do intend to go somewhere with this shortly."

"I'll allow it. But let's move this thing along."

"Thank you. Now, can you tell the court who retained your services? Who hired you?"

"Gordy Rutherford."

"Do you know why he hired you?"

"No. I can't say that I do."

"Is he somehow related to Miss Lee, that you are aware of?"

"I don't know the answer to that."

"Let's go back to this comparison you claimed to have made with the documents to the so-called genuine handwriting samples. How are you able to determine that these genuine samples are indeed genuine?"

"I usually ask the person who hires me ..."

"Gordy Rutherford, in this case."

"Person. Persons."

"All right. Continue."

"I usually ask the person or persons I'm working for to present me with at least three or four signatures that have some sort of formal origination. Like an income tax form, canceled check, that sort of thing. As long as I have a few of those, it's pretty obvious whether or not the other samples they provide are authentic."

"I see. So, you have made the claim that the 1980 will was a fabrication. What drew you to that conclusion?"

"A number of things. Thirty-seven, to be exact."

"Could you briefly tell us about a few of these things?"

Garnet went on to explain some of the mistakes he found, describing them in detail.

"All right. These mistakes. These errors. Is it possible that there could've been an underlying factor that caused them? Are there things that could affect a person's signature to make errors happen?"

"Sure."

"Like what?"

"Well, being drunk. That could affect a person's signature."

"Anything else?"

"The instrument you use to write with. I suppose if it isn't working properly, that could have an effect."

"Any others?"

"The surface you're writing on. If it's bumpy, you know."

"So you've got being drunk, a pen that doesn't work, and a bumpy surface."

"I certainly don't think that a person signing a will is going to approach doing so in such a casual manner that they'd allow any of those things to be a factor."

"In your expert opinion?"

"Yes."

"Okay, now. Refresh my memory. You said that you were certified by two organizations. Is that right?"

"Yes."

"So, all in all, how long would you say you've been examining handwriting?"

"I began studying it back in college in 1957."

"Did you major in that?"

"No. It wasn't something that was offered."

"Let me stop you for a moment. You presumably have a college degree, but not in the field in which you're currently working?"

"I have a degree in Science."

"So, if you didn't study handwriting examinations in college, where did you study it?"

"Well, I began studying it on my own, but ..."

"Thank you. Your Honor, I believe I'm finished with this witness, but I would like to call Mr. Rutherford back to the stand at this time."

Rutherford didn't budge.

"I believe I called Mr. Gordy Rutherford to take the stand."

Again, he remained seated. What he was actually trying to do was give himself enough time to come up with an answer to the question he knew Saunders was calling him back up for.

People in the room began to snicker. Especially those in the general direction of the defendant's table.

"Mr. Rutherford," said Waters, "you're going to have to take the stand."

Suddenly Rutherford twitched his head. "I apologize, Your Honor. The batteries on these dad-blasted hearing aids. You just can't buy anything decent anymore."

Waters, being on the farther side of middle age himself, smiled. "I know what you mean. Why don't you come up and have a seat."

Rutherford took his time walking up. When he got there, he didn't take his eyes off Saunders for a minute.

"Tell us about your relationship with the plaintiff."

"She's a family friend."

"So, she's not related to you?"

"No. Her Daddy worked for me."

"Pretty close, you and her father. Sounds like a nice relationship. So, how do you feel about the defendant? What is your relationship with Earlene Lee?"

"I don't have a relationship with Earlene Lee. Unless she knows something I don't know."

"Well, perhaps in a round about sort of way, you do. Isn't it true that you have a personal prejudice against the defendant's mother?"

"Objection, Your Honor," said Arthur. The defendant's mother has no bearing on this case."

"Mr. Saunders ..."

"Your Honor, I said that I planned to take this somewhere."

"Continue on, then."

"Isn't it true that you refused to hire the defendant's mother when you had half a dozen job openings at your bank thirty years ago?"

"Excuse me, Your Honor. Thirty years ago?"

"I'm leading up to a point, Your Honor."

"I don't know where you're going with this, but if you see me yawn, that means ..."

"You won't have the chance, Your Honor. Trust me. Now, Mr. Rutherford, after you purposely threw out her application for a job that she was more than qualified for, you a few years later tried to use your pull in the community to have her ostracized as an official of the court. Isn't that right, Mr. Rutherford? If my recollection is accurate, you made no secret to the fact that you tried to bribe Arnold Lanford, her predecessor, into concocting alleged illegal documents in order to have her removed from her position. Are you going to deny that, Mr. Rutherford?"

"That was a long time ago."

"But, wouldn't it be fair to say that you oppose and have always opposed having the defendant's mother in her current position?"

"Your Honor, what does Mr. Rutherford's personal opinion of the defendant's mother have to do with this case?" asked Arthur."

"At this point, I'm not so sure."

"Your Honor, this man is well known to have a score to settle with the defendant's mother, and would do just about anything he sets his mind to, to see that she and everyone associated with her, including the defendant, is destroyed. And if it means hiring a handwriting expert with credentials that are ... what were they ... self-taught, then so be it. Therefore, it would be safe to presume that he has a relationship of hatred with the defendant."

"Objection."

"Tell the court, Mr. Rutherford. Whose idea was it to hire George Garnet?"

"Mine."

"Nothing further."

An echo of voices poured through the room, as a flushed faced Rutherford walked to his seat.

Arthur, shocked by Saunders' outlandish commentary, was unfortunately without words. What could he have added to the situation to make it better? It was a known fact that Rutherford hated Margene. And in this case, it was true that his feelings for her passed on to that of her daughter. He only hoped that Judge Waters would have enough common decency to acknowledge the fact that Saunders was merely grasping at straws.

"At this time I'd like to call my first witness," said Saunders.

Leonard Moss, not being capable of perpetrating a mind-blowing finale, was that witness. His testimony was simple, brief, and anything but what he'd sworn on the Bible to tell. And when Saunders finished with him, an anxious Arthur was ready to dig in tooth and nail.

"Mr. Moss, you are aware of the importance of a document such as a will, aren't you?"

"Sure."

"Given that, I'm trying to figure out one thing that doesn't quite add up. I noticed the signature on the 1980 will. Your signature. Looks to me like anyone could practically emulate it. Do you see what I'm talking about here?" Arthur held up a photocopy of the page containing his supposed signature.

"I'm not terribly sure how a person could even make out the name Leonard Moss. You see this? Unless my eyes are starting to give out on me, I'd have to say that your signature looks like a couple of wavy lines. Like something a four-year-old might draw to look like water."

"Objection," said Saunders.

"Your Honor, if you'll allow me to finish here."

"Overruled."

"Thank you. Now, Mr. Moss, do you see what I see? Other than this printed capital L, the rest of it is nothing more than a couple of wavy lines. Mr. Moss, are you by any chance illiterate?"

"What?"

"Do you read and write? Well, excuse me. I guess you must write a little, otherwise there wouldn't be two wavy lines scribbled across the signature line here."

"Objection. Mr. Arthur is badgering this witness."

"Your Honor, I'd like to come to some conclusion as to the competence of this witness."

"Overruled."

"Do you read, Mr. Moss?"

"Whoah ... that's the way I sign my name."

"Mr. Moss, can you read this sentence here?" Arthur placed a sheet of paper in front of him with one sentence typed across it in plain, bold print. "Mr. Moss, can you tell the court what this sentence says?"

"No."

"No? Why is that, Mr. Moss?"

"I can't read."

"You can't read. So this very important document, that one would think should've been taken seriously, was signed by you, a witness, who is illiterate. I can't for the life of me understand why Clinton Lee, or anybody for that matter, would choose someone who couldn't read or write to witness a record of their last wishes. Can you explain why a reasonably intelligent man would've chosen in such a way?"

"Well, we was friends."

"Friends. All right. I'll jot that down. Thank you."

"I'd like to redirect," said Saunders. "Now, Mr. Moss, you say that you were friends with Mr. Lee?"

"Yes, we was."

"And as his friend, would you have considered asking him to witness any will that you wanted to have drawn up?"

"Shore. He was my buddy."

"Even if he was, let's say, illiterate?"

"I don't see why that'd matter."

"So, even if he wasn't able to read, because he was your buddy you would trust him with your most personal affairs? You wouldn't hesitate to ask him to be a witness, would you?"

"Naw. I shore wouldn't."

"Nothin' wrong with bein' impartial."

Darryl couldn't believe what she was hearing. Not just the words of Moss, but those of Saunders as well. It was as though neither knew the difference between telling a lie or telling the truth. Or maybe it was that they just didn't care. One thing was for sure in this case, though. The act of swearing truthfully on the Bible was one that had been thrown straight out the window.

"Couldn't you have said something to him while he was still up there?" she whispered to Arthur.

"Remember, this is just Probate. We don't want to pull out our entire bag of tricks now. If we did, they'd figure out our tactics. Like I told you, we can only pray that this does go to a higher court. That's when we'll surprise them. After they've let their guard down. Trust me."

She wanted to trust him. She wanted to believe that everything would turn out right in the end. But she was impatient. Especially considering that she was forced to watch one liar after another take ownership of the courtroom, all the while being strapped down to do absolutely nothing but let it happen.

"Don't get too bent out of shape with this next witness," he said. "He's a known troublemaker. Let it go in one ear and out the other."

She squeezed her palms together as hard as she could and watched one Troy LeMaster walk into the courtroom from his temporary sequestration.

"Mr. LeMaster," said Saunders, "is this your signature?" He held up a copy of the 1980 will.

"Yes. It is."

"I take it that you, like Mr. Moss, were a good friend of the deceased."

"We was fishin' buddies."

"Well, you must've been more than that if he wanted you to witness his will."

"I don't want to put anybody down here, but Clinton hung around me a good bit o' the time 'cause he said I was a real, down to earth friend. Not like all those highfaultin' banker types that he was around at work."

"So Clinton Lee was just a normal, everyday guy, then."

"A regular Joe."

"And when he asked you to witness his will, did you question him as to the contents of it?"

"I looked over it, but I didn't ask him any questions about it."

"Not even why he would've left one of his children deliberately out of it?"

"Didn't need to. He told me why."

"He actually offered this information to you freely?"

"Yeah. He said that he'd already paid enough to raise Darryl. Said he'd spent a fortune on her, while his other kids just had to make do. Besides that, he said he was ashamed of her."

"Objection. Heresay," said Arthur.

"Your Honor, my witness has sworn to this testimony."

"Overruled."

"Now, did your friend Mr. Lee tell you why he was ashamed of his daughter Darryl?"

"He didn't like the fact that he'd raised her to be proper and she kindly acted rebellious. Wastin' all that college money just to be a musician."

"I see. So, given the fact that he'd raised her with an elaborate upbringing, he expected more of her than to be a musician."

"He said he didn't see much future in it."

"So, he was embarrassed to a certain degree?"

"Ain't no question about it."

"And because she'd been blessed with, let's just face it, the good life, he chose to give his other two children what they'd been left out of for most of their lives."

"Yeah."

"Thank you. I have nothing more."

"Your witness, Mr. Arthur."

"Mr. LeMaster, how well do you know Mr. Moss?"

"Well, I don't really."

"When did you first meet Mr. Moss?"

"The evenin' we signed the will."

"Let me inquire about this evening the three of you signed the will. How did this meeting go about happening? Did Mr. Lee contact you and ask that you meet to sign his will?"

"Naw, nothin' like that. He called me up and asked me if I wanted to come over for dinner. That's all. I didn't know what he had on his mind till I got there."

"When you say 'there,' you mean his house?"

"Yes."

"And where is his house, exactly?"

"On Old Jordan Road."

"And on Old Jordan Road is where you first became acquainted with Mr. Moss?"

"That's right."

"Explain something to me. How is it that you managed to hang around with Clinton Lee, I'm sorry, for how many years was it?"

"A little over three."

"For three years you were friends with the deceased and never once came in contact with or met Mr. Moss before the evening of the will signing. How could that be? I mean, I presume being Clinton Lee's pal and all, you would've had some sort of run in with him before that night."

"I didn't know any of his bank buddies, either."

"That's right. You were his one 'down to earth' buddy. Not like Mr. Moss."

"Your Honor," said Saunders, "he's badgering this witness, and somehow trying to squeeze in a little personal criticism, too."

"Forgive me, Your Honor. There wasn't meant to be any personal insinuations or attacks here. I'm simply trying to determine the actual relationship between this witness and the deceased."

"That's all well and fine, Mr. Arthur, but in the future, try and be a little more tactful."

"Understood. Mr. LeMaster, what color was Clinton Lee's living room?"

"Objection."

"It wasn't really what I'd call a color," LeMaster answered, in spite of his lawyer's opposition. "It was wood. A dark, hardwood."

Darryl began to look frantic. Had the low life trash seated before her and the rest of the room actually been inside Shangri-la?

"How many times, Mr. LeMaster, would you say that you'd been to Clinton Lee's house?"

"I can't really say. A person don't keep track o' things like that, you know."

"I can understand that. And I suppose he came over to your house about as often as you came to his?"

"I guess so, yeah."

"I bet it must've been awkward for you, then, when one of those times was when he had to repossess your vehicle."

"Well, I uhh...."

"Isn't it true that Clinton Lee had to personally come to your home to repossess the truck that you were almost six months behind on the payments of? How did it feel to have your buddy come over and take care of business like that?"

"Business is business. Sometimes a body has to do what they gotta do."

"I'll tell you what, Mr. LeMaster. That there is an attitude we all should have."

"Your Honor!"

"Mr. Arthur, I'm getting' tired of this. That goes for you too, Mr. Saunders. If I didn't know any better, I'd say the two of you are using witnesses to settle a personal score of your own."

"Just one more thing, Your Honor. Mr. LeMaster, you stated that Mr. Lee was embarrassed of his daughter. Is that right?"

"That's what he told me."

"Because...refresh my memory, would you?"

"Because she wanted to be a musician instead o' shootin' for an honest and decent type o' job."

"Embarrassed is a pretty strong word. Are you sure that's what he told you?"

"I'm sure of it."

"Well, I suppose after having married a musician, it would've been humiliating for him to raise one, too. Nothing further."

CHAPTER THIRTY-THREE

It seemed as though there were more people gathered on the courthouse lawn after the hearing than were inside during it.

"Where do these people come from?" asked Darryl. "Does nobody work?"

"Apparently not today," said Arthur. "Let's get out o' here so we can talk. Lunch? Do you want to have lunch?"

"I don't think I have much of an appetite. I probably won't either. Not til the Judge comes to a decision. I just need to be alone right now. Tell everybody 'bye for me, would you?"

She hurried through the crowd, hoping to make it to her car before anyone was able to stop her. Arthur, disappointed by her quick departure, watched to make sure she was able to get there without any harassment.

"Is she gonna be okay?" asked Rutherford.

"She's a tough one. I think she'll be fine."

Whether or not she was going to be fine was the last thought on her mind. In a matter of speaking, she was actually too nauseated to do much thinking. And even more so when the face of Aaron Prouty grazed past her windshield as she drove off.

His was one she'd all but forgotten about until now. What was he doing there? And better yet, who was he there to root for?

Prouty knew better than to talk to her. He knew that she hated him. And worse than that, he'd never quite gotten over the guilt of passing up her case, even though he knew he had done it for the best of reasons. It was just that sitting through what he thought must've been a nightmare for Darryl made him re-think his decision. It certainly did prompt him into doing one thing he should've done all along, attorney to the plaintiff or not. He was going to figure out a way to spill all the information Clinton had filled him up with just before his death.

But first, he was going to spend a little quality time eavesdropping on the lady behind the nightmare.

Since she was nowhere to be seen at the courthouse, he figured one fly could lead to another. So he set his sights on locating Earlene among the crowd. It wasn't easy. Earlene, it seemed, had garnered instant fame from the day's events. She was bombarded by a herd of people with questions and comments. This being the case, he thought it best to keep an eye on her from his car. Being out of the crowd, he wouldn't chance the possibility of getting interrupted in his spying.

He found it odd to see Earlene all smiles. Apparently she was enjoying the attention. Concerned that her giddiness might lead him to follow her to some bar to go let loose instead of to her mother, he feared that he was wasting his time. But he waited. And waited.

Almost two hours passed until she and Earl packed it up and headed for their own vehicle.

"Finally," he said. He followed them just like a professional; close enough to keep up and far enough away to be out of sight.

Inevitably they did lead him to Margene. The only problem was they had led him to Margene's house, which wasn't exactly the most practical place to eavesdrop since it wasn't some sort of public facility. Never mind the fact that it was still broad daylight. Even so, he still kept his patience up.

He waited in his car for the rest of the day, a day that would prove to be of little to no help in finding clues that led to Margene's guilt. But that was all right. Just as long as that day didn't repeat itself the next day when he would try again.

Like Prouty, Darryl too had spent the day in front of a steering wheel. She drove until she was out of gas. Not caring whether she was stranded or not, she sat there in her car as though nothing had happened and watched the day go by.

The next morning she woke to the sound of someone banging on her window.

"Are you all right, Miss?" A strange gentleman stood outside her car.

"I must've nodded off," she yelled, rolling down her window.

The man looked at his watch. "At seven o'clock in the morning?"

"No, no. I mean, I ran out of gas last night. It was dark and I guess I just fell asleep. Never mind. It wouldn't make any sense to you, anyway."

"If you're out of gas, I'd be happy to give you a lift somewhere."

"You sure?"

"Don't be silly. Come on. Where do you want to go?"

The man drove her directly into town and let her out at Arthur's office.

"Are you sure there's someone here to help you with your car?"

"At seven o'clock? There's no question. He's an early bird." She thanked the man, then dragged herself up to the door, still half asleep. She held her hand out, but the door opened before she could ball it up to knock.

"Darryl, where have you been? There've been quite a few people looking for you. Not to mention me being worried to death."

"I drove 'til I ran out o' gas. I've always wondered what that would be like."

"Come sit down. I think you might be a little delirious right now. Have you had any sleep?"

"Yeah. I fell asleep in the car. I've gotta go get it. I need to get some gas."

"Let's go get your car. Then you are gonna go and get some sleep. Let me call your uncle and tell him you're still alive."

She watched in silence as he did what was necessary to organize what she had so cleverly unorganized. When he finished, she walked behind him to the door. "I'm sorry. I uh..."

He put his hand over her mouth. "You don't have to. Nobody's mad at you. Not here, anyway. I just didn't want to see you....oh, never mind. It can wait. We'll talk later."

He helped her gas up her car, then followed behind her to her uncle Martin's.

"Make sure she gets some sleep."

"I'll do it," Martin said, pulling the screen door shut.

Later that day, Arthur showed up again. He had a basket of food on his arm and a smile on his face. Darryl had barely woken up when she saw him appear.

"Food for the wise," he said.

She laughed. "Is that supposed to make sense or something?"

"No. But you've gotta eat. And I know you haven't."

She looked away bashfully, holding the door open for him.

"I thought maybe you might want to go outside. Thus, the basket."

"It does look pretty out."

"Well, let's go catch the day while it's still around."

"Listen, again I'm sorry. Yesterday was a bit of a shock."

"I told you not to apologize. Listen, if I were in your shoes, I may have reacted worse. You're fine. Let's talk about yesterday later."

The two walked out to one of the nearby fields and made themselves at home on the grass. Not used to talking to him about anything other than courtroom issues, she shyly said nothing. Instead she occupied the time by picking at her food. He was amused by her bashfulness, but didn't bother letting her in on the joke. It was obvious that outside of his being her lawyer, she carried some sort of crush on him. She never, ever made direct eye contact with him for more than a second at a time. He didn't mind. In fact, there was only one thing keeping him from acting on his own feelings.

"You're not saying anything."

"Okay. So how did you know my mother was a musician?"

"I guess I'm about to get busted."

"What?"

"I guess it's not really fair, but I do know a good bit about you. My grandmother wasn't exactly the silent type. I think she was really fond of you. She talked about you, your mother, your father. You might say that I know a lot about you and your family."

"You're right. It's not fair. Scary, really. Speaking of scary, do you think Troy LeMaster had been over to our house? Shangri-la?"

"If he had, Darryl, it wasn't through invitation. I can assure you of that. If I had to guess, somebody told him about the inside. I could imagine Margene spending hours with him, telling him everything there was to know about your father."

"Oh, my God! I don't even like to think about her being inside the house."

"Have you been to it lately?"

"No. Too scared to."

"It's probably just as well." Arthur didn't have the heart to tell her that someone was currently residing there. He just wanted to hurry and win her case, so that she could have everything that belonged to her again.

"Margene is gonna be behind bars when it's all over. You can count on that." He paused for a minute. "Would you look at me?"

She looked. For a second.

"That's for me to worry about. You've been through enough. You don't need to worry about that. Which is why I told you not to talk about it."

"It's hard. It's really hard. There's just so much going on in my head. There's so much I want to accomplish. And it's not even for me. It's for Daddy."

"Well then, I'm gonna do everything in my power to make things right. I'll do it for your daddy, but I'm gonna go it for you, too. He would've wanted me to do this for you."

In town, Saunders was pulling out his magic tricks to make things right for his client. Even though in this case she was his client incognito. Margene had made arrangements to meet with him after business hours. After dark, to be exact. In the meantime, she listened to as much as she could absorb from Earl and Earlene about the happenings in court. She was pleased, but not altogether satisfied. Nor would she be until a verdict leaning in their favor came in.

"Did Waters give any clues as to when he would decide?"

"He didn't say," said Earlene.

"He'll take a month, knowin' him. I just want that little bitch off our ass, so we can get this show on the road."

"She didn't look too happy when Troy was on the stand," said Earl. "I was lookin' right at her. She looked like she was gonna cry. I 'bout started laughin'."

"Laugh all you want, but don't let anybody see you do it. You don't wanna look like you're trying to gang up on her. You wanna look legitimate. Like you're trying to take care of business."

"What about that Leonard," said Earlene. "Did you know he couldn't read and write?"

"What?"

"It was embarrassing to me to have him up as a witness."

"You're pullin' my leg, right?"

"You didn't know?"

"Now, how the hell would I know he was illiterate?"

"Mama, I ain't stupid. I know you have some sort of connection with him. You must. Otherwise, his name wouldn't be on the will as a witness. I just can't believe you would choose somebody who couldn't read to get involved in this."

"I told you I didn't know."

"How could you not? I mean, what did you do? Forge his name too?"

"I'm leavin'. And when I get back, I want this place rid of smart asses."

She stormed out of the house and drove off, partly because she was embarrassed, and partly because Earlene had guessed right about the forgery bit.

"Can't read or write? Good Lord." She tried to figure out how she could've overlooked something that basic during her past involvement with Moss. Then she realized that her involvement with him never made it much past the bedroom. Even so, she had seen his signature those many years ago. It's the main reason she came up with it to use for the will. It was an easy name to forge.

"I gotta start doin' my homework better than this." She looked at the clock. It wasn't yet time to have her run in with Saunders. "Guess I got time to go check on my coins." So that's where she headed. She and the two other cars tailing her.

Prouty was at it again, determined that he was going to bust her. What he didn't realize was that somebody was following him follow her.

He stopped some two hundred yards from where Margene had. He waited, watching her through the thicket he'd parked near. When he felt it was safe, he quietly got out of his car to follow her trail. But he stopped.

There was a smell. Something familiar, but one he couldn't place his finger on. It was weird, like incense. And weirder yet to be coming from out of the middle of nowhere.

Suddenly something was thrown over his head. Some sort of cloth. He felt someone grab him from behind. It could've been two people. Maybe more. He didn't know. He opened his mouth to yell, but a round, bulky object was shoved in from outside of the cloth. He squirmed and kicked. It was no use. He was held too tight. Then he felt the pain of all pains from a blow in the torso so hard, he could actually hear the density of the object swing toward him. But he couldn't yell in agony. His mouth was packed too full.

He couldn't fall to the ground, either. He didn't know what was happening or why. He could only feel the mutilation and the dragging of his shoes across the ground.

He was then thrown into a small space. It was only when he heard the ignition start that he realized he was in a car. He listened for voices. There weren't any. Not a slur or a whisper. All he heard was the wind breathing through the cracks in the windows. He was afraid.

What was in essence a short trip felt like a never ending journey to hell. When the car stopped, he was pulled out and forcefully led to some unknown territory. The cloth was then ripped away from his head. It was dark, but he could see the two generic faces staring from either side of him.

"Why are you following Margene Lee?" one of them asked.

He didn't answer. He was too afraid. Another blow to the torso loosened him up. Again, he was asked the same question.

"I'm trying to make things right."

"What are you in on?"

"In on?" Another blow.

"Please! I'm not 'in on' anything. I'm following her because I'm trying to..."

"Tryin' to what?"

"I'm trying to get some information."

"Information for what?"

"I'm trying to prove that she had something to do with Clinton Lee's death."

"What do you know about that?"

"I don't know anything. That's why I'm following her." Another blow.

"What do you know?"

Prouty was out of breath. He could barely feel his lips move.

"I know she came up with a phony will."

"How do you know that?"

"Clinton Lee came to me. He was changing his will. He was gonna leave Margene's two out of it."

"What else?"

"He said they weren't his real children."

There was silence, then a choke hold. "You better know what you're talkin' about."

He couldn't breathe. He started gasping.

"How do you know this?" His neck was released.

He stood slumped over. The wooden object came for him again.

"No! Please don't! I'll tell you what I know." He tried to catch his breath. "He had come from the doctor. Something about blood types were all wrong for Margene's two to be his flesh and blood. Something about one of 'em being conceived on the wrong day. He wasn't with Margene on that date. That's all I know."

"You have proof of this?"

"Yes and no. It's the doctor. He's the one with the proof."

"Here's what you're gonna do. You're gonna get this proof from the doctor and you're gonna get it to Guy Saunders."

"It's not as easy as that."

"Figure out a way to make it easy." Another choke hold. "I'm not givin' you a choice here."

"I understand."

Prouty watched as one of them lit up a cigarette. That's when he figured out the smell. Cloves.

"Get him outta here." The cloth went back over his head.

He was dumped out at his car and ordered not to remove the cover until he'd counted to a hundred. He counted to two hundred.

CHAPTER THIRTY-FOUR

It was definitely an evening of people unaware of their tracks. Margene never even spotted Prouty's car tucked in the bushes while he was out being taken care of. After she left the old well house, she made a beeline straight into town. As planned, she met Saunders at his office after there were no cars left in the parking lot.

"You were right," she said. "Said everybody'd be out by seven thirty."

"I don't guess I need to tell you about the problems we're facing here, do I?"

"Which one? The Garnet guy or the dumb guy?"

"Do you think it's funny?"

"I'm tryin' to have a little piece o' humor about it. Takes my mind off the waitin' game Dickie's forcin' us to sit through. Don't matter though. You're gonna win this. You always do. Matter of fact, I'm right proud o' you. From what the younguns tell me, you blew the lid right off that courtroom. Said you didn't do a damn thing wrong."

"Margene, you know as well as I do that the opposite of wrong isn't always right."

"Who the hell told you that?"

"Do you want to stop horsing around so we can get down to business? There is always that minute possibility that I'll lose your case."

"Does the word 'appeal' mean anything to you?"

"That's why we need to sit down and discuss the details. I hope you weren't planning on going anywhere tonight. We've got a long one ahead of us."

Margene's car remained parked outside his office until the wee hours of the morning.

Prouty's car showed up at the home of Arthur Peterson somewhere around those same hours. The old man was sound asleep when all the banging began. With the time being as it was, trying to wake him was a task reasonably proportionate to that of waking the dead. But a frightened Prouty didn't mind making a commotion.

"What in tarnation are you tryin' to do?" said Peterson, finally flicking his porch light on. "Did you wake up the whole neighborhood or just half? When I heard that banging, I didn't know who it could be. Then I looked out the window. Good thing I know your vehicle."

Peterson hadn't noticed the shape Prouty was in until he walked in the house where things were more visible.

"Good Lord, son. Did you get attacked or something?"

Prouty was still trembling from his earlier episode. Right then and there, Peterson knew he'd been more than attacked. He'd been through something gravely wrong.

"Let me get you to the hospital. There's only so much I can do for you here."

"It's not why I came."

"Well, you need to get some help."

"I'll be fine."

"What's this about, Aaron? If you didn't come here seeking medical attention, then you'd better cut to the chase. What's a goin' on?"

"I know you know about Clinton Lee not being the father of Earl and Earlene."

"I don't know what you're talkin' about."

"You've got to send the information you have to Guy Saunders."

"I think you'd better leave."

"If I leave here without your word that you'll expose the truth, then you'll have only your conscience to blame."

Peterson got ruffled. "I swear, Aaron. This goes away from everything I stand for. You know I'm a 'by the book' all the way person, don't you? Clinton told you, didn't he? I didn't think it would all come down the way it did. So seein' that we're bein' honest here, why don't you give it to me straight? Was he murdered?"

"If I had to guess."

"And these people who did that to you?"

"I don't know. All I know is that they told me I had to get the doctor to send the information on the birth records of Earl and Earlene Lee to Saunders."

"And these people know that the doctor is me?"

"I don't know. I don't think so. All I know is they mean business. They'll be back if they don't get what they want."

"Good Lord! All right. But it'll have to be anonymous."

Peterson sent out the information the next morning. It was as anonymous and to the point as any information could be. The simple, white envelope with no return address held a note inside reading: "Your clients are not the biological children of Clinton Lee. Check the blood record of the girl. If that convinces you, you can have the information on the boy."

The letter landed on Saunders' desk among the rest of the mail that arrived that afternoon. He, being too caught up with other issues, didn't give it a second glance.

In mafia territory, there wasn't a face to be found that was anything other than solemn. Grampus being the leader of the trend.

"And you're sure that's all he was doin'? Just following her?"

"I ain't never seen anybody that scared in all my life," said Little One. "Trust me. He was out to get her just like us."

"You think he'll get the information on to Saunders?"

"Yep."

"As long as that's being taken care of, there's only one other soul to get done."

Shakey and Little One had heard those same words before. It was true that Grampus had his suspicions of Margene from the very start. But after trying to come to grips with the fact that she was holding out on him with the still unsolved coin bit, and then learning that she'd lied about two people who weren't even the flesh and blood of the man he had killed, there was no doubt what he had in store for her.

Like many others he had "taken out," Grampus left no instructions as to how it should happen. Therefore, the sky was the limit to Little One and Shakey.

"What do you think?" asked Little One. "Do we wanna do her nice and quiet like we did her ex-husband?"

"I got somethin' a little better in mind than poisoned tea."

"That woman's either stupid or crazy. Nobody cons Grampus and thinks they're gon' get away with it. She was actin' so pitiful like she was concerned about her ex leavin' his children out o' his will. Some poor little wife. Wife in sheep's clothin' more like it."

"She goes to that well house just about every day, don't she?"

Little One smiled.

"What you got up that sleeve o' yours?"

Late that night, Darryl was barely able to sleep. She tossed and turned to the point that her bed began beating up against the wall. The nightmares in her head were reminiscent of those that she'd had right before each of her parents' deaths. All night long she repeated a pattern of waking up, then falling back asleep. Each time, she could barely distinguish the difference between reality and dream. But when morning came, it was as though her entire night of delirium had never happened. She was alert and reasonably happy, without any clue as to why.

"You're in a good mood today," said Martin.

"Yeah. I guess I am, aren't I?"

"Oh, by the way, Arthur called this morning."

She looked at the clock. "It's only seven-thirty."

"Yeah, it was right around seven when he called. Sounds like news to me." He handed the phone over to her.

"You know what? I think I'll pass on the phone. If it's news, I'd rather hear it in person." She rushed to get ready, hoping that whatever had driven him to call her that early was something good.

When she got to his office, she found him hunched over his desk staring into space.

"Hello?" She tiptoed in not knowing what might come out of his mouth.

"Have you heard?" he said, looking up. "No. How could you have? It hasn't really gone public yet."

"What?"

"Early this morning, Margene's car was seen parked out near an abandoned well house. Car door was open. That's what started the search."

"Search?"

"It appears that her body was found at the bottom of the well."

Darryl went numb.

"Right now, the police are chalking it up to a suicide. What do you think?"

"What do I think? I think I'm gonna have to sit down and absorb what you just said." Darryl sat down, playing copycat to Arthur's original state. In all the time she'd been involved in the catastrophe with Margene, it never occurred to her that the woman could die. It was too farfetched a notion. And too sadistic to wish for.

The postman interrupted by knocking at the door.

"I've gotta get that," he said, and opened the door.

"I'm gonna need a signature," said the postman. "Certified Letter."

Arthur took the letter to his chair and opened it. "Well, I guess today's chock full of surprises. Do you want to read it yourself?"

"I'll let you tell me."

"Judge ruled in favor of the 1970 will."

"They'll appeal, won't they? Earlene and Earl."

"I don't know."

"Listen, would you think it rude of me if I told you that I needed to be alone again?"

"No."

She grabbed her purse to leave.

"Listen, when you figure out what you want to do next, let me know. And other than that, just know that you can come to me anytime. About anything."

"It'll give me something to think about."

He watched her leave, realizing that he could no longer look at her in the way an attorney should look at a client. He knew the next time he saw her, everything would be different.

On her way back out of town, she saw Saunders outside his office building dealing with the same postman who had come to Arthur's office. She couldn't help but chuckle at what his reaction might be.

What Darryl didn't realize was that his reaction to losing would be far less devastating than one would expect.

The fact that his case didn't win was not only his last concern, it was altogether unimportant. Finding that he'd lost his client incognito by a mysterious leap to the bottom of a well was the ticket to freedom he'd long since wanted to purchase. And it took him only thirty years to save up for it.

He held the letter of verdict in his hand and plopped down on top of his desk.

The mail, which he'd allowed to pile up, was right under him. He squirmed a bit, pulling out one letter after another. The last one had no return address. He almost tossed it aside like the others, but something on it caught his eye. It was addressed to one Garfield Saunders. He hadn't been called Garfield since he was a boy. He didn't like it back then, and he surely didn't like it now.

He ripped the letter open in disgust and read it. When he finished, he laid it on his desk and walked out. The words were etched in his brain. He had wasted an entire career representing liars. And it was at that moment he realized that he was no better than any of them.

Just as she reached the edge of town, Darryl shoved her hand in her purse to grab a peppermint. She dug around, but instead of pulling out a piece of candy, she wound up with something else in her hand. It was the key that she'd gotten out of the pitcher on top of the piano at Shangri-la. In all the action, she'd not only forgotten that she had it, but she'd also failed to present it to Rutherford.

She was well aware that Margene had long since collected the contents of the lockbox that the key belonged to. But if she was going to start putting things behind her, now was as good a time as any.

Turning at the next corner, she headed back into town. She drove into the bank parking lot and went straight inside to find Rutherford. He, who was in his office, didn't hesitate to stop what he was doing to tend to her.

"I don't know what you have or haven't heard, but I don't want to talk about Margene, or anything else pertaining to court," she said. "We won, by the way. That's all I feel like saying right now. But I didn't come to tell you that."

She held her hand out and dropped the key on his desk. "This belongs to you. I just wanted to return it."

Rutherford picked it up and looked at it. "I'm lost, here. Where did this come from?"

"It was Daddy's lockbox key."

Rutherford looked at it again. "Darryl, this key goes to a lockbox, but not his."

"How could that be? He always kept his lockbox key in the same place. He told me to look for it if anything were ever to happen to him."

"Darryl, honey, I don't know about this key. Normally I wouldn't remember such a thing, but your daddy picked out his lockbox in accordance to his birthday. His lockbox number was 1122. This one here is 1109."

"That's my birthday, if you're looking at it in terms of dates."

The two immediately rushed to the basement level of the bank where the lock boxes were.

"Here it is," he said. He inserted the key and unlocked the small, hinged door. He pulled out a long metal box and handed it to Darryl. "Do you want me to leave you alone with it?"

"No. Stay." She pulled back the lid and looked inside. In the far corner without so much as a wrapper laid a small coin. Nothing fancy. It wasn't even shiny. She pulled it out and grasped it in her palm.

Rutherford took the empty metal box and pushed it back into the slot.

"Your Daddy sure did have a fondness for coins." He smiled, thinking that Clinton had opened the secret lockbox especially for her. "I bet he was starting a collection for you."

"Probably so." She grinned and took the coin otherwise known as *Die Irrtümliche Münze* and put it in her pocket.

"I'm gonna head to the farm. I'll see you later."

Clinton had never told her about the coin. To her, it was nothing more than a piece of stamped metal. It's sentiment, on the other hand, was everything.